Praise for *The Sleeping and the Dead*

"Crook deftly explores the human fascination with the macabre at the same time he draws attention to the reader's own voyeuristic impulses." —*Publishers Weekly*

"[Crook's] first mystery sets a high standard." —Associated Press

"Want a ghost story/crime story/police procedural/Shakespeare lesson all twisted—really twisted—into one page-turner? See *The Sleeping and the Dead.*" —*Memphis Flyer*

"A suspenseful blend of the supernatural and crime fiction. Jackie Lyons is a strong female detective." —*Mississippi Magazine*

"This series starter should go right to the top of all bestseller lists. It is very well written, with fresh new characters, an unusual atmosphere and setting, and an explosive ending. Crook's voice is well developed although this is his first mystery. . . . An excellent read that you won't be able to put down." —*RT Book Reviews* (Top Pick)

"A dark and creepy mystery with a brave but deeply flawed heroine. A promising series kickoff." —*Kirkus Reviews*

"Crook brings the world of the dead and the living together perfectly in this captivating mystery starring one of the most wonderful, unlikely protagonists I've come across. Jackie Lyons is a flat-out train wreck—an ex-cop turned crime scene photographer battling addiction who happens to see dead people. You will love her, not in spite of her faults and demons, but because of them."

—Jennifer McMahon, *New York Times* bestselling author of *Promise Not to Tell* and *Don't Breathe a Word*

"A fun, spooky ride."

—Tom Franklin, Edgar Award–winning author of *Crooked Letter, Crooked Letter*

"There is no killing me softly in this hard-boiled song from a Southern city sinking into the abyss; a terrific tale hammered down on filthy keys in a lost bar."

—Åke Edwardson, author of *Sail of Stone*

"Read *The Sleeping and the Dead* and you may never buy a camera from a stranger."

—Pieter Aspe, author of *The Square of Revenge*

The
Sleeping
and the
Dead

A JACKIE LYONS MYSTERY

Jeff Crook

Minotaur Books
New York

THE SLEEPING AND THE DEAD. Copyright © 2012 by Jeff Crook. All rights reserved. Printed in the United States of America. For information, address St. Martin's Press, 175 Fifth Avenue, New York, N.Y. 10010.

www.minotaurbooks.com

The Library of Congress has cataloged the hardcover edition as follows:

Crook, Jeff.
    The sleeping and the dead : a mystery / Jeff Crook.—1st ed.
        p.   cm.
    ISBN 978-1-250-00028-6 (hardcover)
    ISBN 978-1-250-01481-8 (e-book)
    1. Murder—Investigation—Fiction.   2. Memphis (Tenn.)—
Fiction.   3. Paranormal fiction.   I. Title.
    PS3553.R5463S57 2012
    813'.54—dc23

                                                2012007789

ISBN 978-1-250-02324-7 (trade paperback)

Minotaur books may be purchased for educational, business, or promotional use. For information on bulk purchases, please contact Macmillan Corporate and Premium Sales Department at 1-800-221-7945 extension 5442 or write specialmarkets@macmillan.com.

First Minotaur Books Paperback Edition: June 2013

10 9 8 7 6 5 4 3 2 1

I will drain him dry as hay:
Sleep shall neither night nor day
Hang upon his penthouse lid;
He shall live a man forbid.
—MACBETH, ACT I, SCENE III

The sleeping and the dead
Are but as pictures: 'tis the eye of childhood
That fears a painted devil.
—MACBETH, ACT II, SCENE II

Monday

1

I SAT AT THE DEEPEST corner of the bar away from the door, trying to get the bartender's attention without my hands shaking. He finally noticed and came over—young kid, obnoxiously cute with his manicured chin stubble, pouty moist bottom lip, lips too pretty for a guy. Lips I'd kill to have. He wore tight jeans with the circle of a snuff can lid worn into the back left pocket. "You got a cigarette?" I asked.

"No smoking. City ordinance," he said. He wiped his hands on a bar towel. He had good hands, no rings, no watch, long fingers, the skin moist and healthy-looking from the lotion he had just applied. But he was way too young. Way too young. But what was too young anymore? He was old enough to serve drinks.

"Waiting for somebody?" he asked.

"A bartender. Seen one?" He laughed at my joke as though he'd heard it before. "How about a beer?"

"What flavor?"

"Whatever's closest."

I took a bar napkin from the stack in front of me and blew my nose into the restaurant's logo. He pushed a pressed cardboard coaster across the bar to me, then drew a glass of Icehouse from the tap and set it in on the coaster. I didn't take it right away. I watched the bubbles rise in the thin yellow beer while I pulled a blister pack from my shirt pocket and shoved the last two red sinus pills through the foil onto the bar, Frisbeed the empty pack into the garbage pail behind the bar, popped the pills into my mouth, washed them down with about half the beer, feeling it burn through the bilge layers coating the back of my throat. I returned the glass carefully to the bar and tried not to suck air while I waited for the shakes to go away.

When the phone rang, I had a couple more beers in me and the sinus pills were starting to kick in. I was back in battery so I answered it. "What's up, Adam?"

"You moved, Jacqueline."

"I got a new place on Summer Avenue across the street from the Methodist church," I replied. "I was going to call you."

"I heard about the fire. I didn't realize it was your apartment until I stopped by and saw the crater." I could hear the sound of his car engine, the radio squawking something unintelligible in the background as he spoke. "I checked with a guy I know in arson. The fire started with a candle in the bathroom. You were using again, Jackie."

"I can't light a match without you thinking I'm sticking needles in my arm!" I was angrier than I should have been. "I'm in control, for once, maybe for the first time in my life. I'm taking things one day at a time, recalibrating my life. I turned the page, Adam." True, I had only turned the page yesterday, but you got to turn it sometime. In the olden days, I would never have dropped two grand on a new camera, like I had just done. That kind of money buys a hell of a lot of bonita.

"So in control you almost killed yourself?" He wouldn't let it go.

"It wasn't that bad."

"Shit, Jackie, they said you were floating so high they had to carry you out. Another three minutes and I'd be going to your funeral."

"Don't hate me because I'm lucky."

"You ain't lucky, Jackie." He stated fact. "You're the unluckiest shit I ever met. You got lucky once and now you think Judas is your friend. You got to come back to NA."

"I'm still going." Adam was my Narcotics Anonymous sponsor, but I hadn't been to a meeting with him in ages. I had made it past the first few of their twelve steps, admitting my life was a hopeless shambles. That was easy, but by that time, I'd been to enough meetings to see even the leaders hadn't done anything more than switch addictions, from drugs to God, whatever got them through the day. Addiction is addiction and I couldn't see the difference, but the court said I had to go, so I went.

"Where's your meetings?"

"Some dump off Tutwiler. Is that why you called?"

"I'm still your sponsor, but that's not why I called." I heard him stop his car, open the door and get out. "I'm calling because you got a job."

"I'm meeting somebody." I winced as the tension over the phone jacked up about eight notches.

"Somebody who?"

I knew what he was thinking. The only people I ever met were ambulance chasers, junkies and dealers. "I'm buying a new camera. I'm meeting the seller to give him the rest of his money."

"Do you want this job or not? Meet me at the Orpheum. I'm there now." He hung up. Adam wasn't usually such a hardass, but hearing he was at the Orpheum gave me a pretty good idea what had put him in high order.

I paid my tab and left. It was pouring outside and I didn't

own an umbrella. The normally busy street looked like a parking lot, a fire truck blocking most of the lanes, cars backed up for miles, cop cars and ambulance lights flashing through the rain. Every exit from the parking lot was blocked and I wasn't going anywhere soon, so I ran to my car and grabbed my Canon from the backseat. The day before, I had dropped two grand on a new Leica M8 digital camera. I still owed five hundred on it, and I had just paid first and last month's rent on a new apartment, so I needed every bit of folding money I could broom together. I barely had enough to pay for the beers. If I could steer a little business toward one of my lawyer friends, he'd pay me for the photos of the accident.

I hurried across the parking lot and started shooting pictures. A Memphis Police Department cruiser had T-boned a white Skylark. The Skylark sat on the sidewalk under a bus-stop canopy advertising personal-injury-lawyer services. The patrol car was folded up on the median strip. I got some shots of blood on the open passenger-side door before the rain completely washed it away. There was blood pooled in the passenger-side seat. The firemen were in no hurry to get their equipment cleared, as the wreckers hadn't showed yet. The cops on the scene looked like they had eaten a shit sandwich. They didn't even try to stop me.

I gave the driver of the Skylark a business card. They had just taken his wife and mother-in-law away in the ambulance. I don't know if they survived. He was an older white guy, dressed in gray slacks, white shirt and blue windbreaker. The front of his shirt was pink with somebody else's blood. He didn't have a scratch on him.

"You need a ride to the hospital?" I asked.

"My cousin's coming to get me," he said.

There were spiderwebs in the cruiser's windshield where

the cop's face had smacked it. I saw him standing alone by his wrecked car with his face torn up and bloody, his uniform shirt hanging open, EKG wires dangling from his chest. I raised my camera to get a picture of him, but he didn't appear on the viewscreen. Just his wrecked cruiser. He wasn't really there.

"You work for a lawyer?" the driver asked.

"Preston Park, like it says on the card." I lowered the camera. The cop wandered over to the curb and sat down. "Do you see that policeman?"

"Hell no, I didn't see him coming. He didn't have his flashers on," the driver explained, misunderstanding my question. "If I had seen him, I never would have pulled out. They said he was responding to a call. He should have had his flashers going."

"Did you see what happened to him after the accident?"

"I don't know. They took him away in the ambulance about ten minutes ago."

I could still see the cop sitting on the curb with his bloody face in his hands. People were walking right past him, not even looking at him. I tried to push him out of my mind. I looked back at the driver and said, "Give Mr. Park a call and I'll forward your pictures."

"I can't pay you." He put the card in his wallet.

"Not a problem." Preston would pay me and add the expense to his share of the settlement.

"How much do you think I'll get from this?" the guy asked.

I didn't bother answering. I took a few more pictures of the scene and left him thoughtfully rubbing his neck. Traffic was starting to inch along. My cell phone was ringing when I got in my car. It was Adam again. I let it ring.

2

I HATED DRIVING IN THE rain at night, but that's all it ever did in Memphis in November. The raindrops sounded like somebody dragging a chain across the roof of my car. The wipers bumped back and forth, streaking the greasy windshield. My phone rang again, but this time it wasn't Adam. I answered it.

"I'm at the bar. The traffic was killer," James said. He was the guy selling me the new camera. We were supposed to be meeting tonight so I could pay him the rest of his money.

"I got called out on a job."

"What kind of job?"

"Crime scene."

"Are you a cop?"

"Not anymore. I just take pictures now. There's a dead body at the Orpheum. It'll be all over the news tonight. You should watch, maybe you'll see me on television."

"That's incredible. When you said you were a photographer, I had no idea you did that kind of . . . thing." I couldn't tell if he sounded pleasantly surprised or scared surprised. Some guys freak when they find out you take pictures of dead people. Why wouldn't they? James St. Michael wouldn't have been the first, but I didn't think that was his particular problem. At least he wasn't pissed that I had stood him up. It was just a dinner date, after all, and not even a real date. That's what I told myself and I almost believed it, too. At the same time, I got the feeling he was in a hurry to hang up. But so was I.

I helped him out. "I'll call you tomorrow."

"OK." We hung up, but there was a new tension between us and I didn't know what it was. I didn't have time to think about it.

The marquee lights of the Orpheum Theatre were dark but Beale Street was lit up like Vegas. I parked beside an MPD squad car in the middle of South Main. The three local news stations had their vans set up across the street. The sidewalk was packed with people, curbs blocked by cop cars, a fire truck and an ambulance idling in front of the main entrance. Busy night for everybody.

I was climbing out of my car when a young male traffic cop grabbed my door and told me I couldn't obscenity park there. "She's with me!" Sergeant Adam McPeake shouted from the front door of the theater. He waved me over. I smiled at the traffic cop as he reluctantly stepped aside, then ducked under the police tape and hurried through the rain. Adam held open the door next to the box office. "Jesus, Jackie. You don't look like shit for once," he snarked, looking me up and down. My friend.

They had all the crystal chandeliers lit up inside, bright as opening night. The lobby was filled with cops dicking the dog and scuffing up the carpet with their wet shoes. Nothing like a murder to flush the bastards out of the walls. I stopped beside the concierge desk and waited while Adam spoke to a guy with bruised shadows in the hollows of his eyes. Adam brought him over and introduced him as the theater manager. "Dave found the victim," he explained. We shook hands. His grip was weak and shaky, his hand hot and damp, like he had just washed it. He had short dark hair combed back from a sharp widow's peak, and thick, close-set eyebrows that drew closer together as he glanced at the cops in the lobby parlor. Some were leaning against a wall decorated with publicity photos of celebrities who'd played the Orpheum over the last umpteen years. The theater was built in 1890, burned to the ground in 1923 during a striptease vaudeville, rebuilt in 1928, and completely refurbished and reopened in 1984, my senior year in high school. I remember my parents bringing me for the grand opening, but not what they were showing that night—I just remember hating it on principle because I was too Fonzie-cool to enjoy anything my parents liked.

Advertisements around the lobby announced several upcoming shows—*Rent* opened the day after Thanksgiving, *High School Musical* in December, and Verdi's opera *Macbeth* in January. I wouldn't have minded seeing *Rent*, or maybe *Holiday Inn*, which was showing just before Christmas, if I'd had money for tickets, which I didn't. I thought about asking the manager if he could hook me up, but I had already forgotten his name.

The doors opened again and Dr. Paul Wiley, city medical examiner, entered lugging two tackle boxes full of equipment. He spotted me right away and glared, his liver spots flushing. He had his own people to take crime-scene photos. I smiled, extended my hand. He stopped but he didn't return the gesture. He smelled like Old Spice and latex.

"Jacqueline," he said. "I hope you don't plan to walk all over my evidence this time."

"I'll try to stay out of your way," I said.

"See that you do."

"If you promise to keep your big head out of my pictures," I added. I had nothing personal against him but he was dreadfully famous old money and didn't like dealing face-to-face with us peons, especially peons of the female persuasion, unless we were dead. Being an early disciple of Spanky and Alfalfa's He-Man Woman Haters Club, he was almost as famous for his militant, anachronistic misogyny as his talent as a professional body snatcher. He refused to be interviewed on air by female reporters and had gotten himself in trouble a few times with the Equal Opportunity bureaucrats. Paul Wiley came from an old Memphis family, mostly surgeons; his great-uncle Ted had been a part of Boss Crump's political machine. Wiley sat on the board of just about everything of consequence, from the hospitals to the utility company to the Memphis Ballet.

Deputy Chief of Investigative Services W. E. Billet swept down the grand stairs from the mezzanine, entering the lobby in his dress blue uniform, polished brass buttons sparkling under the crystal chandeliers. The only person Wiley hated more than me was Billet.

Billet was young, brilliant, black, photogenic, and a favorite of the mayor. He and Wiley had an ongoing feud and were forever seeking new ways to sabotage each other. That's why I was there; that and the deputy chief liked having his own crime-scene pictures. For his part, Wiley was habitually slow with his findings, forcing Billet to wait days for even the most basic forensic test results. Meanwhile, a serial murderer was walking the streets and these two politicians conducted ongoing ratfucking evolutions preparing for the day when one would be named director of the Memphis Police Department and the other forced to retire or run out of town completely.

Sergeant Adam McPeake was my connection to this bag of dicks. He recommended me to Chief Billet four years ago, before the Playhouse Killer had cooked his first victim. McPeake was younger and better-looking than Billet, carved from mahogany so rich he almost glowed, and smart where it counted. Smart enough never to cross his boss or get between him and a camera. I had brought him up from traffic when he was a rookie and introduced him to vice. He made it into homicide through a combination of hard work and the golden horseshoe lodged up his ass. He'd overcome a cocaine addiction that nearly cost him his career, but he was also a shrewd politician and knew how to play the system, so he'd been able to hang on to his job. I had pissed mine away.

Chief Billet trailed Wiley into the theater. Adam and I followed, along with what appeared to be half the police department. "Don't these people have jobs?" I said as I turned on my cameras. I had brought my Canon, my work camera, in addition to the new Leica.

"Everybody thinks it's the Playhouse Killer," Adam said.

"Isn't it?"

"I don't think so." For some reason, I was relieved by that. I had learned a long time ago to treat this like a job, but the Playhouse murders got to me.

From the back of the auditorium, the body looked like a pile of old bedding left on stage. It lay in a pool of white light. Wiley's assistant was already circling it, snapping photos. The victim lay facedown under an old mattress freckled with overlapping liver-colored stains, with only his naked brown legs visible from the knees down. As soon as we got on stage, I secured a flash to the top of my Canon and started shooting.

At the first snap, Dr. Wiley glared up from his open tackle boxes. "Keep her back!" he shouted. Chief Billet smiled and waved me on, so I continued to shoot. I took several photos of the bottoms of the victim's feet, which were black with grime. I saw no signs of blood on either the stage or the mattress.

Dr. Wiley had his techs spread a sheet of plastic next to the body and then lift the mattress aside and lay it on the sheet. Dave, the theater manager, turned green and asked Adam if he could leave. Adam nodded and he hurried up the aisle with one hand over his mouth.

I snapped some shots of the cops standing around the stage in this surreal overhead light, with the darkness stretching up and away behind them. At the rear of the highest balcony, I noticed a young girl standing under an Exit sign, watching us work. I turned my Canon on her and looked at her through the viewfinder, but the screen was empty. I didn't say anything. Nobody else would be able to see her.

Wiley spoke into a digital recorder, describing the state of the victim. "Black male, early twenties, approximately five-ten, one hundred and thirty pounds, nude, discovered lying facedown beneath a mattress. A three-foot length of electrical conduit is lodged in the victim's anus."

"I think the cause of death is obvious," Chief Billet said.

Dr. Wiley laughed once, derisively, as he knelt over the body. I locked myself up cold and tight and kept shooting pictures. Treat it like a specimen, an object of study rather than horror. Focus on the details, the minutiae of visual data. Ignore the person, no matter how familiar he seems. This was a stranger, not a ghost from my past. Luckily, I couldn't see his face.

Wiley continued, "There are no other signs of external trauma. Deep coloration of the buttocks suggests cause of death to be *asphyxiation*." He glared at Chief Billet as he said this.

"Get it?" one of the cops grunted. "Ass-fixiation?" A sophomoric snicker circled the stage. Wiley rolled his bloodshot eyes.

"TOD?" Billet asked.

Wiley extracted a long probe thermometer from the torso and examined it. "Less than four hours."

"What about an ID?"

"He's naked," Wiley said. "If I see his wallet lying around, I'll let you know."

"You don't have to be a smartass, Paul," Billet said. He turned to Adam. "Well, McPeake? Is this the work of our boy?"

"I don't think so."

Several cops groaned or swore. "Why not?" Billet asked.

Adam said, "It's not consistent with his pattern. The Playhouse Killer stages his victims in murder scenes from famous plays."

"You can't get a bigger stage than the Orpheum."

"But it's not from any play I know. Dave agrees." He nodded at the theater manager, who seemed even paler than before. "I think maybe this guy's a copycat."

"Great," Billet said. He paced the stage with his hands behind his back, while Wiley smirked and bagged the victim's hands. "That's just fucking great. That's all we need right now." His voice boomed through the auditorium, resounding in the shadows of the balconies and galleries. I looked for the little girl beneath the Exit sign, but she wasn't there anymore. Two in one day—that was a bad sign.

"I think the killer felt remorse and tried to cover up the body with the mattress," Adam said, but something about this didn't ping. The mattress looked like it had been pulled out of a Dumpster. He must have brought it with him, which meant he had planned it this way, for whatever reason.

"You're the expert, McPeake," Chief Billet said. "Now tell me what I'm supposed to tell the cameras."

Adam shrugged.

"Jesus!" the crime-scene tech swore. Dr. Wiley hurried over with a plastic bag to catch the sludge flowing from the pipe rammed up the victim's anus.

"Flesh is cauterized and fused to the metal," he said as he examined the point of insertion. "It must have been red hot when inserted."

"Marlowe!" I shouted. Everybody stared at me. I had known some of these cops from when I was on the force myself, but most of them wouldn't speak to me now. To them, I was just a junkie mooching off the chief's generosity. A few of them had heard about my bad habit of seeing people who weren't there, and I'm sure they thought I was talking to one of my special friends again.

Billet was one of them. He lifted a curious eyebrow. "Well?"

But I wasn't crazy, not this time. I had read about this scene in an English history course in college. "This is from *Edward the Second* by Christopher Marlowe," I said. "According to Thomas More, Edward was smothered with a mattress, then a red-hot copper pipe was shoved up his butt." The brutality of historical British executions had been one of Professor Cromwell's favorite subjects. Writing about a truly grisly one, like Edward II's, was a good way to get an A in his class.

"Adam?" Billet turned to his expert.

Adam shrugged. "That scene was never in Marlowe's play."

I said, "Edward's death was. The killer's not re-creating, he's interpreting. He's making it his own. Maybe he's a frustrated playwright."

"Write us a book report," Billet said. "What I want to know is why did they shove a pipe up his ass?"

"You ever see the movie *Braveheart*?" Billet nodded that he had. "Edward the Second was Longshanks' gay son."

It was like a light came on over the heads of the cops around me. "That movie's fucking awesome," one said.

"Then this is the work of our killer?" Billet started straightening his tie.

"Provided the victim is gay," Adam said. We wouldn't know for sure until he was identified, but there wasn't much doubt anymore. It fit his pattern. The Playhouse Killer's last victim had been staged in a scene from Shakespeare's *Richard III*, but this was his first murder in a long time, and his boldest and most public staging by far.

Chief Billet winked at me and slipped out to talk to the reporters, while Wiley continued his work in sullen silence. He wouldn't look at me now, not even when I took a picture of him bending over the body. Adam was talking to some guys dusting for fingerprints near the backstage door. It was pretty clear from the placement of the body and the lack of blood that the victim hadn't been killed here. He must have been brought in, but how had he done that in a public place like the Orpheum without being seen?

Adam waved for me to follow him. I started putting my cameras away, but as Wiley and his assistant turned the body over, I almost dropped the Leica.

I hurried across the stage and grabbed Adam by the elbow, pulled him behind some scenery so the other cops wouldn't overhear. "Adam," I said. "I know this kid."

I had met him about five hours ago.

3

A LIGHT MIST WAS FALLING through the sycamore trees. The driveway was packed with cars of all makes, models and conditions, from brand-new Acuras and BMWs to rusted-out junkers with hocked titles and plastic sheeting duct-taped over busted windows. The house rose up in the darkness beyond the driveway, bowed and swollen, light streaming from every window like a house afraid of its own shadows. Adam and I climbed the steps to the porch.

"You met the victim here?" he asked. I nodded and shook the water from my hair. "How do you know Michi Mori?"

"He promised to sponsor an exhibition of my photography."

"Is that why you were here today?"

"Yeah." I couldn't tell him the truth, so I pushed the glowing yellow doorbell button.

"Did you hear about that cop?" he asked as we waited for someone to answer.

"Which one?"

"That accident over on Union."

"What about him?" I knew the one he was talking about, and I knew what Adam was going to say before he said it.

"Died at the scene. Damn shame. He had three kids. He

was a good cop." He checked his cell phone for messages. "I guess the lawyers will be all over it."

"I took some pictures of the accident." I didn't tell him I had seen his dead cop. What was the point? He'd only use it as another excuse to hassle me about coming to meetings.

He said, "Ring the doorbell again." He pointed at the Leica hanging around my neck. "Is that new? Looks expensive."

"It is."

"Where'd you get that kind of money?"

"I got a good deal on it."

"Stolen?"

"No, it isn't stolen. You think I'd buy a hot camera?"

"Just asking."

"Well don't."

The door finally opened and we were greeted by an elderly gentleman, about five feet tall, with a thick wavy pompadour of ivory-white hair sweeping back from his tanned and botoxed forehead. He blinked his dark, almost-Chinese eyes slowly and smiled just with his lips. "May I help y'all?" he drawled.

Adam gave a surprised little suck of air and said, "Jesus! You're Cole Ritter!"

"My reputation precedes me." He wore a red silk smoking jacket, but his legs were naked, bandy as a flyweight boxer's legs, deeply tanned and utterly hairless. His feet were bare, the trimmed nails shiny and healthy. He held a martini glass between the index and middle fingers of his bejeweled left hand.

Adam turned to me. "Jesus, Jackie, this is Cole Ritter! Do you know who he is?"

"Cole Ritter, I presume."

"On the button," Cole said.

Adam grabbed his hand and shook it, almost upsetting his martini. "I've loved your work since *I Can't Remember When!*"

"Much obliged, I'm sure." Cole gradually extracted his hand from Adam's fist. He took a sip of his martini and glanced at me.

"I was a theater major in college," Adam said. "My senior year, I played Sonny in *Forrest Park*."

"Ah yes," Cole smiled at me. "I wrote that play when I was in high school."

"That's what's so incredible about it! Such maturity of style, such depth of characterization! Jackie, do you have any idea who this man is?" Adam was giving a disgusting fanboy performance. I thoroughly enjoyed it.

"I've heard of him," I admitted.

"High praise indeed," Cole said.

"He's only like the American Edward Bond!"

"Thank you ever so much for not calling me the American Tom Stoppard." Cole smiled at me again. "I get that all the time, you know."

"But I rather liked *Cahoot's Macbeth*," I said.

He snorted and nearly dropped his martini. "Dinner theater!"

"Cole's from Memphis," Adam continued. "He went to East High School, and now he's world-famous!"

"Marvelous." I turned on the Leica and looked at him in the viewscreen.

Cole leaned against the doorframe, faux casual, posing as though in one of his own plays. "Do you know, I can hardly walk down the street in Paris without a dozen people stopping me, but in Memphis I can't even get a table at Paulette's."

"It must be tough being you," I said.

He shrugged. "Prophets are not without honor, except in their own country."

Adam took his notepad out of his pocket. "I had no idea you were in town."

"I try not to let the press know my whereabouts," Cole said. He probably called the newspaper from the airport to let them know he had arrived. He took a sip of his martini and looked me up and down once, his eyes lingering momentarily over the camera in my hand; then he turned his moist gaze on Adam. "But I like to come home a couple of times a year just to catch up on the gossip. You're obviously not here for the party, though I'm sure you'd be welcome." His eyes never left Adam as he said this. "Are y'all from the newspaper?"

"No," I said.

"Because I don't sign autographs."

"I'm Detective Sergeant Adam McPeake." The fanboy vanished, quick as that, and I wondered if he hadn't been playing it up just to put this supercilious old pouf off his guard. "We're here to see Mr. Mori."

"Oh my!" Cole drolly exclaimed, one hand quivering over his lips in mock surprise. "A policeman! I had no idea."

"This is Jackie Lyons."

"Michi-san's little photographer?" His teeth were too perfect, a façade of gleaming white caps behind paper-thin lips. "It seems I've heard of you, too."

"Isn't it marvelous how famous we all are?" I said.

"Don't you try to steal my lines."

"May we come in?" Adam asked.

"Of course." Cole stepped back and allowed the door to swing open. "Far be it from me to stand in the way of the police."

We entered and Cole closed the door behind us before continuing, "You'll have to excuse Michi-san. He's entertaining." He took another sip of his martini. A hard driving techno-beat thumped through the ceiling. "I'll see if I can drag him away from his guests. Y'all make yourselves comfortable in the parlor." He pointed to a small, dark room just off the hall, then sauntered away in none too great a hurry.

Adam wandered down the hall without removing his shoes. I stripped off my wet jacket and hung it on the hall tree, then kicked my shoes into the corner beside a wet pair of black high-top sneakers. The walls of the entry hall were grotesque, the trim and crown molding carved into phantasmagoric scenes of orgies between men and animals, the antique wallpaper dripping with scarlet and gold foil, every surface swirled and feathered and coraled. What the Romans called *horror vacui*—the fear of unadorned spaces.

I found Adam standing thunderstruck just inside the parlor door, staring at a hideous clutter of Victorian furnishings and glass curios. Shelf after shelf lined the walls, Lenox and Baccarat figurines sharing space with glass porpoises and seagulls picked up on the Mississippi Riviera. They seemed chosen with absolutely no sense of taste or even apparent consciousness of value.

"Nobody actually lives here, do they?" he asked.

"It's not all this bad. The kitchen's OK. I haven't seen the upstairs." I plopped down on the antique settle.

"I always thought my grandmother's house was a creep show. She collected those realistic, life-size porcelain dolls. But this . . ." He ran a hand over the top of his smooth, shiny brown head. "Whoever put this together, there's something not right with his head."

"I think all this belonged to his wife." I wasn't sure if it did, but sometimes when I visited I saw her sitting in here, polishing her nails. It seemed to be her room.

"Michi was married?" He sat on a Casanova loveseat across from me.

"He's a widower."

We waited in silence, looking at the carpet. I was struck, as always, by the smell of Michi's house. It smelled like money, piles of it, obscene wealth mixed with the spicy odor of ancient lacquer, damp bricks, musty fabric and desertous old carpets, grease and rot and dust and sex and death. *Behind every great fortune there is a crime,* somebody once said. It took me a minute to remember who.

Balzac.

The driving, thumping techno beat never let up the whole time we sat there. It reminded me of that Poe story, "The Fall of the House of Usher"—the ancient dying house rotting beneath the weight of the family's sins, its dark and secret heart bump-bump-bumping to the natural rhythm of a good hard rogering. It occurred to me then, but not for the first time, that Adam and I had never done it, never even made out at a Christmas party. It was strange. Although he was my junior by several years, he was good-looking and certainly desirable enough, but every time I thought about him that way, it gave me the heebs, like wanting to kiss your brother. He'd never shown any interest in me, either, never hit on me, never gave me any vibes at all.

"Sorry about tonight," I said.

He looked up from his wet brogans. "For what?"

"For stepping on your toes with the whole Christopher Marlowe thing. I wanted to say I'm sorry. I just blurted it out."

"You saved my ass from a major rug dance in front of the

chief. Just imagine if some reporter had made the connection instead of you." He was being very gracious, more gracious than I ever would have been in his position. Adam was the MPD's expert on the Playhouse Killer. His theater major from Rhodes College had come in handy when all the criminal-justice graduates were scratching their asses for answers. That jumped him in front of a bunch of more experienced detectives on the investigation. If he could break this case, he'd make captain. He knew it, I knew it, everybody knew it. What was more, he looked good on camera, so they had him on *This Morning Memphis* now and then to talk about the case, and after the last victim, they'd done a cover story on Adam in the *Memphis Flyer*. There was talk of a national news television show doing a special with him. They were hoping to get a Playhouse Killer episode, but our boy never obliged their shooting schedule.

"You're a better person than me," I said as I stood up. I couldn't sit still.

"We already knew that."

I was no longer a passive observer in this investigation. I was part of it now—a witness. For the last four years I had been photographing the Playhouse Killer's crime scenes. I had photographed his first victim before we knew we had a serial killer. Adam got me the gig when I was literally as low as I could get, and he'd broken any number of rules—personal and professional—to do it. At the time, I hadn't worked in months and was almost to the point of hooking for dope money. He got my Canon out of hock at the pawn shop. I still hadn't paid him back for that, four years later. He'd never asked. One more person I owed, one more person I could never repay.

4

ALMOST FIVE HOURS EARLIER, I had pulled up to the curb in front of Michi-san's house and parked under the same dripping sycamore trees. I had known Michi for nearly fifteen years and had been mooching money off him for the last three. If it hadn't been for Michi's generous employment, I don't know if I'd still be around to pollute the earth. He was a sugar daddy who demanded no sugar, daddy to dozens of human derelicts just like me. He had given me the money for the Leica in the first place, but that was before I had been obliged to pay first and last month's rent on a new apartment. I needed more money and I knew just how to get it. So I was a leech, but I had learned a long time ago how to live with that.

I leaned over the backseat of my Nissan and dug through the garbage on the floorboard until I found a plastic grocery bag full of dried-up Kleenex. I rolled down the window and shook the bag out in the rain, and then wrapped it around the camera. The leather camera case alone was worth three hundred dollars and it didn't even belong to me yet. I had to show the Leica to Michi-san if I wanted to get more money. I tucked a thin manila folder under my windbreaker, climbed out and had to slam the rusty door twice to get it shut.

The wide lawn was gray and the house hidden by veils of rain. A couple of cars were parked in the driveway—a white Saab and an old baby-blue Camaro with a faded rainbow apple sticker peeling from the back window. As I ran up the drive through the rain, the house slowly resolved from the mists, a looming pile of rock and timbers, with high mansard roofs steepled by dripping gothic ironwork, beetling windows and a forest of stone chimneys. A broad Italianate porch, deep as a cave, wrapped around the front and north sides of the house. I cut across the yard, splashing through deep puddles that soaked me to the knees, and hurried up the steps.

All the porch furniture was shrouded with white oilcloth, even the tables. Dead ferns hung in plastic flowerpots from the rafters, quietly dripping. A glass ashtray swimming with cigarette soup sat on the porch rail beside the steps. I thumbed the softly glowing doorbell. The door opened while it was still ringing.

"I'm here to see Michi Mori," I said to the young black man who answered it. He looked about twenty, boyishly thin with narrow hips, long wrists and curly black hair that he shook out of his brown eyes when he smiled. His smile glowed and his lips were dark, like an Ethiopian. I had never seen him here before, but he seemed perfectly at home, greeting me at the door in his gym shorts, white socks and naked chest. He looked like a catalog model for boys' underwear, and in less than five hours, he would be dead.

"Come on in," he said. I stepped into the entry hall and onto a thick rubber mat. "You'd better take off your shoes. You can hang your coat up here."

I set the Leica and the manila folder on a table behind the door, then shrugged out of my dripping jacket. "This weather is ruining the floors," he said.

"Sorry," I said.

"I'll see if I can find him." He left, singing "Michi-san!" all the way down the hall. I sat on the edge of a Rococo Revival slipper chair and peeled off my wet socks. The hall tree opposite the chair had five pairs of men's shoes of various sizes tucked neatly underneath it, and three umbrellas hanging from the coat hooks, all dry. I draped my wet socks over the two remaining hooks.

"She didn't tell me her name," the young man said as he returned.

A second voice, reedy and slightly nasal like an oboe, whined, "You let a *strange-ah* into my *hay-youse*?" The owner of that voice tottered around the corner behind his young companion, leaning heavily on a bone-white cane. He was short, round as a boule, with a flat bald head like a rotting pumpkin.

"Oh good lord, child, it's only Jackie," Michi said when he saw me. He stopped and put his hand against the wall to rest. "I thought you said she was a *strange-ah*."

"I never said she was a stranger, Michi-san. I only said I didn't know who she was." He turned aside and pounded up a curving staircase, taking the stairs two at a time.

Michi waved his cane at me. "Come on in my kitchen, honey. I got *thangs* on the stove," he said in his Hollywood version of a South Carolina accent. I took the squat little arm he held out to me and waited while he slowly pivoted around his cane. "Lord have mercy, you are soaked through. Do you think it will ever quit raining? My hip does act up in this *weath-ah*." He played up his accent because it was startling for people to hear a redneck voice coming out of his Japanese face. I didn't know why he still did it with me. He'd drop the accent when it became too much of a burden.

Michi's grandfather had been a taro root farmer in Hawaii

before the war. Michi was only six when his family was moved to the Japanese internment camp in Jerome, Arkansas. After the war, they couldn't afford to move back, they couldn't even afford a train ticket to California, so his father moved them to Greenville, Mississippi, and took the first job he could get—sharecropping cotton for the camp commandant. Most of the local sharecroppers had moved away or joined the army during the war. So Michi grew up speaking Mississippi Delta English. He spoke almost no Japanese because his father insisted his children assimilate and become "real" Americans. Kowtowing to their cracker overlords probably kept them from being destroyed; postwar Mississippi was no place to raise a Japanese family.

The kitchen was recently remodeled and modernized with new stainless-steel appliances, a Viking stove, and white marble countertops imported from Italy. Michi had the builders knock out a wall and construct a big bay window that looked out on the garden and elm forest in his backyard. There wasn't much to see there now, just steel-gray columns of rain. I liked the old kitchen better. It looked like my grandmother's kitchen. Now you could film a cooking show in Michi's kitchen.

Michi pointed me to a chair while he turned up the volume on something hugely operatic playing on his Bose stereo. I sat at the Skovby kitchen table in a chair by Marie-Christine Dorner. Michi always let you know the lineage of his purchases. I pushed the Sunday paper aside to make room for my camera and folder. Michi picked up a large white coffee cup and a cigarette that he'd left burning on the edge of the marble counter. "Shush!" he said as the music pounded toward its finale.

The soothing voice of a public radio announcer came in at the end: "That was 'Nessun Dorma,' from the opera *Turandot*, by Giacomo Puccini, with Jussi Björling, directed by Erich

Leinsdorf." Michi touched a finger to his lips and the announcer continued, "Classical Afternoons are made possible by a generous grant from the Michi Mori Foundation." He smiled and turned down the volume. He paid a lot of money to hear his name over the radio.

He toddled over to his stove, where an eight-quart stockpot quietly steamed and a large iron skillet hissed with onions and celery. "I'm gettin' my *conebread* dressin' ready for Thanksgiving," he said in his exaggerated drawl. He pulled back a chair and sat across from me at the table. "For my family, such as they *ah*. Most of them have nowhere else to eat turkey."

"Isn't it a little early to be cooking Thanksgiving?" I opened the camera case and snapped his picture, the smoke of his cigarette caressing his wizened face. If he ever wrote a book, this photo would go on the back cover. He looked like a merry old Buddha, his sagging pectorals like an old woman's breasts. His silk pajama bottoms and glittering red curly toe slippers, his coffee cup and his perpetual cigarette were as much a part of his left hand as his fat little sausage fingers, and his white skull-headed cane a bony extension of his right arm.

Not that he would ever write a book, unless it was a cookbook, or a dirty book filled with pictures of naked French children.

"You're trying to flatter me, Jackie," he said after a moment. "You got a new camera. May I?" He set aside his cane, took the camera from me and squinted at his picture on the LCD screen on the back.

"It's a Leica."

"And you prefer this to film?" He frowned at his photograph, then set the camera on the table. "God, I look like an old *wrastler*. Do you remember Tojo Yamamoto?"

"Wasn't he an admiral?"

"He used to *wrastle* here in Memphis." He took a long crackling drag on his Winston and squinted one eye against the smoke. "Being Japanese, he usually played the heel. But you should have seen him karate-choppin' all them big sweaty young men—Jerry Lawler, Austin Idol." He sighed and closed both eyes. "Wildfire Tommy Rich."

He took another drag and left the cigarette wedged in the corner of his lip. "Kamala the Ugandan Giant. You wouldn't think I'd care a switch about such lowbrow trash, would you?" He glanced at the manila folder lying on the table between us. "I had me a front-row seat at the Mid-South Coliseum. Season ticket. I was there the night Jerry Lawler broke Andy Kaufman's neck with a pile driver—April 5, 1982. Do you remember Andy Kaufman?"

"Sure," I said. "He was on that show."

"*Taxi.* That was before he started *wrastling* women. It was theater, of course, but what the *hale* did we care? It got your heart to pumping so you wanted to smash somebody with a folding chair. What's in the folder?"

"Some pictures I thought you might like." I removed the rubber band and pushed it across the table to him.

Michi looked at it briefly, then stood up and hobbled to his stove. He picked up a spoon and stirred the skillet. "You look like shit, Jacqueline," he said. I could always count on Michi for this. He wasn't cruel, just honest, like a child who will tell you your breath stinks while they hug your neck.

"I'm OK. All I need is a shower."

"You can use one of mine." He stubbed his cigarette out in an ashtray beside the stove. "I got half a dozen. I got some I ain't seen in five years." He pinched another smoke from a pack beside the ashtray and held it to the blue gas flame until the end caught fire. He blew out the flame and took a long drag and held the smoke in his lungs for a moment.

"I got a new apartment today. I'll be OK."

"Where at?"

"Summer Avenue."

"Is it safe?"

"As safe as anywhere. Nowhere is safe in this city."

He limped slowly back to the table and took my hand. His hand was fat and soft and dry as a pincushion. He squeezed my fingers affectionately. "Let me see your pictures." He opened the manila folder. I took his cigarette and stuck it in my mouth, tasting the coffee residue from his lips. "Oh my," he said, leaning closer to the first photograph. "Honey, this *is* different."

The photo on top was a glossy 8x10 blowup of the remains of Roger and Loeb Simon—high-school brothers who were found three years prior in the ruins of the Warren Academy auditorium. The boys were curled up side by side in a claw-foot iron bathtub. The outside of the tub was charred, but the white enamel inside was only slightly browned. They were naked and partially submerged in their own liquefied fat, like sheep boiled in butter.

"Is this . . . ?"

I nodded. "Playhouse Killer. Victims two and three."

"I didn't know you worked that case." He lifted the first photo and reverently set it aside, revealing the same gruesome scene shot from a slightly different angle. "Why didn't you tell me?"

"They're still open investigations. If the department found out I showed these to anyone, much less sold prints . . ." I inhaled a lung full of Michi's Winston. My grandfather had smoked Winstons. He drank so much coffee and smoked so many cigarettes that his dentures would turn their soak water brown as tea. I had a cousin who said you could catch a buzz drinking it.

It wasn't easy letting these pictures go. As much I hated anything to do with the Playhouse Killer, I hated the idea of profitting by his work even more. I walked to the fridge, opened the massive stainless-steel door, stood in front of the cavernous shelves with the cold flowing out around my naked feet like a ghost. "You got any beer?"

"In the door." He lifted the third grisly photograph and tilted it into the light. I found a Heineken and twisted off the cap. "Do you have more of these?" he asked.

I swallowed and shook my head no at first, then shrugged. "I have pictures from all the murders."

Michi set the photos down and turned in his chair to look at me. "God dammit, you're no different than any of my other little sycophants. You profit by my eccentricities, yet you withhold your best from me. You know I'll buy every picture you bring me, yet you keep these . . ." He turned and reverently touched the four photographs with his outspread fingers. ". . . *masterpieces* of the genre to yourself."

I had been supporting myself over the last four years by selling accident and suicide photos to Michi, catering to his death fetish, but selling these photos was a new low for me.

"I'm taking a huge risk even coming here," I said, suppressing a belch.

"And I pay you well for your risk." He thumped his cane on the floor. "You know I love you, Jacqueline, but why don't you do something positive with your life, instead of sticking every dollar you earn into your arm?"

"I'm not a user," I said.

"Really?" Michi exclaimed. "Yesterday I bought three

thousand dollars' worth of pictures from you, yet here you
come back today in the pouring down rain to sell me some
more. What did you do with it all?"

"You sound like my mother."

The young black man who'd let me into the house entered
the kitchen, suddenly and unannounced. He was dressed in a
loud yellow sports coat and check slacks. He opened the fridge
and fished out a bottle of Evian.

"Where are you off to?" Michi asked him.

"Out," he said as he glanced at his watch.

"With who?"

"Whom with?" The young man twitched a moist lock of
hair from his eye. "If I told you, you'd only have a stroke, Michi-
san." He opened the bottle, took a swig, winked at me and left.
His was a friendly secret smile, shared between us parasites. It
was scary to think that somebody can be that close to death
and not know it, not sense it somehow.

Michi frowned after the boy. "I'm getting old. I can't recall
his name. Chris something, I think. So many boys come through
my house these days, I don't even meet half of them. But I
don't complain because they would just go somewhere else."

"I'm buying the Leica," I said. The boy was already gone
from my mind. I passed the strap over my head and let the
camera's weight rest between my breasts. "This is one of the finest cameras in the world, used by the best photographers, pro-
fessionals like William Eggleston and Huger Foote. I already
paid three thousand for it, but I need another five hundred. A
new Leica would cost twice that."

Michi laid his cigarette on the edge of the table. "Good for
you, honey!" he said. "I always hoped you'd take your art seriously. You're a remarkable photographer. You're wasting yourself with these . . ." He waved his fat hand over the grisly photos

spread across the table. ". . . *things*, though by all means you should continue taking them. They do pay the bills. But if you'll put together a portfolio, I'd love to help you out. I know all the wine-sippers and cheese-nibblers in this shitty town. I can make things happen for you, if you're willing to do the work."

"I appreciate everything you do for me, Michi-san."

"Of course, you'll have to clean yourself up first."

"I already told you, I'm not a user."

"I don't mean that. I mean do something with you—*your-self.* Buy some decent clothes, get your hair done. You're still a good-looking woman. Take advantage of that."

"I'd rather make it on talent."

"Wouldn't we all?" Michi laughed. "But that ain't the way the world works and you know it, honey. God gave you looks, so why waste them? You got to use it while you got it. You won't always got it, and then you'll wish you did." He stubbed his cigarette out and scooped up the four photographs.

"I'll think about it," I said. I stood up, ready to get away from his vinegary smell and the screech of his voice, the nagging and the guilt trips and the fake sincerity. Michi was rich and spent his money freely, giving it away to artistic friends to whom he clung like a tick, growing fat on their creative energy, pulling them back with promises of more money whenever they tried to escape.

Leaving was always the hardest. I hated to ask for the money, but Michi wouldn't let it go until you pried him loose. He always wanted to hang on to you for another minute, to squeeze that last penny out of the soul you sold him. I tossed the empty beer bottle in the trash and bummed a smoke out of Michi's pack. As I stooped to light it off the stove, a shadow passed the kitchen door. I heard footsteps hurrying up a nearby set of stairs. "Who was that?"

"My daughter's son," Michi said.

Michi had a grandson named Noboyuki Endo. I had only seen him once—when he was a gangly, sullen fourteen-year-old boy with thick eyebrows that almost met over his nose. His parents were dead and he had been living with Michi since he was four. He was placed in state custody when I arrested Michi on child-pornography charges. I had always assumed he remained in foster care. "How old is he now?"

"Almost twenty-eight. His birthday is Friday. You're invited to the party, of course." The bitterness in Michi's voice surprised me almost as much as the fact that he had never once mentioned Endo in all the times I'd been here.

"Does he still live with you?"

"No, thank God." He lit another cigarette and looked out the window at the rain. "That boy is the reason I have to walk with a cane."

"I didn't know that."

"After I was acquitted, the state tried to give him back to me. I told them I didn't want the little bastard, but they insisted. He was listening around the corner, like he always does. So one evening dear Endo pours a bottle of olive oil all over the bathroom floor while I'm taking a shower. A good bottle, too, imported from Tuscany, a hundred and twenty bucks a pint. I could've killed the little shit."

"What happened?"

"Oh, I laid on the floor a couple of hours until one of my house guests found me." He sighed a cloud of cigarette smoke and shrugged. "I can't blame Endo. I've never been much of a grandfather to him, but we're the only family either one of us has got."

5

S O THIS CHRIS KID WAS dead and I had seen him alive,
maybe one of the last people to see him before he was murdered by the Playhouse Killer. Six hundred thousand people
live in Memphis, over a million in the greater metropolitan
area. Memphis has the highest rate of violent crime in the
country, one of the highest murder rates, and for the last four
years I had photographed most of them—everything from
cheating wives to gangbangers killed Bonnie-and-Clyde-style
in their pimpmobiles. I don't know how many times I'd heard
people say, *I just saw so-and-so a couple of hours ago, I can't believe
she's dead.* Now I was saying the same words, over and over.
Adam was talking and I hadn't heard a thing he said.

"What?" I tried to catch the thread of his one-sided conversation.

"I said I always heard Michi was a perv."

"He is a perv."

"If he's helping you, he can't be all bad." He winked and
rose to his feet. Michi's nasally whale song preceded him
down the wall.

"But what do they want, Cole?"

"To talk to you."

"Did the neighbors complain again?"

"They're not in uniform. One's a detective, the other is your photographer."

They rounded the corner and Michi stopped, huffing in the doorway and leaning against the frame for support. Cole waited behind him, balancing a silver tray on his fingertips. A glass pitcher and four frosted martini glasses stood on the tray. Michi was dressed in a long formal black kimono with clusters of pink cherries embroidered on the sleeves. His face was flushed and damp, as though he had just washed it in scalding hot water.

"Jackie! What are you doing, bringing the police into my house?"

Cole slid past him and set the tray on the coffee table.

"We just need to ask you a few questions, Mr. Mori," Adam said.

"About what?" Cole asked. He poured four martinis into the glasses. "I'm Michi-san's legal counsel, by the way."

"I didn't know you were a lawyer."

"I'm not. But I've written enough lawyers to fake it. Besides, he needs me to hold his fat little hand." He passed a martini to Michi, who took it, tossed it back and set the empty glass on a side table in almost one motion. Cole offered the next one to Adam, but he declined. Cole passed it to me.

"Now. What's all this about?"

I glanced at Adam and he nodded that I should take over. I took a sip of the martini. It was a good one. "When I was here this afternoon, there was a black kid, about five-ten, thin-boned, curly hair. He answered the door." Michi and Cole looked at one another and Cole shrugged. "He came into the kitchen while you and I were talking, Michi. He said he was going out. You said his name was Chris something."

"Oh, him! Chris Hendricks. You remember Chris," Cole said to Michi. He turned back to Adam. "What's he done?"

"He's dead."

"Oh Jesus!" Michi shrieked and collapsed like a deflating accordion, nearly tipping out of his chair. Adam caught him before he spilled onto the floor. He helped him to the Casanova loveseat. Cole knelt beside him.

"How?" Michi gasped. "Where?"

"They found him at the Orpheum."

"Sweet Jesus." Cole patted Michi's face with a handkerchief. "Oh, sweet Jesus. Which play this time?"

"Nobody said this was a Playhouse Killer case," Adam said.

"Oh please!" Cole patted Michi's hand and looked at me. "Which play?"

"*Edward the Second*," I answered.

"He said he was going out with someone. Do you know who?" Adam asked.

Michi mumbled, "No. No, I don't. There's so many boys, I can't keep up with them. . . ."

Cole dipped his fingers into a martini and flicked gin in Michi's face. "You think somebody here did it? Is that why you're bothering us?"

"No, we're just . . ." I started to say before Michi piped up.

"These are good boys. Good boys!" He turned to Cole. "Oh my God, to think that monster took one of my *boizu*!" He removed a cigarette case from a pocket of his kimono and opened it, tremblingly removed a cigarette and touched it to his lips. His eyes, almost hidden in folds of fat, darted suspiciously around the room, then settled like roulette balls on me. He removed a hideous bronze cigarette lighter from his pocket and looked at it, then up at me. It was cast in the image of two naked prepubescent boys entwined in a carnal act.

Maybe it was the look on my face, or maybe it was the memory of the first time he and I met. His eyes narrowed even more than usual, his forehead collapsing into elephantine folds and ridges. "So *that's* why you're here," he whispered. I noticed a white gob stuck in one of his wrinkles. It looked like geisha makeup or cake icing. It stood out like a wart.

Adam said, "We're trying to trace the victim's movements. If anybody knows who he went out with, we need to talk to them."

"One of the *boizu* at the party might know," Cole said.

"I'll need to talk to everyone." Adam opened his notepad and took a pen from his pocket.

"Hold on there a minute, partner," Cole drawled. "You can't just go busting in, they'll think it's a vice raid. At least give them a minute to put some pants on."

"I don't want anybody bailing before I can question them."

"Nobody's going to bail on you, honey."

Cole departed. He still had his martini. Michi and I stared at one another across the curved divider of the Casanova, while Adam leaned in the doorway watching Cole down the hall. Michi clicked the lighter and touched the flame to the tip of the unlit cigarette still dangling from the corner of his frog-like mouth.

"May I?" I held out my hand to him. He laid the cigarette case across my palm. It was heavy, gold with ivory inlay—an antique, probably real elephant ivory. I opened it and removed a cigarette, lit it with Michi's dirty boy lighter, and inhaled the smoke. I took a sip of my martini. It was perfect, of course. I couldn't imagine a man like Cole Ritter mixing anything less than a perfect gin martini.

"You almost look glamorous, Jacqueline," Michi said as I blew jets of smoke through my nose. His words were friendly, conversational, but his voice was strained, venomous. "You do clean up well."

"Thanks." I wasn't sure what he was getting at. I tried the martini again. It was damned good gin. I couldn't place the brand. Something my father used to drink.

Michi continued, "You really don't belong in your generation. You and my wife would have made quite the pair back in '55, dressed to the nines with your hair done up and your heels, mink stoles from King Furs draped over your arms, leaning against the bar at the Peabody on a Saturday afternoon, smoking Turkish cigarettes and drinking Cosmos and then maybe going upstairs to Alice's private suite for an hour of hot fingerfucking before the picture show."

"Excuse me?" I almost dropped my cigarette. Michi clapped a chubby hand around my wrist and clutched it with a vicious passion. He surprised me with his strength. I tried but I couldn't pull free.

"How dare you bring the police into my house again!" he hissed. "After what you did to me . . ."

"Hey, pal!" Adam grabbed Michi by the back of the neck and pressed his chins against the loveseat divider. It was all he could do to get his fingers around Michi's rolls of fat. Michi let go of my arm, then shrugged off Adam's hand. He picked up the spare martini, but didn't drink it.

"I was just doing my job," I said. My wrist was sore now, but I wasn't about to let him know he'd hurt me.

"Doing your job!" Michi puffed furiously at his cigarette for a moment, not even smoking it, just burning it up as he stared holes into me. Finally, he took a long drag and stubbed the cigarette out in a crystal ashtray shaped like a skull face.

"I'll never forget the first time I saw you." He laughed through the smoke issuing from his toothless mouth. "In that god-awful red Kmart suit with those broad shoulders. And that mullet! Whatever were you thinking? I mistook you for a bull dyke. You hurt me with those handcuffs, you bitch."

"You deserved it," I said.

"That's right. I was going to make your career, wasn't I?" He seemed determined to dredge this shit up.

"You bought a book of kiddie porn."

"Photos of nude boys. *Art.* There is a difference, honey."

Cole had returned by then but he stopped just outside the door. I saw his martini hand go up as he took a drink. Michi shrugged. "In any case, the charges against me were dropped once my condition came out in the newspaper."

"Condition?" Adam asked.

"Michi's a eunuch."

"A what?" Adam's head whipped around in surprise. Cole finally made his entrance. He leaned against the doorjamb and winked at me. Michi frowned at Adam.

"I'm sorry. I had no idea," Adam said.

"Oh good lord, and you call yourself a cop?" Michi flicked his ashes into the ash tray. "Honey, you need to get out more. It's not like it's a state secret."

"Ask anybody working in the Style section at the newspaper," Cole added.

Michi continued, "In 1968 I was skinny-dipping in Maui with a certain male friend *who shall remain nameless*, when I stepped on a stingray. You're familiar with the species? That's what killed that Australian boy that used to be on television all the time. The ray's cruel barb unzipped my scrotum and spilled my gonads into the sea."

"Lost forever!" Cole cried histrionically.

"I never saw my wormy jewels again, alas. Food for fishes, I suppose." Michi stood and spread his arms wide, the huge embroidered sleeves of his kimono nearly draping to the floor. "From the bloody foam I arose, a naked Japanese Aphrodite, flush with her first period."

"Is he serious?" Adam asked me.

Michi returned to his seat and lit a new cigarette from the gold cigarette case. "Naturally at the time I didn't feel gloriously reborn. Frankly, it hurt like Christ on the cross. But I survived. That which does not kill us makes us stronger. Isn't that what the man says?"

Michi caught Adam staring at his crotch. "Would you like to see it?" he asked. He started to unwrap his kimono. Adam shook his head no. "Oh, come on. I'm not shy."

"I am," Adam said.

"Suit yourself. They didn't want to see at the trial, either. Because of my disability, so to speak, I couldn't possibly receive sexual gratification from looking at those pictures. When I threatened to drop my pants and show the court, the DA dropped the charges."

"I wrote that last line for him," Cole noted.

"You got lucky," I said. Michi wasn't fooling anybody. Politics won that trial, not justice. "The law doesn't care whether you've got testicles. You buy a book of kiddie porn, you go to jail. Unless you're rich or famous."

Michi puffed his cigarette and squinted through the smoke at me. "Lucky for me I am both. As I recall, your old photography professor testified as to the book's artistic merit. Not to mention the photographer's international reputation. But then again, he was more than just your former professor, wasn't he? Didn't you almost marry him?" He and Cole shared a laugh. Adam watched me from the corner of his eye. He looked like he didn't even know me. I had never told him any of this. "I heard he fled the church just before the wedding because

Arkansas state troopers were waiting in the parking lot to arrest him for bigamy." Michi laughed again, no longer angry, more like a grandmother recounting the exploits of some precocious grandchild. "Isn't that droll?"

"Very Tennessee Williams," Cole said.

Michi turned to me. "Your failure to brief the DA about your history with the star witness is what got you suspended, wasn't it? It was all downhill from there."

"And straight to the top for you, dear Michi-san," Cole added.

"All my life I wanted to be a luminary. I tried to marry into society. I couldn't buy my way in, not even with my wife's old cotton money. Honest to God I never expected I could *weird* my way in. People had always invited me to their parties because of my money. Write somebody a check and they'll let you sleep anywhere. But after the trial, I became *The Star* of Memphis society. I found out people liked me *because* of my little extravagances. I have Jackie to thank for that. That's why we're such good friends. That's why I always try to help her out. That's why I can't believe she brought the police into my house tonight, after all I have done for her, especially after her divorce. How is dear old Reed, by the way?"

"Fuck you for asking," I said. "Prick."

"Look," Adam interrupted. "We're not here to cause any trouble, Mr. Mori. We're just trying to find out if any of Chris's friends know who he was meeting tonight."

"I can tell you that," Cole said.

"You said you didn't know."

"I didn't know before. I know now."

"How?"

"Because I asked," Cole said.

"Jesus Christ," Adam swore. "I'll ask the questions, if you don't mind."

"Not at all. I just thought I'd save you the trouble. Half them boys won't even talk to you for fear you'll turn their lives into a public spectacle. Like Michi said, they're good boys. They'll talk to me." Cole touched Adam's arm. The old fag could lay the butter on thick when he wanted.

"All the same . . ." Adam began.

"Oh screw that. My word is as good as theirs. Better, and I'll testify to it if need be. Chris was supposed to be rehearsing tonight. He's playing Banquo in a production of that Scottish play at the Lou Hale Theatre. Or I should say *was playing*." Cole finished his martini and looked a little sad and tired around his Cherokee eyes.

"Which Scottish play?" I asked.

"*Macbeth*," Adam said.

"Oh, he is one of us, after all," Cole said to Michi.

"I told Kouyate he shouldn't stage that thing," Michi frowned.

"Why not?" I asked.

Adam answered for him. "Theater people have a lot of superstitions about *Macbeth*, including a fear of speaking his name or quoting lines from the play anywhere but on a stage."

"Bad things happen." Cole touched his nose conspiratorially. "Nothing good ever comes of a production of *Macbeth*." He gasped and clapped a hand over his mouth. "Excuse me. It's late and I really need a drink." He hurried away.

"We should probably talk to the manager at the Lou Hale," Adam said to me.

"You're not staying?" Michi asked.

"No, but I'll need a list of people who knew Chris."

"I'll have Cole arrange it." Michi followed us to the door, leaning heavily on his cane and breathing in wheezing gasps between puffs of his cigarette. I knew the extremity of his decrepitude was just a show for Adam's benefit. Maybe he was trying to make up for grabbing me. My wrist still hurt, the bastard.

Adam opened the door and stepped out on the porch. It had begun raining again. I paused. "One more thing," I said to Michi. "You're on the board of directors at the Lou Hale Theatre, aren't you?" I didn't know for sure, but it was a logical guess.

He flicked his cigarette past me into the rain. "So what? I'm on the board of damn near everything. Is that all?"

"That's all," Adam said. "For now."

"Well, goodbye then. Don't be a *strange-ah,*" Michi drawled. Adam started down the steps.

As I leaned close to give Michi a peck on his flabby cheek, just to show him we were still friends, I whispered in his ear, "You missed a drop, Michi-san." I pointed at the white blob still stuck in one of his forehead wrinkles. He touched it, paled, then flushed pink as a piglet and slammed the door in my face.

6

ADAM DELIVERED ME BACK TO the Orpheum and dropped me off at my car before somebody towed it away. A news van and a fire engine were still parked in front of the theater. Adam was going to be up all night working on the case.

I drove home in the pouring rain, thinking things over, and before I knew what I was doing, I found myself turning into the lot at my old apartment. Blue plastic sheeting covered the smashed-out windows, but the rain hadn't washed away the smudges of soot going up from the windows to the roof. This place was only the latest in a long string of personal disasters going back almost five years. The starting point was when I ruined my marriage and left my husband, Reed Lyons. I had a tendency to destroy everything I touched, nothing lasted once I got my claws into it, whether it was a career or a relationship or even something as innocent as a car or an apartment. That was my problem—I had a destructive genie, too much fiery yang. I couldn't help it. It wasn't anything I did. It just happened.

But it didn't *just happen*, I usually made it happen. I left the barn door open and the stove on and the cigarette burning. I cheated on my husband, shirked my responsibilities, slept with my bosses and hooked myself on pills and smack. For a while, the Police Department acted like they were interested in keeping me on the payroll, but they were only following the prescribed steps so the police union wouldn't get all up in their kitchen when they eventually fired me. So they sent me to talk to a counselor who asked me about my father and told me I harbored a morbid fear of success. Any time I seemed to be getting my life together, I'd do something stupid to bring it all crashing down again. Any time I got close to someone, I'd drive them away; Adam was the exception. God knows I'd done my best to run him off, but he didn't seem to care. Maybe he was just a stubborn ass. Maybe he felt like he had to save me. I didn't particularly want saving. What was it the man said?— Life is nasty, brutish and short.

After they rescued me from the fire, I ran into my landlord standing in the rainy parking lot looking up at the smoke and steam still pouring out of the broken windows. He said, "What the fuck, Jackie? Ain't no blackened catfish this time. I hope you got some goddamn insurance."

I didn't. He had insurance, he just didn't want the insurance company coming in and setting minimum standards for the people he rented to, to make him run credit checks and collect security deposits that half his clientele couldn't pass or pay, most of them Mexicans without Social Security numbers and living six or eight to a bedroom. His insurance company would triple his rates and price him right out of business. I knew I could use that against him. The smoke and water damage and the busted doors and windows added up to more than I owned in the world. So while he was talking to the fire chief, I took all I could salvage and split. He was going to have to sue me, provided he could find me.

Sitting in the parking lot, seeing my burned-out apartment

and thinking about how easily I could have died and the innocent people I might have taken with me, I suddenly wanted more than I had in a long time to push a big fat needle in my arm and be done with it, ride that magic carpet so far away I could never find my way home. Sayonara, you fucked-up old world, y'all are better off without me. Instead, I turned around and drove out of the apartment complex before the landlord spotted me sitting there feeling sorry for myself, mooning over my miserable life. He used to watch out the windows. He never caught a single burglar or car thief, but he always knew you were home when you were behind on your rent.

Money was going to be tight after tonight. I had probably ruined my relationship with Michi. Not that I particularly cared for him. I never was convinced the old perv wasn't a pedophile, no matter what the DA thought. I had busted Michi for buying a book of photos of nude boys. *Art*, they said, but what kind of art was that? If Michi wanted art, couldn't he find something that didn't skate along the edge of kiddie porn? And what about his *boizu*—those college-age young men who lived out of his house like gypsies and alley cats? He gave them money and a place to stay in exchange for their participation in his rites. Being physically incapable of engaging in a sexual act didn't stop him from entertaining the most profound sexual perversions. The least of these, to my knowledge, involved his infamous Monday-night bukkake parties with eleven young men dressed up in football uniforms. That's what we had interrupted tonight.

But Michi's *boizu* were adults, if only just, and they were willing participants, so who was I to judge them or, for that matter, him? They probably needed Michi's money as much as I needed it. I hated my need, but maybe they hated it, too. For several years now, Michi had been buying my photos of the dead. He always paid more for violent deaths. He paid best for suicides, especially hangings, and especially if they were still hanging. I don't know what he got out of it, but in some way I could almost understand—he had seen too much and hurt too much and now the only things he could feel through the numb calluses on his perverted heart would blast the eyes of any ordinary mortal. It wasn't sex. It was far deeper, darker, gone beyond simple fetishism or even carnal depravity, down to a place where the acts performed in the conjuring chambers of his seven-gabled house might actually summon The Devil Himself to watch and sing along. Or so I sometimes imagined. Honestly, I didn't know what he did, and I didn't want to know. But I needed his money just to keep my head above water, so I catered to his death fetish and sold him the graven images for his midnight sabbaths, even if it damned my soul.

It was all too easy to forget the people I had photographed, all the bodies and parts of bodies, the human wreckage of so many lives thrown away. I had become numb to them, except the Playhouse Killer victims. For most of the others, it was a job. I took the pictures and sold them to Chief Billet, to insurance companies, to people with lawsuits and personal injury lawyers, and to Michi Mori. Meanwhile, every drowned baby and every bloody smear on the road chipped away at me until almost nothing remained but a cold lizard brain, flicking its tongue and tasting an opportunity to make a buck. The money took the pain away for an hour or two. I couldn't stand to see a dead dog on the side of the road but it was nothing to shoot photographs of some bum cut in half on a train track, because I knew Michi would write me a fat check. But no matter how I tried to kill the horror—with drugs, sex, oblivion—it never went away.

They never went away, either, but sometimes they weren't so bad. Sometimes they were bad. Sometimes very bad. November never was a good month for me.

There was this thirteen-year-old girl who hung herself. I couldn't remember her name, not even if I wanted to. I had cut her name out of my memory with a heroin needle, but I couldn't forget her face. I couldn't forget her parents, who wanted a photo of their dead daughter to print on posters, because after the funeral they were traveling to Washington to demonstrate in front of the FDA who approved the antidepressant that had driven their baby girl to suicide. I still woke up nights thinking about those people and the enormity of their grief. They had sent their daughter to the doctor to help her, they had forced her to continue taking her meds even though she told them something was wrong and begged them to let her quit. They had killed her trying to save her from being a normal, dysfunctional teenager.

With the murder victims and the car crashes, a corpse was just an object to me. There was a purpose to my work then—to record the event, to provide evidence for the trial or the settlement. But that girl and her parents, furiously determined that her death should have some meaning, haunted me like no other. They lived on Central Avenue near the Pink Palace Museum, and I used to drive past their house on my way to Preston's office, where I sold most of my accident pictures. I would see her sometimes, standing in her yard beneath the elm tree where she hung herself. She wasn't looking at anything. I don't even know if she was real or just something left over from another time, like a photograph.

She wasn't the only one who still haunted me. There were others, plenty of others, some whose corpses I had photographed, others I had never seen before. And there were some I wanted to see again but never could. On bad days the bad ones would crowd around so, it got hard to tell people apart, who you could talk to and who you couldn't. I could photograph the dead all day long, because they're just meat, but I couldn't deal with the grief of the dead. They brought the grave near enough to see myself in it. It was too much. But without grief, you aren't human. That's what separates people from monsters.

Tonight, as I was driving home, Adam was headed to Whitehaven to tell Chris Hendricks's parents their son was dead. I didn't allow myself to imagine that scene. I didn't need to imagine it because I had lived it. Instead, I drove home to my new apartment and unlocked the door. It was a heavy, solid door with stout bolts and brass screws driven into real wood, not plywood, not some flimsy fifty-dollar piece of cardboard and glue that some crackhead could kick in. This building, old as it was, had good bones.

I unstrapped my cameras, hung up my jacket and peeled off my wet clothes. My socks were still soaked. There was an old steam radiator in one corner, no longer hooked up to steam but it made a good place to to dry my jeans. I was still hungry but what I really wanted was a fix.

I resisted. To take my mind off it, I downloaded the photos from the Orpheum and burned them to a CD. I didn't examine them except to make sure I wasn't sending crappy pictures to Chief Billet. While the CD was burning, I opened my last quart can of Tecate beer. I put the finished CD in a brown envelope, addressed it to Chief Billet and set it on the kitchen counter. It was too late to call a courier.

I plugged the Leica into my laptop and opened Photoshop to view the pictures, but the camera's brand-new memory card appeared empty. I unplugged the camera and checked the review feature. The photos were there. I plugged it back into my laptop and examined the memory card. The files were there, but my computer wasn't able to recognize the Leica image file format.

Luckily, I knew where I could get the right software. I had already planned to drop the camera off at Marks Camera Repair to make sure everything was working before I took full possession. Deiter Marks was one the best camera gurus in the country. His shop wasn't even open to the general public. He catered almost exclusively to professional photographers, numbering the top pros among his select clientele.

I shut down my computer, took a quick shower, checked the door and climbed into bed. I always slept commando. It was only a little after midnight—an early night for me. I lay in bed and watched the lights play across the ceiling and the brick wall, getting the feel of the place. It was my first night there.

My apartment was the largest of six in an old converted bakery on Summer Avenue, west of Highland. All the apartments were on the second floor, with four shop bays fronting the street below, including a launderette and a tae kwon do school. My place was above a mercado on the corner. It came furnished, two rooms plus a bathroom. A Formica dinette table with four cheap wooden chairs for a kitchen, a sagging couch divided the room into a den. Avocado-green electric stove, equally ancient fridge, a drawer full of old silverware and knives, including one butcher knife sharp enough to split a hare, wood-frame bed and a dresser. Bathroom not much bigger than a linen closet. There was a big bay window in the bedroom that faced the traffic light and the Methodist church across the street.

The industrial gothic interior of the apartment begged to be photographed, but what it really needed was a model to bring out its character. It needed someone sitting at the cheap dinette table or staring out the bedroom window, dressed in panties with a white tube top and her hair wrapped in a towel, cigarette smoke curling like a rough hand across her cheek as she listened to the sinoidal honking of some distant lovesick saxophone and the tearing silk sound of wet tires on wet pavement, while George Clooney narrated the depths of her loneliness and the hard ugly carapace of horn into which she retreated, nightly, to keep from tying a rope around the closet rod and kicking over the chair.

Sure.

The Leica sat on the dresser, its dark round camera eye pointed at me as I lay in bed. I remembered lying on another bed in another town and another time while my college photography professor took roll after roll of black-and-white nudes with his Leica MP. Only 402 MPs were ever made. Being photographed by an MP was like being painted by Raphael.

Raphael had lied about his divorce.

I couldn't sleep in a room with the door open. I got up and locked the door, then wished I'd remembered to buy cigarettes. It would have been nice to lie in bed and watch the smoke hang lazily in the Christmas greens and reds of the traffic light outside my window. I liked to smoke in bed. When I was in high school and my parents were out of town, I used to smoke in their bed and watch *The Tonight Show* and fall asleep with the television on because I didn't like being alone in our old house on Schoonover Street. I didn't like being alone pretty much anywhere.

But I was tired and I had gone two nights now without a fix and no withdrawals. It was a good sign. I rolled over and pulled the covers up to my chin and tried not to think about the dead.

I woke up about oh-dark-thirty with a woman sitting on the end of my bed. She had short, straight dark hair and no face above the lips. Her mouth was moving as though she was trying to say something but couldn't get the words out. I rolled over and sat up and there was nobody there.

I grabbed my brother's baseball bat from under the bed. The weather had changed again and it had stopped raining. The bedroom was cold and the window panes fogged over, tinted a solid sheet of red from the traffic light. The bedroom door was still locked and there was no closet for anybody to hide in, nothing but dust and my own empty suitcases under the bed.

I tried to remember what I had been dreaming before I woke up. The woman reminded me of someone. I thought maybe one of the neighbors, maybe the Korean lady I had seen downstairs in the mercado. I always had nightmares when I slept in a new bed. I told myself this was no different. It had to be something reasonable. I was used to my special friends hanging around, haunting dark corners and stairwells and old elevators, but when they sat on the end of the bed, that was different. Seeing three in one day was also a bad sign. All the really horrible parts of my life had started this way. Or maybe when I was counting down to self-destruct, I started seeing ghosts. That's what the police counselor told me.

I rolled over facing away from the window. I could almost feel her weight still there on the end of the bed, pressing down the sheets. I didn't think I would gonk because I was shaking with the cold, but I did, with the baseball bat beside me in the bed.

The next morning, the bedroom door stood wide open. My sneakers were sprawled like a dead animal on the floor, tied together by their shoestrings.

Tuesday

7

IT WAS ELEVEN O'CLOCK BEFORE I made it to Marks Camera. As usual, the door was locked so I knocked. On my way over, I bought a sausage biscuit at Mrs. Winner's. A light rain pattered on the hood of my jacket. While I waited, I ate my brunch. Sometimes it took a while for Deiter to answer his door. Sometimes you had to call and tell him you were outside because he would be out back dismantling some three-hundred-thousand-dollar lens for NASA and wouldn't hear it if a SWAT team kicked down his door. Finally, he opened it a crack and squinted out like he was afraid to get wet. I don't think he recognized me at first.

I shoved the uneaten half of my biscuit in his face. "Oh, you got the Leica!" He accepted my food offering and opened the door.

Deiter's place was a ranch-style house built around 1960 and converted, like all the other houses on his street, into retail or office space sometime in the late seventies. The front room of his shop looked like it had been recently burglarized, but it always looked like that, just as Deiter always looked like he had just crawled out of a hayloft. You half expected to see straw in his hair and sheep shit down the front of his paisley pajamas. He wore no pajama top and had tits bigger than mine, though his sagged like something out of a *National Geographic* magazine. He sported greasy blond hair and a bushy hay-colored Viking beard littered with enough yellow crumbs to reconstruct a whole Twinkie.

Once upon a time, his shop had been a dentist's office. Even with all the cameras and other equipment, I could still smell burning teeth and hear the whine of the drill. No other place in the world smells like a dentist's office.

Deiter lived in a single room off the back. The rest of the shop was given over to photography equipment, storage, computers and offices for his myriad other ventures. Sometimes you'd see police cars parked in front of his place, and sometimes you'd see other types of cars, mostly rentals, with men in dark suits and sunglasses sitting behind the wheel, whispering into their coat sleeves.

I followed him back to his workshop, which looked like a lawyer's office, except instead of stacks of filings and depositions and folders, there were piles of laundry and empty Doritos bags, as well as technical manuals and photography magazines. He was regularly published in most of the best ones. I noticed several had most of their pages ripped out. "I use them for toilet paper," he said.

"Why?"

"They are so full of shit. Sit down."

"Where?" Other than the chair behind his desk and a loveseat buried in garbage, there was nowhere to sit.

"OK, stand up. See if I care."

I passed the camera strap over my head and let him take it. "So, you got the M8," he said. He turned it over in his hands, swiftly examining it with his genius eye for detail, showing me a dent I hadn't noticed and a couple of tiny scratches I had. "How much did you pay?"

"Twenty-five."

"It's practically brand new. Is it stolen?"

"Not that I'm aware of."

"If you wanted a Leica, you should have asked me. I can get you a used R9 for that price and you could shoot digital or film. The R9's a good camera."

"What's wrong with the M8?"

"Have you looked at your pictures?" He opened a drawer and removed a USB cable and a package of powdered doughnuts.

"I couldn't open the files."

"That's the first problem with the M8. What software do you use?"

"I still have the Photoshop you gave me."

He shook his head. Crumbs drifted down his naked belly and into his lap. "Photoshop 5.5 is a focking dinosaur. The old versions can't convert Leica DNG files." He picked up a Power-book laptop from a pile of laundry on the floor and opened it on his desk, then plugged my camera into it. "Leica included a copy of Capture One LE in the box. The seller didn't give you the disk?"

"He probably didn't know about it."

"I'll give you a copy of the Adobe Lightroom." He opened the camera files and pulled up the first picture I had taken—a self-portrait shot in the parking lot at Best Buy right after I bought the new memory card. The image was strangely sur-real. My black T-shirt looked almost purple.

"There's your second problem," Deiter said.

"What's wrong with the color?"

"It's not the color, it's the light." He peeled the wrapper off the powdered doughnuts and shoved one into his mouth, then continued talking while he chewed. "The M8 is supersensitive to infrared. Deep blacks, especially dark fabrics, show up as magenta. Sometimes the whole image will have a magenta wash."

He cycled through the photos of my new apartment, the intersection outside my bedroom window, the gothic church across the street, and the photo I'd taken of Michi. Each one was tinted a sickening shade of purple, and with each picture he opened, I felt just a little more like I had swallowed a wasp. I began to think that the two grand I'd given James St. Michael had been spent on a one-way ticket out of town. I'd fallen for it because he looked like a pilot and acted interested in me even though I hadn't bathed, smelled like a fireman's boot, looked like a turd on a biscuit and was probably ten years older than the oldest woman he'd ever consider dating. And didn't he get nervous last night when he found out about my connection to the police?

I met James St. Michael the previous Sunday. I had been at the hospital taking photographs of an old lady whose back was eaten up with bedsores. I usually took pictures of the dead. This woman should have been dead, the way they treated her.

I recognized James when he walked through the door by the leather camera case slung over his shoulder. He was younger than I'd guessed from our phone conversation, late twenties to early thirties, wearing a University of Memphis ball cap, a blue jacket, new dark blue jeans and a pair of worn out Nikes with brand-new white shoelaces tied in double knots like a kindergartener. He slid onto the stool beside me and set the camera case on the bar. "Sorry I'm late," he said. "The rain."

"Jackie Lyons," I said. He shook my hand as though shaking a man's hand. He had a grip like a Norse god. There wasn't a ring on his finger, but there had been, not long ago.

"James St. Michael."

His name was so familiar it startled me. I sat there staring at him and holding his hand, trying to remember where I'd heard his name before, and now that I looked at him I thought I recognized him from somewhere, maybe from television, but I couldn't remember. I said, "With a name like that, you should be flying helicopters."

"I am a pilot," he laughed, surprised, but also a little nervous. He let go of my hand. "How did you know that?"

I didn't. It just went with his face. He looked like a pilot. "Squint lines around your eyes. Young face plus old eyes equals pilot."

"I didn't realize my eyes were old." They were blue, hard and clear as gems, but a little sad. He looked at himself in the mirror behind the bar, examining his face from different angles. He hadn't shaved.

"I didn't mean it that way," I said. "I mean you look like you spend a lot of time staring a long way off."

He turned on his stool and rested an elbow on the bar. "Now it's my turn." He rubbed his chin and looked at me. "I think you're aaaaaay . . . photographer."

I smiled despite myself. "How'd you guess?"

"Squint lines." He reached up and almost touched my right eye. "You look like you go through life with one eye shut."

I picked up my beer and held it to my lips without drinking. My breath fogged the glass. That was a pretty accurate description, I had to admit. This guy was some kind of philosopher.

"Or maybe it's because a person wanting to take vacation photos isn't about to drop three grand on a camera."

"Only if I like it." I sipped my beer.

"What's not to like?" He pulled the case closer and unsnapped it. I set my beer down and lifted the camera from its leather sheath, cupping it reverently in my palms like a splinter of the true cross. When I spotted the ad for a Leica M8 in the *Memphis Flyer*, I called the number immediately and offered to pay the asking price in cash, even though I couldn't nearly afford it. I'd asked James for a few days to get it together.

I still couldn't afford this camera. But now that I had cradled it like a newborn child in my hand, I couldn't let it go. It felt heavy and solid for its size, the black parts gleamed, the silver parts shone, and when I turned it on, the little LCD image on the back was as clear and crisp as the HD television picture above the bar.

I released the locking toggle to uncover the bottom. "There's no memory card," James said. "I didn't know that when I listed it in the paper. I'll knock fifty off the price for that." I nodded and removed the 50mm Leica lens and looked inside the camera body. It seemed to be in perfect condition. I replaced the lens and turned the camera on again, looked through the viewfinder, caught him checking out my tits.

I turned the camera off and set it on the bar. "I'm sorry. I really wish I could, but things have changed since we talked. I got kicked out of my apartment and I have to find a new place, so I can't afford to buy this, not even at your very generous asking price."

"What happened?" he asked.

"To what?"

"Your apartment."

I tucked a strand of dirty blond hair behind my left ear, wincing inwardly at how filthy it felt. "I set it on fire."

"Jesus," he smiled and covered his mouth with his hand.

"It was an accident. So, as much as I'd like to . . ."

"Twenty-five hundred," he said. "I know a guy who will give me twenty-five for her. If you can match that, she's yours."

"I don't know. . . ." I hadn't expected him to come down so easily. He must have been desperate. I was tempted to find out how much lower he would go.

"I'd rather sell her to you, anyway," he said with a shy smile.

So that was it.

I knew I could get the money from Michi, but I'd already gone to that well once too often lately. I looked through the camera again and knew I had to have it. I couldn't part with it now. "Can you wait until tomorrow?" I asked. He was definitely interested and it took every scrap of my remaining dignity not to lay it on sweet and thick and let him get ideas. He seemed like a nice enough guy. He was already willing to come down five hundred. I could have put my hand on his knee and talked him down another couple hundred, but I didn't want it that way. I liked him for some reason. "I'm pretty sure I can get you the full twenty-five if you give me until tomorrow. I know somebody who might buy some pictures."

He scoured his lightly stubbled chin with his palm. I watched him mentally calculate something, reject it, rethink it, recalculate. I picked up my beer and polished it off. The bartender started over, but I put my hand over the top of the glass.

"Do you have two right now?" he asked.

"Yeah. . . ." I wasn't about to buy a Leica M8 for two thousand. If he sold it for two, it was either ganked or busted. I might as well throw two grand off the Harahan Bridge.

"OK," he said. He set his hand flat on the bar and stared at it. He was nervous about something. I thought he must have stolen it and was now desperate to get rid of it. He seemed too nice to be a thief, but then again, what was a thief supposed to look like?

"How about you give me the two now," he said without looking at me, "and the other five hundred tomorrow night." He still didn't look at me.

"Tomorrow night?"

"We could have dinner, drinks, whatever."

Oh Jesus, I thought. "Whatever?"

"Anywhere you want to go. But I need at least two grand today." He looked at me finally. He was blushing. Christ. He was shy.

"You're asking me out?"

"I guess." Not looking at me again, his face pink. Morbidly shy.

"I'm married." I showed him my hand with the wedding ring.

"Oh." His blush deepened to a flaming Irish red. "I'm sorry. I didn't see . . . it." Morbidly shy and clueless. I liked him now more than ever. My mother always said I got my mean streak from my grandfather—the dentist. I let James dangle for a bit, slowly twisting on his bar stool like a worm on a hook. He started to pack the camera away. I hated to let it go. I'd never get another chance to buy a Leica at this price, but I wasn't about to trade myself for it. No matter how much I liked the guy.

He snapped the case shut, set it on the bar again, and looked at me, no longer blushing. "OK. If you can get me the other five tomorrow, you can keep her."

"Keep it?"

"Sure. Go ahead and take her with you." He pushed it toward me. "That's what car salesmen do, isn't it? Let you take her for a test drive, get used to the idea she's yours."

"Well . . . thanks." He was a salesman after all. He had me nailed. I dug the envelope with the two grand from my pocket and put it in his hand.

He tucked it away without even looking to see what was inside. He said, "Just don't forget where you got it."

"I won't." Smiling now. "I promise." I shook his hand again, warmly, and took the camera. What did I care if it was stolen? It was a Leica! I dropped a five on the bar and James followed me out into the parking lot.

He opened a big black umbrella just outside the door. The rain hammered on the taut fabric like a bucket full of marbles. "I'll call you tomorrow," he said.

I grabbed one of Deiter's doughnuts and crammed it in my mouth. He stopped on the first picture I'd taken of the cops onstage at the Orpheum. "What's this?" he asked. "Shit, this is from last night?"

I nodded and took another doughnut. He clicked through the photos. I couldn't stand to look at them anymore. "Christ. Two thousand bucks down the shitter."

"What are these?" He clicked through a series of eight or ten grainy purple images of nothing.

"No idea."

"Let's see." He converted one of the images to grayscale and everything changed. The darkness came alive with textures, tones and shades. It was a photo of the backstage area of the Orpheum, but I hadn't taken it on purpose. My finger must have touched the shutter between shots, maybe when I was running back to tell Adam that I recognized the victim.

"The M8 is easy to turn on by accident," he said as he clicked through the next few photos. "It's a known bug. You should always carry an extra battery."

"Great." One more fault to love about it.

"Don't be pissed, Jackie. The M8 is a damn good camera, and there are workarounds, plug-ins can fix the color problems. It's worth every pfennig you paid. Black-and-white and infra-red photography is where the M8 really stands out. It's superior to just about anything on the market." He tweaked the settings, bringing out even more detail in the otherwise empty scene. I leaned over his shoulder to watch him work his voodoo.

"That's incredible." In one photo there was a huge piece of castle scenery that I hadn't noticed even though I walked right past it.

"There's somebody standing back there," Deiter said. It was only a hint—an outline of a shoulder, an arm and part of a head, leaning out. I couldn't make out the face, but it wasn't one of the cops, I could tell. This person, whoever he was, was short, almost like a kid. It was difficult to judge his height for sure. It might have been another piece of scenery, some cardboard-cutout figure, but my gut told me differently. There had been somebody hiding backstage the whole time.

"Can you pull out any more detail?" I asked.

Deiter shrugged. "Maybe. It'll take time. I'm too busy today. Maybe tomorrow or Friday."

"It's important, OK?"

"Sure. You think maybe he's the killer?"

"Maybe." Wishing, hoping to God I should be so lucky.

"It could be a ghost," he said.

I laughed, but he was deadly serious. "Do you believe in ghosts, Deiter?"

"Of course. The Orpheum has lots of ghosts. Look at this." He opened a file on his computer and pulled up an image named Orpheum_ghost_girl. It was a picture of a blob of light hanging over one of the balcony seats. "That's Mary, seat C-5, the most famous Orpheum ghost. This is the only known photo of her. I took it myself with a Hasselblad 503CW mounted with an Imacon digital camera back."

To me, it looked like a flash reflecting off a speck of dust in the air. But in the background I could see the Exit sign where I had seen the girl standing last night.

"Of course, it's only an orb, not a full-body apparition," Deiter continued. "You have to be careful with orbs. Most of the time they're just bits of dust, but I've analyzed this photo every possible way and there is no physical explanation for it." He opened a drawer, tossed me a black baseball cap. The letters GMPI were printed in white block letters on the front of the cap.

"Grant-Marks Paranormal Investigations. That's why I'm so busy right now. We're doing a tour Friday night at Magnolia Manor out in Bolivar, then we're headed over to the old mental hospital. You want to come? You could bring your Leica."

"I had no idea you were into this kind of thing."

"Yah, it is important work. You can keep the cap."

"Maybe you could check out my place sometime." I don't know why I said it. Just making conversation.

"Do you have a ghost, Jackie?"

So I told him about the faceless woman on my bed, but I failed to mention my other special friends. Crazy as he was, I didn't want him to think I was crazy, too.

"A full-body apparition!" he sighed. "That's damn cool. And it's a rare haunting, maybe one in a thousand where you get a spirit actually interacting with the environment, unlocking doors, tying knots. I'd love to see her. Maybe we can come over tonight?"

"I don't know. I mean, it's not like *Ghostbusters*, is it?"

"No, nothing like that," he laughed.

"Because I'm at a good place in my life. I don't want anybody bringing Ouija boards or conducting séances or anything like that." I had enough problems in that department without a bunch of freaks stirring my personal pot of demons.

"We're scientists, Jackie, not mediums. We'll take pictures, maybe some digital video with infrared, EVPs, check for EM fields, temperature fluctuations, that sort of thing." He unplugged my Leica and showed me how to mount the infrared filter, then gave me a copy of Adobe Lightroom. He didn't charge me for any of it.

"So, what do you say?"

"I'll think about it," I said.

He walked me to the door. "One more thing. If the seller wasn't a pro, I doubt he knew about the infrared problems with the Leica. He wasn't trying to rip you off."

"Thanks, Deiter." Maybe he was right. I hoped so, anyway. I liked James and didn't want to write him off as a thief.

I ran through the rain to my car. Deiter stood in the doorway in his ratty pajama bottoms and watched me drive away.

8

AFTER I LEFT DEITER'S, I got a call from Preston
Park to photograph a wreck on I-240 involving a tractor-
trailer and a motorcycle. The biker earlied-out beneath the
trailer, doing an estimated buck-twenty. There wasn't much left
of him above the zipper except a big red dent on the trailer's
back door. His mother called Preston Park wanting to sue the
truck driver, the trucking company, the city of Memphis and
maybe God Himself for making it rain. The scene was jacked
up on epic scale, traffic jammed for eight miles, car after car
full of Adam Henrys trolling for a look at the corpse folded up
under the truck axle. It was enough to make you hate people on
principle, but I was happy not to see the motorcyclist anywhere.
He hadn't hung around and I was starting to think God had let
this cup pass from me.

The rain was coming down in a gray veil and the air was
steadily getting colder. I took about two dozen pictures of the
accident. The job only paid fifty bucks, but it wasn't just for that
fifty bucks, it was for every fifty bucks to come after. Besides,
Preston was a friend and a decent man, something you wouldn't
expect from a personal-injury lawyer. He passed on more cases
than he took, and he wouldn't take a case unless it was clear his

client was a victim and not some leech trying to get paid for a hangnail. Some lawyers I wouldn't cross the street for, not if they were giving out diamond nose rings.

As I sat at the corner intersection waiting to turn in to his office parking lot, I spotted James St. Michael coming out of Preston's office with a black banker's umbrella under his arm. He got into a silver Lexus, backed out and drove away before the light changed. I honked but he didn't hear me.

I found Preston sitting behind his desk in his dinky office. His receptionist was also his wife, a gorgeous blonde of Cuban descent named Leta. She waved me through while drying her nails and babbling into a telephone crooked against the side of her face. Preston greeted me at the door, pulling me into his office with his gentle hands. I was soaked to the bone and shivering. He coaxed me into a warm, clean leather chair near the heater.

"How have you been, Jackie?" he asked as he sat. There was one file on his desk, about five inches thick, wrapped with a rubber band. "Have you eaten?"

"I had a bag of Fritos," I said.

"We were just about to order lunch from Central Barbecue. Would you like a sandwich?"

"Thanks, no." I took a disk of photos from my back pocket and slid it across his desk. When I was out on an insurance job, I usually took my laptop with me so I could burn the disk and save my employer the cost of a courier.

"I think I'll save this until after lunch," he said.

"Good idea. It's a mess."

"That's a shame. His poor mother."

"Can you do me a favor?"

"Sure." He folded his hands on the desk and waited while I

wrestled a wad of papers from my jacket. "That's my divorce. Could you take a look at it before I sign it?"

"Of course." He took the divorce papers, unfolded them and carefully spread them out. "Finally ready to cut loose?" he asked.

"Something like that."

While he bent over the papers and gave his meticulous attention to every word, I wandered back out to the reception area. The rain was really coming down now, so hard I could barely see the cars passing on the street outside. Leta Park was just hanging up the telephone. "Do you think it will ever quit raining?" she asked with a pretty shiver. She was gorgeous, statuesque, with a head full of honey-blond hair that tumbled halfway down her back. Three children had only improved her figure. They were beautiful kids, their pictures hanging on the wall behind her desk between a pair of palmettos. Leta shaded Preston by at least twelve inches, but she looked even taller, towering over men and women alike with the withering radiative power of her sexual kung fu. People said that when Leta crossed her legs, Jesus wept. She was on the cover of at least one local society magazine every year.

"Was that James St. Michael I saw leaving here a few minutes ago?" I asked. She nodded. "What's his case?"

She leaned forward, her blouse falling open and half exposing her tremendous boobs. "You know I can't talk about another client," she whispered. "Preston would keel me!"

"I won't tell." I winked, just between us girls, but she shook her head no. "Well, what can you tell me?"

"So you know James?"

"I'm buying a camera from him."

"Yes, it is so terribly sad, isn't it? And he is so young and handsome."

Before I could ask what she meant, Preston stepped out with my divorce papers neatly paper-clipped and tucked away inside a clean new manila folder. His familiar smile was gone. "Have you read these?" he said so sternly it surprised me. He sounded like my father on the few occasions when he actually tried to be a father.

I said, "Of course."

"I can't advise you to sign this."

"Why not?"

"*Why not?* You realize you get nothing."

"I know."

"No alimony. No part of his estate. Nothing."

"I don't want anything from Reed," I said.

"He is worth several millions," Preston said.

"Oh Jackie!" Leta gasped. "You can't!"

"You could set yourself up nicely," Preston said. "Are you sure you want to give that up?"

"I don't need the hassle." I took the folder from him and he shrugged. Leta clucked her tongue as she counted out the money for the motorcycle pictures, fifty dollars in cash. I took the bills and stuck them in my back pocket, then pulled Deiter's GMPI cap tight over my eyes.

"You're a fool, Jackie Lyons," Leta said as I opened the door. I didn't need her to tell me that.

9

BY THE TIME I MADE it home, it was doing a little bit of everything outside—sleet, rain, even a little snow swirling, none of it sticking, not even to my windshield. Other drivers on the roads had lost their minds. I passed half a dozen accidents just in the four miles between Preston's office and my apartment, but I didn't stop to shoot any of them. Instead of going straight upstairs, I headed for the mercado to buy some food and sinus pills.

It was always the same short Hispanic guy standing behind the counter. He had never once looked me in the eyes. He had a dark round Mesoamerican face with almost no trace of European in it, a face you might see looking sideways at you from the wall of a pyramid. I grabbed a shopping basket and rolled to the coolers in back, loaded up with four quarts of Tecate beer, and a twelve-pack of Diet Coke. I grabbed some limes, a block of queso blanco and a pack of fresh tortillas. The sinus pills were behind the bulletproof glass at the cash register.

By the time I made it to the front of the store, our landlord, Walter Pinch, was leaning against the counter. "Afternoon, Miss Jackie," he almost sang. He shook my hand with his moist, bony one, then unloaded my basket, setting everything on the counter.

Walter Pinch was a black man no bigger than a twelve-year-old boy. He dressed like a COGIC preacher in a black three-piece Italian suit, red silk tie and red handkerchief sticking three inches up from his top pocket, half a pound of gold on his bony knuckles and a diamond as big as a split pea in his grill. He used hair straighteners and walked on his toes like he was walking onto a stage.

This close to him, I could smell the gin on his breath. I instantly grokked his plight—a straight gin man with a mickey in the back pocket, never got drunk, just a nip now and then until the end of the day when the pint was empty and his liver was another day harder with the sclerosis that would ultimately lay him dick-up in the earth. I liked him the first time I met him, when he rented me the apartment and offered to carry up my stuff, weak and feeble as he was.

He introduced me to the man behind the counter. "This here is Jackie Lyons. She's taken the apartment upstairs," Walter said. "Jackie, this here is Nachos."

"Happy to meet you," Nachos said. He finally looked at me and smiled.

"She just moved in," Walter continued. "This is Nachos's store. He's been here about six years now, ain't it?"

He nodded and said, "*Siete*."

"Nachos is good folk. You need anything, Nachos has got it. If he ain't got it, he'll get it."

"That's good to know," I said. "You look like you're having yourself a fine day, Mr. Pinch."

"Every day is a fine day, Miss Jackie. Life is too short to have shitty days."

"Sometimes life gives you shitty days."

"That's true enough," Walter agreed. "All the more reason not to make shitty ones yourself." He squeezed my arm as he staggered by, headed toward the beer coolers at the back. Nachos rang up my stuff.

"So what's your real name?" I asked him.

"Mynor."

"Is this your place?"

"I'm just the manager. I started out sweeping floors here, now I still sweep floors, but I'm the manager. The owner lives in Singapore. So you live upstairs?" I nodded. "The music, is it too loud?"

"It's OK," I said. I barely even noticed the Tejano music anymore.

"I can turn it down. My wife listens to it."

"I don't mind." He seemed to like that I didn't mind. He smiled as he rang up my beer. He had perhaps the worst set of teeth I'd ever seen in my life. He looked like someone had dipped his teeth in acid and stuck them back into his face to rot.

"Where are you from?"

"Arizona," he said. "But my parents are from Guatemala."

Walter returned from the back with a quart of Miller Genuine High-Life tucked under his scarecrow arm. "By God, you do clean up nice, Miss Jackie," he said, sucking his diamond tooth and looking me up and down. He edged up beside me and breathed some gin fumes my way. "I honest to God thought sure enough you was a junkie." He touched my arm just above the elbow. "But God damn if you ain't looking fine today."

"You rent to junkies, Mr. Pinch?"

"When they pay cash money," he said. "Beggars can't be choosers, I always say. What you say, Nachos?"

"She is very pretty," Mynor said without looking at me. He bagged each quart of Tecate in its own brown paper sack, as though I were going to drink them outside on the curb. "A little skinny." He shrugged apologetically.

"Shit, I like skinny women. You could've pushed my ex-wife through a keyhole, God rest her soul." Walter screwed off the top of his quart bottle and took a swig, looking at me with one eye closed, then sat heavily in an old split-cane chair in the corner by the door. It looked like it had been placed there just for his use. "I like your hat. What's GMPI? Is that the police?"

I gave Mynor two of my tens. "You've been here seven years?" He nodded and handed me my change. "You ever see any ghosts?"

"No, but we get a lot of shoplifters."

"You seen a ghost, Miss Jackie?" Walter asked.

"I don't know. Maybe."

"I lived in that apartment near eight years, I never saw nothing," he said. He looked like he was scared I might ask for my money back.

"You ever have trouble with that bedroom door coming open by itself, Mr. Pinch?"

"No, but I kept it open most times. Living all by myself, you know," he said. His rheumy yellow eyes narrowed and he leaned forward in his chair. "But this ain't the first time. You seen one before, ain't you?" He leaned the chair back against the wall and put his hand on the pocket where he kept that bottle of gin. "Was you born with a caul over your face?"

"A what?"

"A caul. A veil over your head. My granny always said a child born with a veil can see the dead."

"It's true," Mynor said. "My mother says it's also a sign of good luck, and that you won't die from drowning. She was born with a veil." He slid my bags across the counter but I didn't pick them up. What Mynor said had given me a chill. Back in my rescue training days in the Coast Guard, the instructors used to call me "unsinkable." I wasn't the biggest or the strongest, and I sure as hell wasn't the best swimmer, but every time it looked like I was about to go under for the last time, I'd pop back up and keep going. That's the only reason I graduated from that course.

"That's just crazy, Nachos. A woman with a caul ain't got no good luck. It just means she haunted," Walter said. He took another swig of Miller like he needed it in the worst way, then wiped his mouth with his handkerchief. "I had an auntie born with a veil—dead folk coming round drove her so crazy she hung herself in a closet. Left three babies my mama had to take care of."

"My mother never said anything about a caul," I said. I took my bags. I didn't want to talk about it. It had been my experience that talking about my special friends sometimes made them appear. I hadn't said my grandfather's name aloud in twenty years.

"Me, I got no truck with the dead," Walter said to the air above his head. He downed another slug of beer and wiped his mouth on the sleeve of his pinstriped suit. "I knowed a down-low man was staying in a Holiday Inn in Jackson Missippi one night about 1976 when a ghost comes in his room and tells him to get the fuck out, nigger. Just like that—get the fuck out, nigger. He say the man had on a Confederate uniform, so he thought it was the Klan. Time he jumped out of bed, weren't nothing there but a smell he say he ain't never smelled but once, and he wouldn't say where."

"What did he do?" Mynor asked.

"Got the hell out! Slept in his car the rest of the night. Said it was the best night of sleep he ever got." I nodded to them and left. As the door shut behind me, Walter said, "He's dead now. The AIDS got him 'bout five year ago."

I awoke some time in the night shivering in bed, thinking that the heat was broken. I sat up and saw a cloud of smoke seeping under the closed bedroom door. I threw back the covers and stood up in bed. It didn't look like normal smoke, the kind of smoke that might have come from a fire I had set by accident again. It was too white and it pooled like water in front of the door instead of spreading out or rising up.

Sometimes I had nightmares. Not normal nightmares. That's why I locked my door at night. I told myself to wake up. I whacked my forearm against the brick wall beside my bed. It hurt like hell and it didn't wake me up. I didn't really expect it to.

The pool of smoke grew into a pale white column that so-lidified into the shape of a woman. She had no face, just a mouth, as though she was wearing a veil over her eyes. She turned and opened the door and floated into the kitchen. I stood on the bed, my shivering shaking the whole bed.

When she didn't return, I slipped to the floor and tiptoed to the door, but the kitchen was dark and the den empty. Rain slid in sheets down the bay window behind me. It looked like the glass was melting. I could almost believe it was a dream, if not for the open door. I tried to convince myself that I was dreaming again or that it was the heroin purging from my sys-tem, but I didn't believe my excuses any more this time than I had last night or any of the other times. She hadn't even used the key to unlock the door, this ghostly figment of a dream, this undigested bit of queso. Apparently she didn't like me closing my bedroom door.

I returned to bed and pulled the covers up. I took the Leica with me this time, rested it on my stomach and waited to see if the woman would reappear. I waited maybe an hour. Hard to say how long I lasted before I gonked. But the next morning, I woke up in almost the same position, the camera lying beside me in the bed, my sneakers sprawled in the middle of the floor with the shoestrings knotted together again.

I called Deiter. He answered on the first ring.

"What time can you be here?"

Wednesday

10

THREE GUYS SAT AROUND MY kitchen table playing with their toys. It was early, a couple of minutes after 6 p.m., and the rain was coming down harder than ever, rattling like fingers across the bay window in the bedroom. Deiter's GMPI ball cap was turned around backward on his hayrick of hair. It was the first time I'd seen him in any anything but pajamas. He checked the battery charge on a Panasonic RR-DR60 digital audio recorder.

Next to Deiter sat a guy about my age, square-faced like a book, with short dark hair and a toothy smile. He wore a black GMPI shirt that clung like cellophane to his muscles. He had forearms like a gorilla and hands big enough to palm a sixteen-pound bowling ball. There were two pieces of equipment in front of him—a Sony NightShot digital infrared camcorder and a K-11 Safe Range EMF meter. His name was Grant. He and Deiter founded Grant-Marks Paranormal Investigators about ten years ago.

"Anybody want a beer?" I looked at my dwindling cache. My last remaining quart of Tecate wasn't nearly enough for three grown men.

"We don't drink alcohol during an investigation," said

Trey, the third guy at my table. He was about twenty-two, five-ten, a shade over 140 pounds, dressed in dirty overalls and a pair of rubber hip waders folded down to his knees. He had just gotten off work locating buried cables—he was the Call Before You Dig man. His investigative equipment consisted of a pair of brass rods housed in an old flute case. His left cheek stuck out like he had a golf ball in his mouth.

"Sometimes we drink plenty after we're done," Deiter laughed.

"What happens first?" I asked.

Deiter nodded at Grant and turned on the digital camcorder. Grant said, "First thing we do is make a sweep of the area with the EMF reader." He turned on his machine and began moving slowly around the room, stopping at each point where the meter registered a change. "I'm getting a small increase near the stove," he said. "And the refrigerator. They're both ancient, so there's nothing unusual about that. Point one, point two, not enough to notice."

"Not enough to notice what?"

"A strong EMF field can sometimes generate the sensation of being watched, or feelings of fear or anxiety."

"I've never felt uncomfortable here," I said.

I took a picture of Grant coming out of the bathroom with his EMF meter. He passed me on his way into the bedroom, then stopped and scanned me with the meter.

"Do you have a cell phone?" he asked.

"Yeah."

"Turn it off." I did.

He finished his sweep of the bedroom and returned to the kitchen. Deiter set a Sharp MD-SR60 MiniDisc audio recorder at the center of the table, then set his EMF meter next to it. Grant stood by the refrigerator and started filming. I recounted everything I had experienced since moving into the apartment. When I was finished, Grant turned off the lights.

"Now we introduce ourselves." Deiter raised his voice slightly. "I am now addressing any spirits or entities who may be present. My name is Deiter Marks. Also present is Grant Lauderdale, Trey Monroe, and Jackie Lyons. We are not here to harm or frighten you. We only want to find out if anyone is here, who you are, and if you are willing to talk to us."

Trey waited and listened, but nothing happened. "Can you knock on something, like this?" He rapped on the table with his knuckles three times. All I heard was the Tejano music downstairs.

"If you are here, we would really like to get to know you better," Deiter spoke into the darkness. One whole side of his face and beard was green from the traffic light outside. He looked like a Viking berserk. "Can you make the lights on our meter flash?"

The EMF meter remained dark.

"I only ever saw anything late at night," I said in a low voice. "One or two o'clock in the morning."

"Sometimes it takes a while for them to get comfortable enough with us to make themselves known. We should just be quiet and listen." We listened for about two minutes to the Tejano music, the quiet roar of the rain on the roof and the peeling of tires on the wet pavement. I learned that the faucet in the shower had a slow drip and that the floors creaked like a wooden sailing ship whenever the heat came on. Deiter's belly muttered like an old man talking to himself. Grant filmed the whole thing, all nothing of it, as patiently and quietly as my father stalking a bass on Lake Charles back home. Trey chewed his tobacco with the regularity and monotony of a ticking clock. I never saw him spit.

"Maybe Trey should do his thing now," Deiter suggested.

Trey opened his case and took out a pair of brass rods. The rods were shaped like the letter L. He picked one up in each hand, holding the short leg of the L loosely in his fist, with his arms about chest height and his hands out like he was holding a steering wheel. The rods swayed randomly side to side. "Y'all gimme some room here," he said.

The rest of us backed away from him. Trey walked slowly around the table one time, then stopped. The rods in his hands swung together, making an X, then swung apart again. "They ain't nothing here," he said.

"Try the bedroom," Deiter said.

Trey walked into the bedroom and came back out again, stopping just outside the bedroom door. The rods were perfectly still in his hands. He turned slowly in a circle, shuffling his feet in tiny steps like an old man, and as he came back around the rods moved together as though magnetized. He followed the direction where they pointed, stopping every second step, until he was standing right in front of me. The tips of the rods were touching together, about two inches from my left tit.

"It's her."

"What's that mean?" I asked.

"It's you."

"What's me?"

"Your ghost," he said.

I looked at Deiter. He shrugged and asked, "Have you ever experienced any poltergeist activity? Things flying off shelves? Banging doors? Lights turning on or off? Unexplained fires?"

"No," I said before I even thought about it. Nothing like that had ever happened, except for the fire a few days ago. Adam had told me it started with a candle in the bathroom and I had no reason not to believe him. I didn't remember leaving a candle burning, but I barely remembered anything about that night up until the moment a fireman flopped me over his shoulder.

I said, "Just what I told you before. There was a woman sitting on my bed. The next night, she came in under the door, then opened the door and went out."

"Where are your shoes?" Trey asked.

"I'm wearing them."

"Take one off and put it in the middle of the floor." I did. He held his rods over them for a minute and nothing happened, but when he turned away, the rods swung around and pointed at me again. "It's definitely her."

"I don't understand."

"It's something about you." Trey laid the brass rods in his flute case. "I don't know what. I don't interpret. I just go where the rods point."

They packed up their stuff. I followed them into the hall and closed and locked the door behind me.

Mrs. Kim down the hall stuck her head out for a second, then disappeared without saying anything. She looked like she was expecting somebody.

11

M RS. MYNOR WAS IN THE back cooking and there
was a fine, spicy fried smell. Trey was standing by the
phone-card advertisements with a greasy paper plate piled high
with empanadas, quietly and methodically chewing. Mynor was
talking in bubbling Spanish to a short, round woman with two
short, round children clutching her skirts and eyeing Trey as
though he'd just stepped off the mothership from Zambodia.

Walter Pinch sat in his split-cane chair by the door. He
stood up as I came in and swayed on his feet. He smelled like a
wrecked gin truck. "Mrs. Jackie Lyons," he slurred, and leaned
toward me so I had to catch him. I set him back in his chair,
trying to avoid his groping hands. There was a quart bottle in a
paper bag by the wall next to his foot. Walter was an old-school
drunk, a man who walked himself home no matter how drunk
he was and who called any business that sold wine a liquor store.
I liked him. Lonely as he was, he seemed to have come to a place
of quiet peace I had never known. He wasn't drinking to kill
anything. He drank because he liked it.

"Whose yo friends?" he said slowly, his neck already half
rubber. I introduced them as ghost hunters and Walter shook
their hands politely without standing up. "What you doin',

Jackie Lyons?" Walter asked when they had gone. "Don't you be stirring up no ghost shit. Not in my building."

"They're not stirring anything up, Mr. Pinch."

"What they here for, then?"

"They just want to see if I have a ghost."

"See? See how?"

"They have cameras and meters and stuff. Trey is a dowser."

"A dowser? What's he dowse for?"

Trey was close enough to hear us. "Spirits," he said. "Spiritual residues, energy—dark and light, gates and portals between this world and the hereafter. But y'all ain't got nothin' to worry about. That apartment has ugly memories, but there ain't no spirits, except what this lady brung with her."

"You ever dowse for water?" Walter asked.

Trey nodded. "Water. Lost shit. Whatever you want."

"I had an uncle used to dowse with a stick." Despite the differences in their skin color and upbringing and just about everything else, Walter and Trey were kin. They shared the same folk mythologies. "Once he found a mason jar full of silver dollars somebody had buried and forgot. Maybe you can do me a favor," he said to Trey. He leaned forward and shifted his weight to his feet, then slowly straightened up. "My tenants say the elevator in this building is haunted. Maybe you can check it out."

"Sure."

"I can't pay you."

"That's OK." Trey picked up his flute case and took Walter's arm, and the two of them headed out the front door like old friends. Deiter and I hurried after them, which wasn't hard to do. Walter's top speed was a Parkinson's shuffle. We caught up before they were past the tae kwon do school. The bay between the school and the Laundromat was empty and dark,

the windows dusty with a For Rent sign, a female child mannequin leaning its bald head against one window as though
trying to see down the street.

Nobody was in the Laundromat, but one of the dryers was
running, tube socks and underwear curling around and falling
down like an endless ocean breaker trapped in a magic bottle.
Walter led us to the back, into a narrow, L-shaped hall. The elevator was at the end of the long leg of the L, the tenants' private laundry room was at the end of the short leg, where a bare
light bulb hung from a wire over an old coin-operated washer.
The elevator had an accordion cage door, lacquered wood, Chi-
nese silk-screened panels and a worn brass lever that made the
thing go up and down. It was also claustrophobically tiny and
creepy as a coffin. Whoever put it in this building had strange
ideas.

Walter pulled back the elevator's accordion door and Trey
entered with his divining rods. "You need to keep back," he
said to me. "I can already feel the rods trying to pull to you. I
can't get an honest read."

I smoked a cigarette outside by the front door. The rain mixed
with sleet and snow was coming down hard just at the edge of
the curb, and the cars driving by threw up fans of water from
the swollen gutters. The smoke felt good going down, scratching that old itch that never goes away. I thought about Adam,
somewhere out there in the city, maybe standing in the same
rain, trying to chase down his own ghosts. Sure enough, my
phone rang.

"Hey Jack," he said. He sounded like he had just woken up,
or maybe not slept at all. Times like these I was glad I was no

longer a cop, no matter how poor I might be. I liked being able to sleep regular hours. Regular for me, anyway. He said, "I talked to the director of that Scottish play at the Lou Hale. The vic didn't make rehearsals Monday."

"Maybe he had a date with the killer."

"Or maybe the killer got to him before his date, or after his date. If he even had a date and wasn't lying to Michi. We're canvassing the usual places just in case, see if anybody saw him."

"Anything else?"

"Chief Billet got your photos. He said to thank you."

"He can thank me by paying me." A bus bucketed by, sheeting water onto the sidewalk. "How'd it go last night?"

"You mean the parents?"

"Yeah."

"They said their son wasn't gay." That didn't surprise me, but the bitterness in Adam's voice did. The world is full of parents who can't admit their kids are gay. "They said they sent him to a Christian camp run by Reverend T. Roy Howard to have the demon of homosexuality exorcised from his soul through SSA therapy. They said he was cured and had a girlfriend from Abuja."

"Don't tell me you believe them."

"Doesn't matter I think. They believed it." He yawned into the phone.

"Have you been to bed yet?"

"I think I slept an hour this morning. I can't wrap my head around this killer, Jackie. The body, the pipe, the mattress—everything was clean, no fingerprints, no physical evidence at all, nothing, nada. He's getting better at this and we're still just treading water."

I didn't tell Adam about the backstage photos Deiter found

on my Leica. I wanted Deiter to pull out more detail before I said anything, just in case it turned out to be nothing. I didn't want to get Adam's hopes up. "Wiley's working fast this time, running that evidence. It's not like him to share his results so quick."

"Director Boykin's riding everybody's ass." A car passed slowly, rap music vibrating the trunk so deep the rain danced on the surface. "The media is crawling all over the place. Why do you think I haven't slept?"

I told him to get some sleep and let him get back to his work. I don't know why he called. He didn't even harass me about going to NA. I hadn't even got the phone back in my pocket before it rang again. I never used to be this popular.

"Hi," I said to James. "I have your money."

"Fantastic. I'm at the airport," he answered. "I'm headed down to Biloxi to pick up an Embraer Ipanema." I heard a door open onto the sound of a passing bus.

"Isn't that a song?"

"It's a Brazilian airplane—a type of crop duster. It runs on alcohol."

"So you're a crop duster pilot."

"Yeah. For the time being."

"Isn't crop-dusting a little dangerous?"

"Only if you get careless. Listen, this job just came up. I'm running behind and I've got to catch a flight. I'll be out of town for a couple of days. I was wondering if you have family in town." He didn't wait for me to answer. "Because I don't have any family here and I thought if you weren't doing anything, we could have Thanksgiving dinner together after I get back."

I couldn't tell if he was asking me over to his place for Thanksgiving, or if he expected me to cook for him. When I didn't answer, he said, "Of course, the only place that'll be open is Cracker Barrel."

"Cracker Barrel is fine." He made it easy to say yes.

"Fantastic!" he said. That was two fantastics in one phone call. He was nervous about something, but I didn't know what. I hoped it was just me. "I'll call you when I get back Thursday."

I gave him my address and told him to pick me up at six o'clock.

"I'm about to go through security so I have to hang up."

So hang up. Instead, I said, "Have a safe flight."

"Thanks. Bye." He finally hung up. I tried to picture James's face. Mostly, I remembered how young he looked. He didn't sound young on the phone. I felt a little guilty about being so attracted to him. But only a little.

I found Trey and Deiter digging through a garbage can at the back of the Laundromat, spreading garbage on the floor while Grant filmed them. Walter was leaning against a dryer with his mouth hanging open. As I came in, Trey looked up and pointed for me to stay at the door, as though I had a communicable disease.

"What's up?"

"They is something in the garbage," Trey said.

"What is it?"

"Garbage. Hell if I know."

"Them little sticks crossed over the top of the can," Walter said, looking spooked. He rubbed his mouth with the back of one hand while he reached for his back pocket with the other.

"Y'all stand back." Trey waved his divining wands over the spread of garbage, pacing a circle around it. His circle became an oval that narrowed with each pass, until finally the rods crossed and stuck, as though drawn together by magnets. Deiter stooped under them and picked up a crumpled fast-food bag. Grant pushed the camera in while he opened it.

Deiter looked up and said, "I don't get it." He tipped the bag over and a cell phone slid out.

"Y'all gonna clean this shit up now, right?" Walter said.

12

D EITER LOOKED DEEPLY AND EARNESTLY into my eyes. "Ghost hunting is not an exact science. Sometimes you get a hit and sometimes you don't. Just because we didn't see anything tonight doesn't mean there's nothing there. I just want you to know I believe you."

"I appreciate that," I said.

"And if you experience anything else, you can call me, night or day."

I shook his big, warm hand. "I will."

"If you see anything, try to get a picture with your Leica."

"And you call me if you find anything on those Orpheum images."

After dawdling around the hall and offering several more apologies, he dragged his flip-flops out the door. I closed and locked it, then turned and looked at the room. It still smelled like Trey's chewing tobacco and Deiter's Viking barn funk. I could also smell the faint, sweet reek of garbage, like a fairground on a summer day.

I got the last quart of beer out of the fridge, sat down and turned on the television. I didn't have cable, but a Vincent Price movie, *Theater of Blood*, was still in the DVD player. I listened to the movie without really watching, distracted by the cell phone they had found in the trash. The cell-phone battery was dead. I had the same brand of phone, so I plugged it in to let it charge.

Trey said the phone didn't have anything to do with Walter's haunted elevator. There was something else about it that had drawn his divining rods, but he couldn't say what. I got the feeling he didn't like me much. I jammed his frequencies. I did that to lots of people.

When the movie was over, I turned the phone on to see what I could find out about the owner. The photos indicated a woman. The phone was full of pictures of women at parties and bars, your standard self-portait with your friends. One seemed familiar to me for some reason, but I couldn't put a name with her face—a gorgeous, photogenic blonde. The person consistently holding the phone was a young, pretty brunette, so I guessed it had belonged to her. She had probably thrown the phone away with her lunch.

I checked the last number she called and pressed Redial. After three rings, a woman answered, no hello, just a hostile "Who is this?"

"I found this phone. I'm just trying to contact the owner."

"Jenny, somebody found your phone," the voice said. Music played in the background, something by John Hiatt, and women talking loudly over the din of a crowded bar.

After a few seconds, another woman took over. "Hey, you found my phone!" She had to shout over the noise.

"In a Laundromat on Summer." I didn't try to explain how I found it.

She said, "Somebody stole my purse from a party last night."

"I didn't see your purse. All I found was the phone. Sorry."

"That's OK. I canceled all my credit cards but I was going to call the cell-phone company tomorrow. I'm glad you found it."

"I can call the cops, if you want me to," I said.

"I'd rather just get my stuff back, especially my pictures. Where are you?"

I didn't want her coming over to my place. One look at this dump and she'd think I was setting her up to rob her. "I can meet you."

I needed to splice the mainbrace anyway, so I agreed to meet her at Bosco's.

Bosco's was a brew pub off Madison in Overton Square. The Square was Memphis's seventies-era attempt at re-creating Bourbon Street without all the junkies and whores. The Square had once been the center of Memphis nightlife, before Beale Street was pulled up out of its dilapidation and forced to earn a profit. After that, the party shifted downtown, leaving Overton Square struggling to survive, but there were still a few places around to get drunk and maybe pick up a decent meal. Bosco's had a good restaurant, not your typical bar and grill, and their beer was brewed on the premises. I had only been there once, with Reed, back when I had a life and more than two dollars in my pocket.

My last quart of Tecate was dying to come out. I skipped the bar and was headed straight for the ladies' can when Jenny spotted me and called me over. I don't know how she picked me out of that crowd. Maybe I looked as pathetic as I sounded on the phone. She and her friends were sitting in a deep booth big enough for eight people at a squeeze. They had two big artichoke-and-eggplant pizzas, a bunch of empty beer and margarita glasses cluttering up the table, and no sign of a man, except the ones sitting with their backs to the bar trying to get the four ladies' attention. The place was noisy and beery without being obnoxious, but best of all there were no families, no shrieking children, just a lot of people wanting to get laid on a Wednesday night. With the Thanksgiving holiday coming up, it was practically Friday night for people with regular jobs. For those of us without jobs, it was always Friday night.

Jenny and her posse were older than I thought they'd be. Jenny looked early thirties, brunette, with a thin healthy face pretty enough to make me look like a junkie. She was wearing a tangerine-colored silk blouse that probably cost more than my rent. She waved me over to their table and after asking my name again, introduced me to her friends. I forgot their names as soon as I heard them. They didn't appear to notice me long enough to hear my name, so we were even. There were two redheads, probably sisters, and a brunette with blond highlights and a nose like a pug. She reminded me of a girl I had once tried to drown.

My original plan was to deliver her phone, but Jenny invited me to sit down. The booth was big enough for us to sit at one end and almost be alone. Her friends spent most of their time whining about how stupid everybody was at work. I remembered why I didn't have any girl friends.

"Where did you find it again?" she asked.

This time I told her about the garbage. "I live above the store at the other end of the building." She wrinkled her razor-thin nose as she took it. Her nose was the worst thing about her face. She didn't ask what I was doing digging through the garbage in a Laundromat. She was a little drunk, but then again I was a bit one-eyed myself.

A waiter came by. Before I could say anything, Jenny ordered a drink for me. "It's the least I can do. I have a lot of important pictures in here. I've been meaning to move them to my computer, but you know how it is."

I nodded and lit a cigarette.

"I'm sorry ma'am, you can't smoke in here," the waiter said before he left.

I dropped it on the floor under the table and stubbed it out with my foot. It was my last cigarette, a good time to quit again.

"You want to know something weird?" she asked.

I nodded.

"I kind of knew it would turn up. I think that's why I didn't call my cell-phone company. I know it sounds crazy, but I'm actually kind of psychic, you know? God!" She brushed her hand through her hair and glanced at her friends. "They think I'm nuts."

They would. "Maybe we're both nuts," I laughed. What the hell, I finally told her the whole story about my evening with Grant-Marks Paranormal Investigation and how I had come to find her phone in the trash can in a Laundromat. I don't know why I told her everything about it, even the ghostly woman in my bedroom. Maybe she was an agony aunt—one of those people who put off that vibe that says, hey, dump your problems in my lap.

"That is so weird," she said when I was finished. At least she didn't ask me to leave. "I wonder what it means."

"I don't think it means anything at all. It's just a coincidence."

"I don't think so." She nervously tapped the edge of her empty glass with her wedding ring. "It has to mean something. It's like we were meant to meet each other."

"Do you think so?" As fascinating as this was, my bladder could wait no longer. I smiled and excused myself to visit the head.

13

I HAD TO WAIT FOR a stall. The ladies' room was full of tipsy ladies enjoying a communal piss. Somebody was having a birthday party. At least the facilities were clean and my Kegel muscles strong enough to hold back the flood while they chatted and texted, oblivious to my urgency. I looked at myself in the mirror while I waited, measuring myself against the other women. Except for my thrift-store clothes and my heroin pallor, not one of these darlings had a thing on me. Several obviously envied my svelte form. Honey, it took six years on the junk to achieve this famine-victim body. I was going to have to watch my weight again, now that I was off the stuff. I didn't have the money for a new wardrobe, though a pound or two, here and there, wouldn't have killed me.

Finally a toilet cleared. As I sat, I listened to the asthmatic wheeze of the bathroom door as the last girl departed and I was finally, thankfully alone.

My phone rang. I didn't really want to talk to my mother while sitting on a public toilet, and I didn't have to answer to know she wanted me to come home for Thanksgiving. No matter how many years I avoided her calls and made promises that

I didn't keep, she always called the Wednesday before Thanksgiving to tell me what she was cooking and how much she was looking forward to having me home, trying to pretend that I had already promised to be there. It never worked, but she always tried.

I knew I'd have to call her eventually. At least this time I had a good excuse for going AWOL.

I was just finishing up when I noticed a pair of men's black high-top Reeboks beneath the stall door. I looked up to see a man's eye pasted to the crack, the blackest eye I had ever seen. His skin was a dark reddish-brown. He looked Hispanic. I hadn't heard the bathroom door open, hadn't heard footsteps, but I was fairly certain he wasn't one of my special friends. I could smell his breath—minty, like he had just brushed. My heart was thumping. I didn't know what he was going to do, but I wasn't about to wait for him to try. I pulled up my jeans and yanked the door open without even bothering to zip, but he was already gone. Again, not even the sound of the door opening.

I headed back into the bar, scanning the crowd as I worked my way to Jenny's table. This wasn't the first time somebody had peeked at me in a public restroom, but it was the first time a man had followed me into the john to watch me pee. I was so wired on adrenaline, everybody in the room looked like a suspect. There were dozens of men with dark hair and skin, and they all seemed to be staring at me, smiling like wolves, fucking me with their eyes, but none as black and flat and cold as the eye I'd seen, an eye with nothing behind it, no life, no humanity—a mannequin's eye.

It must have shown on my face because when I sat down Jenny asked, "What happened? Are you OK?"

"Some guy followed me into the bathroom."

Her friends heard that. Now they were all ears, my sympathy sisters, sliding down the benches toward us. "Oh my God!" one of the redheads said. "What did he do?"

"Nothing. Just watched."

"Get the manager!" another said.

"Fuck that! Call the cops," the third shrieked.

"I can't give a full description. All I saw was about this much of his face." I demonstrated the gap in the door by pinching it with my fingers. I used to be a cop, and like they say in all the cop shows we're specially trained in the techniques of observation. Of course, that's bullshit designed to give our testimony more weight in court. A cop is as vulnerable to mistakes as anybody else, and sometimes more so, as any cop who's been on the job for very long carries a gorilla of prejudices. If the only tool in your shed is a sledgehammer, every problem looks like a watermelon.

I tried to play the whole thing hopeless, but I knew if I saw him again I would recognize the bastard. After that, plans got fuzzy.

"That's just too creepy," the brunette said. "Especially after what happened to Ashley. I wish we didn't have to do this here."

"Well I'm not staying," one of the girls complained. "Let's go to Newby's."

"Not until we've had our toast," Jenny said. Our drinks had arrived while I was in the toilet. She lifted her glass and nodded at my beer. "Join us?"

"Sure." I picked up my glass. They raised theirs, and for the moment, I was one of them, though I didn't know why.

"To Ashley," Jenny toasted.

We drank in silence and left our glasses on the table. The

ladies were strangely somber. As I stood up to let the others out, I asked Jenny, "Who is Ashley?"

"An old friend . . ." but before she could finish, a passing waiter bumped her into me and I sat back in the booth to keep from falling. The waiter apologized, but I barely heard him. I had spotted a pair of black Reeboks moving through the crowd of feet near the bar. I shoved the waiter out of the way, but I couldn't see my guy, just his shoes, and only then in flashes through people's legs. He must have been the shortest guy in the room, and he was heading for the door in a big damn hurry.

"What's wrong?" Jenny asked, tagging along behind me. She grabbed my hand and wouldn't let go. It wasn't easy plunging through the crowd dragging her behind.

"It's *him*." I jerked free.

On the sidewalk outside, I saw a short, dark-haired man split off from a group of umbrellas and disappear around the corner of the building. I ran after him, acutely aware that I had no weapon, no backup, and no options if he was armed. However, he was smaller than me, and as long as I was able to get the drop on him, I was fairly confident I could take him, even if he had a gun. The trick was not letting him know he was being followed. I slowed up as I reached the corner, then walked casually by and glanced between the buildings. Bosco's had a large deck on that side, but because of the weather it was closed up, the table umbrellas folded and the chairs stacked upside down. I didn't see my stalker in the alley or on the deck, but I spotted a dark head moving between the cars in the parking lot behind.

"Jackie!" Jenny called out behind me. She was just coming out the door with her friends. I waved at her to shut up and dove down the alley, running low, splashing through the puddles.

My bathroom buddy wasn't easy to follow. I wasn't sure if he was aware of me, but he seemed nervous and kept looking over his shoulder, forcing me to duck and wait for him to move on.

Finally he stopped by a silver Mercedes. I was running with a radar lock on the back of his head. The noise of cars leaving the parking lot helped cover the sound of my footsteps, but at the last second I splashed in a deep puddle. He turned, and even before I hit him I knew he wasn't my guy at all. He was a chick with a short black crew cut, but I couldn't stop myself. I nailed her just behind the right ear with my elbow. As our bodies smashed into the door of the Mercedes, I heard a satisfying crack of ribs that didn't belong to me. I was on my feet again in a second, but she wasn't. She lay on the pavement with her head in a puddle, little bubbles appearing around her submerged nose. She was wearing a white sweater, jeans, and black Adidas that looked similar to the black Reeboks I had seen.

This had turned into one serious bag of dicks. Somebody was shouting to call the police. It was time to clear datum, but first I pulled her out of the puddle so she wouldn't drown, then ran ducking between the cars until I made it to my Nissan. Despite the cold and the rain, I was calving buckets of sweat. I climbed in through the passenger door, started her up and eased her out of the space as casually and quickly as possible.

As I turned out of the lot onto Madison Avenue, I passed Jenny and her friends standing on the corner under their umbrellas. Jenny looked straight at me with absolutely no expression on her face, as I though I was invisible, or a total stranger. That's exactly what I was to her—a total stranger. Maybe she didn't recognize me in my car. Maybe she couldn't see my face behind the wet glass. I hardly recognized myself anymore. I only hoped she would forget my name.

Thanksgiving

14

I WOKE UP ON THE floor in front of the couch with a syringe hanging out of my arm. The candle beside me had burned down to a waxy black hole in the rug, but that was nothing compared to the charred crater in my self-esteem. And after all that back-patting, too. Little Miss Got It All Together, one little mistake, one innocent victim of her rage and she's running home to Mr. Brownstone. Apparently she can't leave the guy, no matter how much he beats her.

I felt like a bag of smashed asshole. I figured at least two days had passed, maybe three, I didn't know. I crawled to the bathroom and into the shower, turned on the water with my clothes still on. I stunk and my clothes needed washing anyway. Water spurted out in a nearly frozen slush that roused me somewhat. I wondered if the customers downstairs could hear me scream.

The weather must have really turned cold while I was larking. After a few minutes I noticed vomit swirling down the drain and realized it was washing off of me from somewhere. I hoped it was my own vomit. I stripped down and picked the bigger chunks of ralph out of my hair, checked my pubes for evidence, found none, and thanked God for small favors. The water had gradually heated up to the temperature of warm spit by the time I turned it off.

I opened the shower door and found myself face-to-face with *her*, not five feet away. Dank blond hair, dank and stringy, hanging over her face like a drowned woman, breasts sagging over skeletal ribs, face like a skull, sunken cheeks and eye holes hollow and dark, mouth hanging open. It took me a minute to recognize myself in the foggy mirror.

I sat on the edge of the john and toweled my hair. The television was on in the den. I didn't remember the television being on when I woke up, but then again, I barely remembered waking up. I walked naked and dripping to the kitchen, grabbed a beer, wondered where it came from and thanked God again that I hadn't drunk it all. I sat on the couch to let my hair dry. The commercial for laundry detergent ended and I was confronted by the Macy's Thanksgiving Day parade and a giant Bart Simpson balloon floating around the corner at West Thirty-fourth.

So there I was on Thanksgiving morning, naked, cold and sick, drinking a beer on the couch at nine in the morning after a smack bender, no turkey in the fridge, no turkey in my future. They say you have to hit rock bottom, and I thought I'd hit it too many times already, but before this I didn't know the meaning of rock, much less bottom. All the times before had been mere rest stops on the journey to the smoking cracks of today's fresh new hell.

I poured the rest of the beer into the toilet and forced myself into some clean underwear, then lay on the couch for half the day waiting to die. When that didn't happen, I searched the apartment until I found the stash under the couch. I still had three decks. It wasn't like me to leave any gato for tomorrow once I was going good. I dumped the whole thing into a paper bag, rolled up the bag and pushed it to the bottom of my garbage can. I hadn't hocked my cameras or my laptop to pay for more, so that was a plus. I finished dressing, then checked the pockets of my wet jeans. Michi's five hundred dollars— James's five hundred if you wanted to get technical about it— was gone. I searched through dirty laundry and drawers, unpacked boxes, in the ashtrays and under the seats of my car until I scraped together four bucks. Flush with cash, I went to see if the mercado was open.

Apparently it wasn't Thanksgiving in Mexico. Mynor looked up as I entered and smiled his friendly disaster of rotten teeth. It was good to have a friend somewhere. I bought a pack of Marlboro Light 100s, the brand I smoked when I was in college. *Might as well go back to the beginning and start over*, I thought.

"Everything OK?" he asked as I counted out pennies.

"Yeah." Something strange about the way he asked. Maybe he'd seen me last night. Maybe I'd come in here and forgot I knew him. Or worse. "Why?"

"Just wondering." He was trying not to look at me again. I wondered what I had done.

"What happened?"

"Well." He glanced at the ceiling. "You were pretty loud."

"I was?"

"I could hear," he said, embarrassed. He pointed at the ceiling. "You were arguing with some woman. Shouting."

"I'm sorry. Did you see her?"

He shook his head. "I knock on your door for a long time this morning, but you don't answer. Was she your sister?"

I said she was. I couldn't imagine who had been with me in my apartment. Maybe another junkie. I couldn't remember.

"Me and my sisters used to fight like that sometimes," he said.

"Pretty bad, huh?" I took my smokes. "I hope we weren't too loud."

"It was nothing. Wait until Mrs. Kim's husband gets back from Korea. You'll hear loud."

I thanked him and hurried out the door.

I stopped at the top of the stairs to open the pack and light one. The smoke seemed to burn through all the cobwebs. In the silence of the hall I heard a woman softly crying. I touched my ear to my door and listened, but the crying came from nowhere in particular, or maybe from inside my own skull.

The accordion elevator door at the end of the hall rattled open and Walter Pinch stepped out. He paused and for a moment he looked like he didn't really want to see me. I tried to be jovial. "Morning, Mr. Pinch."

"Please! Call me Walter." He resumed his usual golden treasure of a smile. A specter of gin fumes preceded him down the hall.

"I just want to apologize about yesterday," I said.

He waved it away and reached for his back pocket, but checked himself midswing. I unlocked my door. The woman had stopped crying. I opened the door and the cold seemed to flow out in a wave. Walter stepped back and bumped his head against the wall.

"Is your heat broke?" He looked past me as though he expected to see a ghost in my apartment.

"Seems so." I closed the door so the old man could dip into his pocket gin. He looked like he needed it.

I stood with my back to the door staring around my apartment. For the first time since I'd moved in, I felt like a stranger. I said "Hello?" to the empty room. I don't know who I expected to answer. Nothing happened except the heat kicked on. The air suddenly smelled of burning dust bunnies.

I tried to be rational about this. Mynor had heard two women arguing. Assuming I was one of them, I thumbed through my mental Rolodex for any female friends who might have shared a scream fest with me. I came up empty. I had no female friends. Those female acquaintances I once had I gave up when I left Reed. Maybe one of them stopped by late last night to try to talk me into going back with my husband. It would have been just like Reed to send one of our old church friends around to talk me out of signing the divorce papers I'd been sitting on since forever.

I checked the messages on my cell phone. I had seven: four from Adam, one last night from my mother, and a couple from a personal-injury lawyer I sometimes worked for. While trying to decide who I should call back first, the phone rang in my hand.

"Hey!" James shouted over the high-pitched whine of a propeller engine.

"Hey. What's up?"

"Me," he said. "Go outside."

"Why?"

"Trick or treat. Just go outside and look up." He hung up.

I had nothing better to do on Thanksgiving Day except to call my mother and tell her I wouldn't be home for dinner again this year. Or call Adam and explain to him why I didn't show up to take pictures of whoever got killed while I was strung out in my own apartment arguing with a total stranger nobody had seen and I couldn't remember.

It had finally stopped raining and the puddles were rippling in the sharp north wind. I looked up, squinting into a painfully gray sky, shading my eyes with my hand. I almost

preferred the drudgery of rain. The sun was up there somewhere running across a blue sky I barely remembered. And
somewhere up there with it buzzed a small single-engine air-
craft. I followed the sound as it came over the roof.

Down out of the clouds dropped this tiny, very red airplane,
red as a drop of blood, with upswept wingtips and the green and
gold of the Brazilian flag painted on its tail fin. As it swung toward me, it wagged its wings side to side, so I knew it was James.
It passed low over the building and my cell phone rang again.

"That was pretty cool," I said.

"It's a great little plane," he shouted over the whine of the
engine. "I can't talk now. I've got to get this thing to the airport before I get dinged by the FAA. I just wanted to make
sure we're still on for dinner tonight."

Sure you did, I thought.

"Are we still on for six?"

"Sure."

"OK. Gotta go." He hung up. I heard him coming back for
another pass, so I stood there in the cold hugging my arms and
waved as he flew over. He wagged his wings again; then, as he
climbed up into the clouds, he performed a quick barrel roll. He
was showing off for me. It was so adolescent and stupidly dangerous, I couldn't help but smile. At the same time, I thought,
*if life were a movie, this would be the moment where I watch in
horror as he clips a power line and crashes in a ball of fire.*

I sat on the couch. There was a football game on television
and the perky sideline announcer looked like she was feeling
her age as well as the cold. *It must be depressing to be an old
cheerleader*, I thought, and that made me feel a little better
about myself. Or perhaps it was the cigarette I burned that
cleared me out. Maybe it was the stupid silliness of my im-
pending date with the pilot. I should probably have curled up

on the couch hugging a pillow, but I still felt vaguely ill about the future and about myself, as though I were only putting off an eventual rug dance in the captain's cabin. Sooner or later I was going to have to go to a meeting and come clean about what I had just done to myself, though I'd probably leave out the part about the felonious assault of an innocent stranger. And there was still my mother to call and explain why I wouldn't be home for Thanksgiving. Again.

At least this year I had an excuse she could understand. I didn't know if she would believe it. "I have a date," I said when I finally called her.

"On Thanksgiving?" Mom asked. I could hear my father in the background wondering where she put the bourbon. Daddy was a drunk in the finest old Southern tradition. He liked his toddy about four in the afternoon, sooner on special occasions, eggnog on Christmas morning with his ham and eggs, which just shows that I came by it honest. He never seemed drunk, but I couldn't remember an evening when he didn't have a glass of something in his hand. Some fathers smelled like Old Spice; my old man smelled like whiskey and spearmint.

"What kind of person goes on a date on Thanksgiving?"

"You and Dad got married on Thanksgiving."

"That's because it's a long holiday weekend," she said. "It was the only time he could get off work."

"I'll come up tomorrow morning. I promise."

"But I've cooked." She said it as though I hadn't considered that possibility.

"He doesn't have family in town."

"Well, bring him here then. You know I always cook more than we can eat, and there are plenty of spare bedrooms." I heard my father in the background ask why she cooked so much since they always spent Thanksgiving alone.

"It's a little early for that. This is only our first date." Which was technically true.

"Oh!" she said in that unreadable way that drove me crazy. She might have been thrilled or disappointed or merely reacting to something on television. Either way, it didn't matter. I wasn't coming home for Thanksgiving and she was cooking a twenty-pound turkey.

I heard my father ask for my date's name. I told Mom.

"Isn't he that man on that TV show?" she asked.

"He's a pilot."

"A pilot!" Now I could hear the wedding wheels cranking up in her head, wondering if I'd wear the same dress as the last two times and who she could get to cater it. I could also hear my father, the retired architect, wondering if he was obligated to pay for this one. "A pilot! Well!" Mom sighed happily. I thought she'd be reasonable once she found out about the pilot part. "What's his name again?" I told her. "He sounds so familiar. Well. You probably need to get ready for your date. Where is he taking you?"

"Cracker Barrel." I didn't tell her he was a crop duster pilot. When she was sixteen, Mom's boyfriend had been a crop duster pilot ten years her senior. He was an ex Navy fighter pilot, ace of WWII, the Big One, forever fighting the Japs. She had defied her family over him and ran around behind everybody's back, until he flipped his biplane on a runway outside Egypt, Arkansas, and spent the rest of his short, furious life confined to a wheelchair watching other people's planes take off through the bottom of a whiskey bottle. "Tom" had been the great romantic tragedy that sustained Mom through a lifetime of ordinary.

Ordinary is entirely underrated.

15

I HAD BEEN READY FOR nearly an hour when James knocked on my door. Six o'clock, as promised, and I only had three cigarettes left out of the pack I'd bought three hours ago. A gray pall of smoke hung at lamp height like a London fog. James wore dark blue Dockers, a gray University of Memphis polo, and clean white Nikes with neon red shoestrings. I had decided on a bulky pullover sweater and the tightest pair of Levi's I owned. I didn't want to give him the idea I was trying to impress him, because I wasn't, but I also didn't want him to lose interest. He seemed profoundly relieved when I opened the door. In any case, I smoked in those jeans, especially when I wore my black heels.

He drove a five-year-old silver Lexus SC 430, which meant once upon a time he'd had money, but not enough now to trade it in for a new model. Sinking into the leather seat was like sliding your hand into a kidskin glove. It certainly beat the crap out of my '92 POS. I hadn't ridden in a car this expensive since I left Reed. James obviously hadn't always been a crop duster pilot, unless he was dusting crops in Guatemala for the CIA. I didn't ask. I liked him enough already to not want to know, just in case I didn't like the answer. With my luck, I wouldn't.

The Cracker Barrel was packed, but it was always packed, and being virtually the only restaurant open on Thanksgiving assured a long wait. We sat outside in the hokey rocking chairs, shivering in the cold and watching cars circle the parking lot waiting for a space. At least we were out of the rain. I smoked and James watched me. I had let him buy me a new pack of Marlboros. You had to like a guy who not only doesn't judge your habits, he'd even spring for them.

Not even twelve hours on the flip side of a dope bender, I didn't feel much like eating anything, but I followed dutifully when his name was called over the PA. He held my hand as we trailed the harried hostess to our table. *Sweet, sweet boy, you wouldn't touch this hand if you knew where it's been.* It felt like everybody was staring at me, though of course they weren't, except for the ones who were. *Do I look too old for this young sky hero?* I silently asked them. *What if we just go home and screw? Is it too soon?*

James sat next to a gilt-framed Victorian advertisement for a carpet sweeper. I sat under a giant rusty scythe. On the wall between us hung a classic Flexible Flyer sled exactly like the one that still hung in my parents' attic.

"I used to have one of these," James said of the Flyer.

"Didn't everyone?" He laughed just the proper amount of time for a first date. A harried waitress, more harried even than the hostess, arrived to take our orders. We decided on the turkey and dressing. She wrote it down on her little pad. She looked like all she wanted to do was lay down for a year.

"So," James said after she had gone. "You used to be a cop. What city?"

"Memphis."

"What did you do?"

"My last post was in vice. I was a detective."

"I bet that was interesting." I smiled and hoped it didn't look too fake. He wanted to hear cop stories. OK. I had one or two.

"One time, I busted this madame. An old lady, she must have been near seventy, named Mary Lewis. She ran a real estate agency as a front for the swankiest house in town. All her whores had realtor licenses. She had been open for business for about three years when I got the first tip from a guy who was getting his ass handed to him in the mayor's race, behind about twenty points to the incumbent. He had some shit on her and the mayor and about half the city council. He wanted to see if it would stick. So I started digging around, not because I owed him anything, you know. I found out the old lady had this one property listed—a big, six-bedroom affair in midtown near the zoo. She had been listing the place for years. The owner was listed as her husband, who was supposed to be dead. She ran a legitimate realty business on the front, but that one house seemed damned suspicious. So I called and acted like I wanted to see it. They told me they had just gotten an offer on it that morning, so I had one of my guys, Adam, call and they agreed to show him the place that afternoon. When he asked how much she charged for a viewing, she said if you have to ask, you can't afford it, and hung up. This woman would have one of her 'agents' show the house to the john for about two grand a pop, with sometimes four or five different agents showing the house on any given day."

"So you busted her?" he asked.

"Eventually. With high-dollar whores like that, you can imagine who her clients were. And let me tell you that old lady kept meticulous records. Her son was an accountant. I started getting calls telling me to shit can the whole investigation, then the Channel Five news got wind of it somehow, if you know what I mean, so I had no choice but to bust her. She was pleasant about the whole thing, kept calling me ma'am as I put the handcuffs on her."

"So what happened?"

"Never made it to trial. There was no way they were going to let her start naming her clients in court. It was a lot easier for them to just get rid of me. So that's what they did. I'm surprised you never heard about it. It was all over the news."

"We . . . I've only been in Memphis a little over five years," he said.

We? Who is we? I noticed the slightest indentation of a wedding ring on his finger. Apparently he was still taking it off for my benefit. I wondered whether he had left it in the glove compartment or at home. Probably at home. I might have accidentally looked in the glove compartment. The waitress brought our iced tea.

"And now you take photos of traffic accidents," James said.

What a way to start a date—Cracker Barrel psychotherapy. What's next, the symbolism of the scythe hanging over my head?

A different waitress brought us a heaping plate of biscuits in which to drown our hillbilly sorrows. "So," I said as I buttered one. "You're kind of shy."

"It's been a long time since I dated." He looked up, blushing. "Not that this is a date or anything."

"Is it a date?"

"Maybe." *Depends on how it ends* was what he was thinking. That's what I was thinking, anyway.

"When was your last date?"

"High school."

"You're kidding."

"I only ever asked out one girl in tenth grade and she turned me down. So when my wife, my future wife (*he admits it*), started hanging around me senior year, I didn't think she was for real. She was so beautiful and popular, it took me a long time just to come to terms with the fact she was interested in a guy like me. I kept waiting for everybody to start laughing at the joke. They never did. She was serious."

"So you're married."

"Was. We married the summer after we graduated. She passed away two years ago."

What do you say to that? I hoped he was lying. I hoped she was still alive somewhere and he was cheating on her, because now, this beached whale of a confession lay between us. Lies I could handle. Lies I could respect and live with. But these chains of grief he secretly bore going on two years now? I could see them in the ghostly indentation of the wedding ring he still wore except when he was with me, and in the way he switched from easy familiarity, almost too easy and too familiar, to the ridiculously sophomoric shyness of a man unused to or afraid of being attracted to another woman. Being with me probably felt like cheating to him. It certainly felt like cheating to me. I could help a man cheat on his living wife, but I wasn't sure if I could do it with a dead one.

"Read any good books lately?" I asked. It was cruel and cowardly. Maybe he wanted to open up to me, but I couldn't deal with that much heavy, not without some kind of prologue. I barely had a handle on my own fragged emotions.

But he laughed.

"I'm sorry," I apologized. "Sorry for your loss. I don't know what to say."

"It's OK," he said. He seemed to relax a bit, allowing his shyness to slip. "Sometimes I don't know what to say, either."

Aw God. Can't I just kiss this man? I laid my hand across his on the table between us and he looked up at me with those glittering blue bits of ice that were his gorgeous eyes, swimming ever so slightly with moisture, maybe tears. *God, why does it have to be so easy?*

Our food arrived, the waitress practically throwing the plates at us. She had forgotten the cranberry sauce. James picked up his knife and began meticulously slicing his turkey into precise squares about the size of postage stamps.

"So what was the last book you read?" he asked.

"I don't remember."

"Come on!"

"I haven't read a book in like ten years." I used to be a reader. I used to have books, but I had spent the last ten years of my life stoned or trying to score my next high, little enough time to read anything more than magazines in waiting rooms. And when you move as often as I had, and lived in the places where I've lived, sometimes all you can take with you is what you can carry in a suitcase. I don't remember what happened to my books.

I shrugged and said, "The last book I *remember* reading was *The Alchemist* by Paulo Coelho."

"What's it about?" James asked.

"It's about this Spanish kid who has a dream telling him to go to the pyramids and find a treasure. So he goes and has some adventures along the way, falls in love, meets the Alchemist and finds the pyramids, only to discover the treasure he sought is back home where he started."

"Sounds like a kid's book."

"It's very philosophical. It's about trying."

"Is that all?"

Jesus, what is this, a third-grade book report? No, it's date talk, safe talk over dinner. No politics. No religion. No com-plaining about work. Books and movies. I went on as though there were nothing in the least artificial about this whole con-versation. "It's also about following your Personal Legend and allowing yourself to succeed." My police counselor recom-mended I read it.

"What's a Personal Legend?" Larry King asked.

"I think it's about living the story of your life as though you are reading it instead of living it."

"So in other words, don't avoid the bad parts, just trust that the good parts will follow? Without the bad parts, it wouldn't make a good story."

"When you put it that way, it does sound a bit Panglos-sian," I said. *Whose ass did I pull that word from?*

"But did you like the book?"

"It's not important whether I liked it or not."

"Sure it is. It's the only thing that matters. Everything else is bunk."

"I don't have strong opinions about books. Or bunk. It was an OK book. I thought it was somewhat overrated." My coun-selor thought it would change my life. Obviously, it didn't.

"I guess we're not book people, are we?" James asked.

"I guess not." I smiled and shrugged. This was getting stupid.

"So what do you do with your time?"

What could I say, with my mouth full of turkey? "I stay busy." I had the feeling I was a test subject for an article in some men's magazine—"Six Simple Steps to Getting Laid on the First Date." Step One: *Pretend you're interested. Get her to talk about herself. Chicks love it when you act interested in the ordi-nary bullshit of their lives.*

"What do you do for fun?" I asked him.

"I fly model airplanes."

"So you fly for a living, and when you're not working, you pretend to fly?"

"Pretty much. Flying's all I ever wanted to do." The way he said it, I knew he wasn't kidding. But he was hiding something, some pain, some lost dream.

"My mom dated a crop duster pilot once." I didn't know why I was bringing this up. Maybe it was the dentist coming out in me again. "He was in an accident."

"Fatal?"

"Eventually."

"It happens."

"Even if you're careful?"

"You're flying along and you flush a covey of quail. Or you get a freak gust of wind. Or just about anything you don't expect. When your number's up . . ."

"I don't believe in fate," I said.

"You know the Red Baron?"

"Sure. He makes frozen pizzas."

"Manfred von Richthofen. Greatest fighter pilot of the First World War. You know how he died?"

"Downed by Snoopy in his Sopwith Camel?"

"A bullet through the heart. A one-in-a-million shot by a soldier on the ground. His number was up."

"Well, I guess that's settled," I said. "No point arguing about it."

James shrugged and ate a mouthful of potatoes. I shredded a biscuit on my plate. He said, "It all depends on what you want out of life. I take comfort in the idea that some things are just meant to be. Nothing you can do or say will change what is supposed to happen."

Our waitress stopped by with the check. "Y'all want dessert?"

"Not me." James didn't want anything, either. The waitress seemed relieved to drop the check on the table and disappear.

"I don't know about you," I said, "but I love Snoopy."

He balled up his napkin and laughed.

16

WHY DID WE COME HERE, anyway? This wasn't Thanksgiving dinner. Not a real one. We might as well have popped a bag of popcorn, made toast, and watched a movie. My mother was right—who goes on a date on Thanksgiving?

On our way out, I stopped in front of the giant fireplace to feel its heat. James stood beside me, staring into the fire. What was he thinking now? I used to be a good judge of these things. I could watch a guy for a little while and tell what he was thinking, like Holmes or Dupin, deducing his thoughts in a way that almost seemed like mind reading. I wasn't so good at it anymore. His face was a blank to me. I was having a hard time penetrating this man of such stark contrasts. Did the smell of a winter fire make him sentimental, or just mental? Was he having second thoughts about this whole thing?

Finally, he looked at me and asked, "Ready to go?"

I followed him out to the country store area of the restaurant. While he stood in line to the pay the bill, I examined a shelf of retro Cracker Jacks and tins of Charles Chips. We met by the John Deere merchandise display and James excused himself to visit the men's room. I browsed the retro Coca-Cola merchandise. While examining a Howdy Doody cap gun, I almost tripped over my husband Reed squatting behind a bin of plastic toys. He acted like he was tying his shoe, but he was wearing loafers.

"Jesus, Reed, what are you doing here?" I hissed, gooselike, at him. He stood up. He still looked like a Republican governor with presidential aspirations—tall, broad-shouldered, dark hair graying at the temples. Mr. Fantastic himself, able to bend in impossible contortions to make that million-dollar sale. I saw his face wherever I went in town—on billboards, For Sale signs in people's yards, even advertisements on grocery carts. It was impossible to escape him. But I never expected to find him hiding in a Cracker Barrel.

He assumed an air of injured dignity. "What am I doing here? What are you doing here?"

"Having Thanksgiving dinner. At least I have an excuse. Are you following me?" His whole shitty family lived in town. They were old Germantown money. All two hundred of them. They didn't need to visit a tourist trap on Thanksgiving.

"As a matter of fact, I'm buying a pumpkin pie," he said. "I saw you coming out. I was just trying to avoid a confrontation."

"You never could bullshit me, Reed." If he was following me, it stood to reason that the person watching me pee at Bosco's might be working for him, too. What didn't stand was why he'd follow me at all. We'd been separated for four years.

"You always were a paranoid bitch." He tried to laugh and move past me, but I shoved him into the corner. He was easy to push around, even though he was a good eighteen inches taller than me.

"I'm not paranoid," I said. "I just want to know if you're following me. Did you send one of your sisters over to my apartment last night?"

"Don't be ridiculous, Jacqueline!"

"Excuse me," said an old lady who had come up behind me. She was about five feet tall and looked like the woman who used to babysit me and my brother. She was the official Cracker Barrel house detective, there to keep an eye on the kitsch so the rednecks wouldn't walk off with a refrigerator pig. "Is there a problem?"

"No problem." I stepped back from Reed. "Except this jackass is following me."

"I'm not following her. She's my wife." Reed smiled, turning on the salesman charm. The old woman almost flushed. She had probably seen his commercials on television.

"We're separated, asshole!" I shouted at him.

"Ma'am, this is a family restaurant. If you don't lower your voice, I'm going to have to ask you to leave," the old biddy warned in a pleasant voice.

"I'm just waiting for the pumpkin pie I ordered," Reed told her.

"I was leaving anyway. If he follows me, call the cops," I said to the old woman. She looked soft and grandmotherly, but she had the eyes of somebody who'd seen it all. She wasn't about to take any shit off me.

James exited the bathroom and spotted us in the corner. He sidled up beside me and took my hand. "Are you OK?" he asked in a low voice.

"This is my estranged husband, Reed Lyons."

"I know who he is." He didn't sound especially friendly, either.

Reed turned up his thin, supercilious nose. "Is this your *date*?" he asked me.

"Him? Not exactly. He's my john. He bought me dinner. I'm going to blow him for dessert."

Reed rolled his eyes, and the old lady shouted "Ma'am!" in a schoolteacher voice that brought everybody up short. She grabbed my elbow with her marshmallow fingers.

"I'm leaving." I tried not to look at James. I didn't want to see the mortification on his face. "If I catch you following me again, Reed, I'll have you busted. I still have friends in the department."

"One friend, from what I hear, Jacqueline. Just one."

"One is enough to pop your buttons. Come, James." I pulled my arm out of Grandma's death grip and headed for the door.

17

We walked to James's car, dodging the traffic still circling the parking lot, and climbed in without either of us saying a word. He backed out of the parking space, though they barely gave him room to back up, and we drove away to the sound of angry honking as some interloper dove into our empty spot.

We were on the interstate before I was cool enough to speak. I tried to apologize. "'S OK." He shrugged.

"No really. I'm sorry, Reed just . . ." *Slow down. Slow down.* Not too much. This guy was still damaged merchandise. He didn't need me adding to his troubles. "He gets to me," I finally said.

"I could see that." He drove awhile. There wasn't much traffic, but it was slow going because of the rain. "You want to talk about what happened?"

"What's there to talk about?"

"I just thought . . ."

"I left him about four years ago. Maybe five. I don't remember. He won't let me go."

"What happened? Did you catch him cheating?"

"He caught me cheating."

"You left him because he caught you cheating?"

"No, I left him because he wouldn't let it go. He didn't want a divorce, but he wouldn't let me forget what I did, either. Every time I'd complain that he forgot to set out the hamburger for dinner, or he hadn't paid the lawn service, or whatever, he'd say, *Well, at least I wasn't fucking your best friend behind your back.*"

"I can see how that would get old," James said.

"No shit." We pulled into the parking lot behind my apartment. He turned off the engine and twisted in his seat to face me. I couldn't look at him. Sometimes this black rage would well up, from where I don't know. It was tooth-bared, nostrils-flared, lurking along the jungle trail down to the water hole. I wanted to get back at Reed. I wanted to see him wither.

I tried to put on a nice face and make a joke. "I've had a wonderful evening," I said. "But this wasn't it."

"Groucho Marx?" he asked. I shrugged. It wasn't very funny and he was being way too nice about it.

"If you don't mind my asking, how old are you?" I asked.

"Twenty-nine."

Christ. "So I could have been your babysitter."

"I'd have liked that."

"You wouldn't have liked me then. I was fat. You want to come upstairs?"

"For dessert?"

"You're hilarious." I put my hand on the door handle, but he didn't move. He just sat there, looking at me. "I'm sorry if I embarrassed you."

"You didn't. Honestly, I thought it was pretty funny."

"What was funny?"

"You're like some kind of little fice or something."

"What's a fice?"

"It's a type of a little dog that isn't afraid of anything."

"So I'm a bitch," I said.

"That's not what I said."

"I know I'm a bitch. I'm a Cunt with a capital C. If you were me, you'd be one, too." I tried to open the door but it was locked. I couldn't find the button to unlock it. I pressed one and the window went down.

"That's not what I said," he repeated. He unlocked the doors from his side. "I thought I was going to have to pull you off his face."

"Or maybe you thought it was cute. Do you think it's cute when I'm confronting my stalker?" What was I trying to do, run this guy off? That's what the police department counselor would have said. I opened the door and got out. It was pouring now, the hardest I'd seen it rain in a long time. I was soaked through in about three seconds. He sat in the car and looked at me through the windshield, his face distorted by the rain sheeting down the glass, like a portrait by Salvador Dalí, melted by time.

"Are you coming up or what?" I shouted.

He followed me inside. We stood soaked and dripping in the entryway under the yellow bug light, looking like drowned tourists. The entry was no bigger than a closet. I stood on the bottom step and my eyes were even with his. He shook the water out of his hair. I wanted to grab him and kiss him, rip off his wet clothes, but it smelled like an alley in there, so I started up.

At the top of the stairs I heard music playing. It wasn't the usual Tejano music from the mercado. It took me a minute to recognize it. I stopped at my door, because the sound was coming from my apartment—a grinding heavy-metal beat, and someone crying "*No! No!*" in a high-pitched voice. James's face was utterly inscrutable. I wondered if I was the only one hearing it.

But as I opened the door, Rob Halford loosed a primordial glass-shattering castrato scream in our faces. After an echoing pause, my stereo launched into the first metal-up-your-ass riff of the next track.

I hurried inside and grabbed the remote off the kitchen table. On the third push of the power button, the music shut off midscream. "What was that?" James asked as he closed the door.

"Old CD." I tossed the remote on the table.

"Do you always go off and leave your music playing?"

I hadn't turned on my stereo in nearly two years. I didn't even know it was plugged in. It was a nice Pioneer system, not too big, with a five-disk changer, purchased during one of my flush periods when I was trying to get my shit together. For some reason, I had never pawned it.

"It must have turned itself on," James said. "My garage door does that sometimes. I'll come home and it's standing wide open."

As he looked around my little apartment, I began to see it with his eyes, how shabby it must look to somebody who drives a Lexus, even if it is five years old. The ratty old couch and the kitchen table with its chipped Formica and rusting legs, and the way the bathroom door wouldn't close all the way. I suddenly remembered I had left my clothes in the shower that morning and hoped he wouldn't ask to use the bathroom before I had a chance to bag them.

But what did I care? This is my life. It sucks, but it's all I have. If he doesn't like it, too bad. Like he never crawled into the shower to wash the vomit from his hair. Well, maybe not, but we all have our moments.

"Is it always this cold in here?" he asked.

"Only when it's this cold outside. You want to get out of those wet clothes?"

"Do you have something I can wear?"

"Not really." I went in the bathroom and stripped and threw my wet clothes in the shower with the others. I toweled off as best I could with a cold damp towel I found on the floor. When I came out, he didn't look surprised by my nakedness.

I went in the bedroom to get the Leica. When I came out again, he was still standing there in his wet polo and dockers shivering. "Here." I gave him the camera he'd sold me, or almost sold me.

"I thought you said you had the money." There was a crack of panic in his voice.

I walked over to the couch and bent over with my elbows resting on the back, then looked at him over my shoulder. "Take a picture of me."

"I'm not a photographer." He set the Leica on the kitchen table, gently, almost reverently.

"You don't have to be a photographer. Just push the button on top." I moved up close to him and started unbuckling his pants. "I want you to take my picture so I can send it to that husband of mine."

"Stop," James breathed.

"I want you take my picture while I blow you." I unzipped him and reached my hand inside his pants. He grabbed my wrist and I grabbed his dick. It was limp and cold as a dead fish.

"Please don't."

"You want to screw instead?"

"I can't do this." He extracted my hand and stepped back, zipped and buckled, a look of profound betrayal on his face.

"I thought you wanted to. I thought you wanted dessert."

"I just can't. Not like this."

"How then?" It really was cold in the apartment. The heat

was busted again, but I didn't care. I could heat things up eventually. "What do you like to do?"

"Not this. It's not right." He was scared now, backing toward the door.

"How can I make it right?" I felt like a used-car salesman.

"I don't know." He was just a kid after all. He was scared. Of me. I wasn't the woman he thought I was. Well screw that, that's what he gets for thinking. Maybe he was old-fashioned or something. But I never met a man who wouldn't take a hummer if offered freely, no strings attached. Even old-fashioned men, even preachers. Especially preachers. And there was no way he was gay.

"Maybe you'd better just give me the other part of the money and I'll go," he said.

I walked over to the table and grabbed a cigarette. I lit it while he watched, turned and rested my ass on the edge of the table so he could get a good look at what he was missing. I didn't have his money. I had spent it all on my bender, or lost it, or been robbed. Maybe all three. I couldn't remember. All I had was twenty-seven cents.

"I don't have your money," I said.

"You said you did."

I took a drag, held it, then let the smoke out through my nose. "Something came up." *Now he really knows what kind of bitch I am.* He was easy to read. I didn't need a sixth sense.

He walked to the door, then stopped. "Can you get it?"

"Eventually." I took another long, crackling drag. He looked like I'd told him he had cancer. I felt bad for the guy. This wasn't his fault. I was a scary bitch, no doubt about it, scary, unreliable, irresponsible, an all-too-willing accomplice to the worst angels of my nature. "Give me a few days," I said, relenting.

"I don't have a few days." He left and closed the door. I listened to his footsteps going down the stairs. I went to the bedroom window and after a couple of minutes watched his car turn onto Summer Avenue.

"To hell with this," I said to no one.

Black Friday

18

I WOKE UP WHEN MY cell phone started ringing under the cushions of the couch. My blood felt like day-old gravy pushing through my veins. I was naked and the apartment was frigid as a morgue. I knew who was calling without looking, but I dug it out anyway and answered it. I deserved that much penance.

"Don't you answer your phone anymore?" Adam asked.

"I answered it this time, didn't I?"

"I've been calling for two days. Stopped by last night about seven."

"I had a date."

"With who?"

"Whom with," I corrected his grammar. This conversation sounded sickeningly familiar. "I had dinner with the guy who sold me the Leica." Or almost sold me the Leica. His camera was still on the table. He hadn't taken it with him.

"Well grab your shit and get over here. We got another body. Playhouse Killer for sure this time."

I stood beside Adam, looking at the pair of naked feet sticking out of a rolled-up tapestry lying on a stage. We were at the public amphitheater known as the Overton Park Shell, located behind the Brooks Museum of Art, near the golf course and the zoo. A sword was pinned through the tapestry like a cocktail skewer through a roll of ham; all that was missing was a giant olive. The body lay at the back of the stage beneath an enormous faded rainbow painted across the inside of the acoustic concrete shell.

It was the brightest, sunniest, coldest November morning in living memory. The air made my lungs hurt. The sky was so blue, the inside of my skull ached. The tapestry and the sword hilt were white with frost. The victim had been lying there awhile. I lit a cigarette and started snapping photos.

"Hamlet stabbed Polonius through the arras," Adam said. I paused long enough to watch a couple of officers exchange some money. There wasn't much to see other than the rolled-up body. No footprints across the concrete stage, no pool of frozen blood, not even a cigarette butt or cigar ash or dull penknife. Nothing but the barren semicircle of painted concrete, the frosty barefoot pig in a blanket, and the arched and peeling rainbow above him. At least it wasn't the side of a road. At least he wasn't dragged behind a pickup to mask the cause of death and left in a ditch somewhere for the possums and dogs to tear to pieces. The killer cared enough to make a spectacle.

I slung the Leica behind my back and knelt beside the body to get some close-ups with my Canon. The sword hilt looked like some kind of cavalry saber, with an ivory grip and worn silver guard and quillons. The roll of tapestry wasn't much larger than if there'd been no one in it at all.

Dr. Wiley arrived with his cohort of grim technicians, all lugging tackle boxes. He looked like we had interrupted his Christmas shopping. News vans were parked along the street running beside the art museum. The air was so cold and thin, you could hear the zoo's siamang gibbons tuning up with their distinctive *mo-mo-mo* calls, while lions and tigers roared over their morning beef. "The jungle is restless," Adam observed.

"*Ungawa, simba.*" The zoo noises made for an atmosphere infinitely more surreal than any of the killer's previous stagings.

Without Chief Billet running interference for me, Dr. Wiley's arrival made it impossible to continue my work. Billet was in Chicago visiting relatives for the weekend, so Wiley quickly ran me off. I moved to the edge of the stage and lit another cigarette to try and kill the hot tickle at the back of my throat.

The Overton Park Shell had been closed three years for renovations. They were ripping out the old bench seating and replacing it with landscaped lawn on which midtown's finest would one day nibble pre-cubed cheese and sip boxed Chardonnay from plastic glasses, pretending they were actually in Central Park. Right now it looked like a bomb crater. I scanned it through the Leica's viewfinder and snapped off a few pictures of the rubble and the line of trees at the top of the hill.

Dr. Wiley withdrew the sword from the body and bagged it. He needed a big bag, like a bread sleeve. While we watched him do his thing from a safe distance, Adam asked, "Did you go out Wednesday night, too?"

"Yeah. For a while."

"To the Square?"

"You know I don't have money for that." I didn't look at him, but I could feel his eyes trying to peel me apart. "Why do you ask?"

"A woman fitting your description assaulted another woman in the parking lot behind Playhouse on the Square."

Oh yeah. How could I have forgotten. I tried to appear professionally curious and asked, "Robbery?"

"Nothing taken."

"How's the vic?"

"Couple of broke ribs and a concussion. Nothing serious."

"That's good."

He stepped in front of me and looked down at my face with his brown eyes. He looked so disappointed, but honestly I don't know what he expected. I always let him down. It wasn't his job to save me. I didn't hire him for that.

"Something's not right," I said.

"I know."

"The killer has never done two murders this close together."

"Hamlet thought it was his uncle Claudius eavesdropping."

"Revenge?"

"Maybe. Or punishment."

"For what?"

Wiley and his goons slowly unrolled the body, stopping at every turn to shoot photographs and lint-roll the tapestry for evidence.

"Maybe this one really is a copycat," I suggested. "Any idiot can do Hamlet. Even Mel Gibson." Adam laughed, his mouth a straight line under his nose. He looked worse than I did, but he came by his death mask honest. He was one hell of a cop. He'd been busting his balls on this case for five straight days. All he needed now was a copycat killer chumming the waters. I could tell he was dreading the news cameras this morning.

"I'm hoping we'll find a print," he said. I didn't bother pointing out that they already had plenty of prints, but maybe he was hoping a fingerprint would definitively tie this victim to the previous murders and eliminate the possibility of a copycat. Or maybe he was just hoping for a fresh break.

"So what's his name?" he asked.

"Whose name?"

"Your date. Last night."

"James St. Michael."

"Isn't he on television or something?"

"That's what everybody says. Actually, he flies crop dusters."

"I didn't know people still did that." He looked up at the sky as though he expected to see one. The air was so cold, I could barely breathe.

"They do. Are we done here?"

"You got another date?"

"With my parents."

"That's good. I'm glad you're going home. Only, go back to your apartment first and clean up because you look like shit, Jackie."

"Thanks for noticing. Can I borrow forty bucks for gas?"

Adam took out his wallet and passed me a couple of twenties, with the unspoken understanding that I wouldn't go and stick it in my arm. He was paying me to go to an NA meeting. Clever boy, that Adam. He knew how to play me. I noticed several of his cop friends watching our exchange, so I smiled at them with my unshaved teeth. They pretended to be looking at something else.

"Sergeant!" Wiley barked. Adam hurried over. He and Wiley were still on speaking terms, because Adam was good at being everybody's friend, even friends with swinging dicks like Wiley. I dropped my cig and ground it out under my shoe, because I liked making enemies. It was the only thing I was any good at. I was free to go, but I waited to thank Adam.

He walked back while they were still zipping up the body. He didn't look at me. He didn't look at anything. He looked like somebody had opened a vein in his neck. I grabbed his arm before he walked off the edge of the stage.

"What's wrong?"

"It's Cole Ritter," he said.

19

I PUT THIRTY OF ADAM'S forty in the tank and bought
two packs of cigarettes, a can of Mountain Dew, and a
scratch-off. I won two dollars and that's all the money I had in
my pocket when I sat down in a room at the adult learning
school to hear people talk about staying off the junk. I tried to
care and they pretended to understand my backsliding twice
just since my last meeting on Sunday. I also tried not to notice
the two men sitting at the back of the room, weeping and chewing their hands, doomed to pay for the sin of their mortal addictions in the eternal hell of Narcotics Anonymous.

I promised I would show up for next Sunday afternoon's
meeting, and as shitty as I felt at the moment, I really meant it.
I put my life in the hands of a higher power and drove over the
Hernando DeSoto Bridge a little after lunch time. Despite days
of rain, the river was low, the muddy water beige with the sand
bars standing out like an old man's ribs. There were dead people
walking on the waters—a whole continent's worth of mob hits,
flood victims, suicides and boating accidents. The clear blue of
the sky had given over to high gray clouds. At least it wasn't
raining, but now they were talking on the radio about snow to
the north.

In West Memphis, Arkansas, I took I-55 north and was soon driving through farm country, the river delta, the rice and cotton and soybean fields shaved naked and brown, the land as flat and featureless as the sky, and a sharp north wind blustering across the barren land, rippling the rain puddles and knocking my little Nissan around like a punk in a locker room. My throat felt acid raw and hot. The highway was lined with shuffling pedestrians from the other side. They tried to wave me down as I drove by. Maybe they were trying to stop me, warn me, hop a cab to heaven, I don't know. I ignored them.

The old two-lane Highway 67 had been supplanted by a vast stretch of Nazca-straight four-lanes atop which you could land whole fleets of bombers when the Russkies invaded. I drove past rotting barns and abandoned school buses slowing rusting in untilled meadows, past the fields and farms of my youth where we used to throw empty beer bottles at mailboxes for fun. The landscape seemed smaller and meaner than the last time, the poverty a little deeper, the dilapidation a little more advanced. Nothing had changed except to fall into ruin. I thought I might have to pull over and puke. I was shaking so bad I could barely hold the wheel.

The road rose and it began to snow as I crossed the bridge over the Black River and drove up into Pocahontas, my own private Mayberry. My grandfather's dental office had been on the square for forty years by the time I was born. Our house, my parents' house, was on Schoonover Street, about five blocks from the square. The house had belonged to my grandfather. When I was a little girl, he still lived in a smelly room off the back and wore a waistcoat and a pocket watch and walked to work at his dentist office every day except Sunday. He died one

June afternoon the summer of my tenth birthday. They found him on Bland Street with a half-eaten peach in one hand and an old newspaper in the other.

I drove by the Masonic Cemetery where he was buried beside his wife, a woman unknown to me save in grainy photographs, with all around them the graves of all the Pastors, except Uncle Dexter, the hero of the Great War, whose lost and shattered bones still lay beneath the buttercups in some unknown Flanders field.

The Pastors populated an entire corner of the cemetery—Pastor Corner; the earliest of them spelled his name *Pasteur*. My grandfather was thirty-one years in the ground now, yet I could still smell the dirty yellow ashtray breath of him, the mothball reek of his woolen winter suits, and the soapy taste of his clean dentist's fingers crawling around inside my mouth. In the years following his death, my brother and I believed his ghost was still wandering, like Hamlet's father, through all the precincts of the third-floor attic of our Victorian manse. Sometimes at night I'd wake up and hear the ticking of his pocket watch, as though he were leaning over my bed in the pitch dark.

Neither he nor any of my relatives were hanging around for judgment day today. The cemetery was eerily empty, unlike the roads and fields and towns I had driven through to get here. I have found cemeteries to be the least populated of all places. The dead seem to dislike them as much as the living.

I pulled into my parents' driveway, climbed out of the car and stood in the softly falling snow. Already you could hear the quiet. The tiny flakes of snow touched my flushed, upturned face and melted with an almost audible hiss. I climbed the steps and rang the doorbell like a stranger. Mama opened the door, drew me inside and led me straight to my old bed, where I lay down with a fever of a hundred and two, eyes of blue, and oh what those blue eyes could do.

Saturday

20

I LAY IN THE LONELY narrow single bed of my childhood, beneath a red and black comforter bearing the Arkansas State University logo. My parents had always meant for this room to serve as summer hotel accommodations for some future granddaughter. As with most other aspects of my life, I had disappointed them.

I felt shaky but strangely alert, no longer feverish thanks to my mother's quiet ministrations and a double dollop of NyQuil. But I was sore and my sheets were damp and twisted about my body, as though I had wrestled all night with the angel of the Lord.

Mom opened the door and looked in on me. "You're awake," she said. She had cooked country ham for breakfast. She didn't often cook a full breakfast anymore. She came back a few minutes later with my clothes washed and folded. My suitcase lay at the foot of the bed. We were nothing alike, she and I. We were strangers to one another, always had been. I had never been able to understand this quiet giant of a woman, who seemed so content within these four walls and a bit of garden. She never could quite wrap her considerable, though underemployed, mental powers around short little Jackie Pastor, who couldn't wait to get out of her house and leap, with eyes and teeth bared, onto the first train out of town. This girl who stripped off her pretty dresses at the age of four for the freedom of panties and a bare naked chest. Who had always run with boys and outrun them, ridden with boys and outridden them, fought with boys and sent them home bloody-nosed and crying, and finally screwed those same boys just as joyfully. All the boys liked me because I gave tremendous head. I never had any girl friends, only accomplices. I would climb out my window after midnight and climb back in before sunup—the female incarnation of Huck Finn. I had never fooled my mother, though she never actually caught me with my pants down.

My father, on the other hand, was willfully clueless, and for that I cherished him. He wanted no part of the daily chore of rearing children. To him children were a source of entertainment, subjects of experiment and study, as though he were Adam and had never been a child himself. I used to ask him after Sunday school, *Did Adam have a belly button?*

What's a belly button? he'd say. I'd show him mine and he'd say, *That's just the scar where the stem broke off. We found you under a persimmon tree and had to dig you up by the roots.* Then he'd send me off to the kitchen to make him a banana sandwich.

You're a banana sandwich, I'd say.

You're a tom boy.

You're a roly-poly.

You're a codfish.

I sat up in bed and gazed through the window curtains upon a world transformed. Snow lay three inches deep upon the windowsill. The sky seemed to hang just above the trees. My car in the driveway lay under a white blanket, and the driveway, the yard and the road were all one, all lines and boundaries erased. A man in a parka vest and red knit cap slid by on cross-country skis. I had awoken in Pocahontas, Norway.

In the kitchen, Dad was already pulling on his boots over three pairs of socks. He looked like he was preparing to search for the Northwest Passage. Mom was setting plates on the table.

"I am," Dad said, continuing their conversation. "As soon as I finish my ham."

"Your father is going to buy whiskey," Mom said. "In this weather."

He pulled his chair up to the table and waited for me to sit. The smell of the frying ham was just about to kill me. Mom had also made biscuits and grits, and there were pink grape-fruit halves sitting in bowls. As I sat down, she slid a plain egg omelet onto my plate. Dad screwed off the top of the pepper shaker and handed it to me. I dusted my eggs for prints.

"You ruin them," Mom said as she sat. She was dressed. She never cooked in her housecoat and fuzzy slippers. She bowed her head and waited for me to stop eating.

"Can I go with you?" I asked my father after Mom had thanked God for ham and eggs.

"Of course."

"You shouldn't go out," Mom said, sprinkling a spoonful of sugar over her grapefruit.

"I feel fine."

"You look terrible. You haven't been eating. Do you take calcium?"

"I'm fine, really," I said.

"If you don't take care of your bones, by the time you're my age you won't be able to straighten your back."

———

I met my father at the truck. He had already started the engine and let it warm up. He never drove anywhere without letting the engine warm up. I finished my cigarette and climbed in.

"Since when did you start smoking?" he asked.

"I've been smoking for years. Where are we going?" Pocahontas was in Randolf County, a dry county in the middle of a bunch of dry counties. Paragould, in Greene County, was the closest place to buy liquor, but that was an hour away, minimum. In this snow, and with him driving like an old man, closer to two.

"You told me you quit smoking."

"I did," I said. "Lots of times."

He drove slowly toward the town square rather than the highway, so I knew he wanted to talk.

"Your mother cooked a twenty-pound turkey. I was up until midnight carving it. The fridge is full. You should take some home with you."

"I will," I said.

"You couldn't have come home for Thanksgiving?"

I changed the subject. "You should have told me you were out of whiskey. I would have brought you a case from Memphis."

"Like you have money to buy a case of liquor. How much do you have right now?"

"I have money."

"You have two dollars."

I stared out the window, trying not to be pissed, because he was my old man and he wasn't doing or saying anything I didn't already know he would do or say. He said, "I emptied your pockets last night so your mother could wash your clothes. Two bucks and some change and a pack and half of cigarettes."

I rolled down the window. He had the heat cranked up to a hundred and forty. The snow was already starting to melt off the roads. "Your grandmother died of emphysema, you know."

"I know."

"Where did you get the money for gas?" He turned south on Marr Street, past the drugstore where I used to skip school and read books without paying for them. Pretending I had money was a waste of time with my old man. He knew I didn't have a checking account and couldn't get a checking account. He didn't have to search my pockets to know I didn't have any money, not after all these years of me calling him up at midnight, begging for fifty bucks just to keep the lights on. Yet still he searched my pockets to see how much I had. And still I lied about having more.

"I'm working," I said.

"For whom?"

"Lots of people. I did some work for the police yesterday morning. They still owe me for work I did last Monday."

"Still doing the photography thing, then," he said with a nod at my new camera.

"It's not a photography *thing*."

"But wouldn't you rather have a steady paycheck?"

"Doing what?"

"Well, you could teach. You majored in history. The schools around here are dying for good teachers."

"I'm a photographer," I said. I couldn't imagine standing in front of a bunch of punk-ass delinquents trying to get them interested in what a bunch of old men did two hundred years ago. If it wasn't about the Civil War or the glory days of the Southwest Conference, Arkansas kids didn't give a rat's ass about history.

"Yeah, but what kind of future is there in what you're do-ing? I mean, I don't see you saving any money, and you aren't getting any younger."

"Thanks for noticing, Dad."

"Do you have a retirement plan at all?"

"Sure. I'm waiting for you to kick the bucket so I can pawn the family jewels." He didn't laugh. "I've been saving money. Look, I'm buying this camera. It's a Leica." I said it like he should know what that meant.

"Buying," he repeated in the fatherly voice he so rarely used, save in moments when he thought I was trying to bor-row money.

"I've already paid two thousand on it."

He turned with a surprised expression, and here was a man who was never surprised. "Two thousand dollars? For that?" But it wasn't the price. He was surprised that I had two grand to spend on anything. "May I see it?"

I pulled the strap over my head and gave it to him at the next stop sign. He turned it over in his hands, mystified by its simplicity. For two grand, you want bells and whistles, you want it to scroll out a sheet of French linen and wipe your ass for you. "What's wrong with your other camera, the one we bought you?"

"This one's better," I said.

"How?"

"It just is. It's a Leica."

"What's a Leica? Canon is a good camera."

"It's the difference between a Mustang and a Maserati." I was speaking his language now. Cars he could understand. "I need it for my work," I continued. Lubricating the conversa-tion with truth made lying easier. "I spent all I had on it."

I couldn't put one over on my old man. Not completely, not when it came to money. "How much do you still need?"

"Only five hundred more."

"Only." He looked out the side window so long I thought he was going to crash into something.

"You know, five hundred dollars will last your mother and me two months."

He turned at the next corner. We slipped and skidded in painfully slow motion down Everett Street. Somehow, he managed to turn onto a side street and glide to a stop against the curb without hitting anything. I pried my fingers from the dash while he opened the door and hopped out.

"Where are you going?"

"Back in a jiff." He crossed the street and disappeared into an alley between two old brick warehouses that didn't even have the charm of dilapidation. I rolled the window down a crack, lit a cigarette, and pulled out the ashtray. It was virgin steel inside, ashless and buttless, because my father, the sociable lush, had never once touched tobacco. He arrogantly turned up his nose at drunks like myself who did. I was, in fact, violating one of his commandments just by lighting up in his automotive sanctuary. But he would never say anything to me. I had long ago got the bulge on this man and could extract from him any concession I desired simply by dropping one of several names.

I was twelve years old the first time I caught him cheating on my mother. First time of many, so many I sometimes had trouble remembering he was my father and not just another guy—older, fatter, but no different. Yet different nonetheless because I've never known a man, before or since, who got more pussy than my pop. I don't know what it was about him.

Maybe he had *it*, whatever *it* is, or maybe *it* was his money.
His architecture firm mostly designed for the state government,
which meant there was never any shortage of work as long as he
made nice with both political parties. He supplied the liquor
and women and the government contracts appeared like manna
in the morning. So there were always women hanging around
his office, women who would do things for money or power or
just for the hell of it, mostly smartass country girls trying to
be city.

That first time, I had come home from school with an early
period to find my old man in the den with my best friend's
mom kneeling between his legs, her head bobbing like a Singer
sewing machine. She looked up just as my father was having
his moment, as they used to say, to see me crouched on the
front porch watching through the window in mute horror and
(admittedly) Freudian fascination.

I circled the house and crept in through the back door to
reach the stairs without having to confront them, unaware that
they had already beat a hasty retreat through the front door.
That night, my father entered my bedroom and asked me what
I thought I had seen. I told him I was fairly certain of what I
had seen, at which point he got down on his knees and tear-
fully begged me to not to tell my mother, promising me anything.

What a flush of power that was. The whole world opened
like a magnolia blossom. He was lucky I was only twelve. Had
I been sixteen, there was nothing I wouldn't have extorted
from him—money, cars, an apartment of my own. He was
only saved by the limits of my pre-teen imagination. That, and
it sickened me to see him grovel. At that moment, all I really
wanted was my daddy back and to be his little girl again. That
never happened, of course.

What is seen cannot be unseen, innocence lost is lost for-ever, but in that there is no crime except, perhaps, against time. Eventually we became accomplices, Dad and I. He cov-ered for me when I skipped school and I covered for him when I caught him with a woman. Any time he tried to reassert his parental authority over me, all I needed was to say I had seen Tammy Albright at the post office or the grocery store and he would smile and nod like the genial fellow thief he had be-come. Eventually I forgave him, as we must eventually forgive everyone, even ourselves. Wisdom just arrived a little earlier for me, as did most of the disappointments in my life.

It occured to me how similar were my father and Michi Mori. It was frightening to think I had never noticed before.

My phone started to ring. It was Adam, but the call dropped before I had a chance to answer. My battery was dead.

Dad returned as I was flicking my butt out the window. It stuck like a dart in a drift of snow. He climbed in and set a paper bag on the seat between us. "It is Thanksgiving, after all," he said.

I opened it and lifted out a jug of Wild Turkey 101. He started the truck and spun the tires. "Nice," I said. My father was a bootlegger, too.

21

AFTER LUNCH, DAD AND I headed back out in the snow. "I'm just going to grab a couple of beers," he said. He had a little fridge in the garage. He may have been a lush, but he was never a lush before four o'clock, except on holidays.

We opened our beers in the garage and watched the icicles drip. I thought about Cole Ritter's frozen body thawing on an outdoor stage in Memphis. I wondered if his ghost was still hanging around the wings, waiting for someone to applaud. I almost told Dad about the Playhouse murders, then decided against it. It was too close to home. He'd want to know why I was involved. He'd remind me that I couldn't make it right again. He'd tell me to let the dead lie.

But the dead don't lie. They stay with you. I hadn't talked about ghosts in his presence since I was a little girl. The one time I did mention my special friends, he looked at me as though he didn't know who I was.

Dad gave me a bag of corn cobs. "We're feeding squirrels now," he said as he loaded up a bucket with bird seed. Though the clouds hadn't lifted, the snow had mostly melted away already, leaving the backyard a slippery sloping hell of mud. He showed me how to set a corn cob on the wooden feeder so the squirrels couldn't steal the whole thing. "They take it eventually, but it feels better to make them work for it. I ain't running no welfare office!" he shouted at the trees, which were full of chickadees and snowbirds. "We mostly get grackles," he said. He rehung the last of the feeders and spread some seed on the ground for the little birds who couldn't compete. He stood at the edge of my mother's dead garden, sucking his beer, looking down the slope of the backyard toward the neighbors' house barely visible through the woods.

"This spring, that whole slope will come up in field corn," he said.

I smoked a cigarette, trying to imagine the hillside covered with tall green stalks rustling in the wind. "Squirrels bury most of the corn we put out. Sometimes I wonder if this is how people first discovered agriculture—watching squirrels. When a squirrel buries a nut or an acorn or a corn kernel, he's ensuring he has food in the future, whether he digs it up and eats it, or forgets it and it sprouts into a new oak or pecan tree or corn plant."

"He's not ensuring anything," I said. "It's instinct."

"Is it? Or does a squirrel plan for the future?" He shrugged and folded up the top of the seed bag. "Squirrels are pretty smart. Man has yet to invent a bird feeder they can't crack. It's like an arms race between bird feeders and squirrels. That's why we put out corn—to keep them off the bird feeders, because they wreck them."

"Does the corn work?"

"Not really. I think they get tired of the same thing every day."

"I don't think squirrels are smart enough to grow their own food," I said.

"Does it matter?" He gazed at me with a strange earnestness.

"At the end of the day, does it matter whether they plan for it or it just happens? The result is the same. The squirrel is providing for his future and the future of his children and grandchildren."

I got the feeling he was trying to tell me something, but I didn't know what the hell it was. I didn't have the energy to try to puzzle it out. If I played dense about his parable, he'd eventually tell me straight up what it was he wanted me to know.

My parents were both being too mysterious for my comfort. Mom hardly spoke during lunch. I suspected they were setting me up. I wondered if I should cut out and head back to Memphis before they sprung their trap, but when I found Mom in the kitchen preparing Thanksgiving dinner all over again, I knew I couldn't leave. I stopped to appreciate the smells, which made her smile, but then she gazed at me sadly as though I were already a memory.

I went upstairs to change out of my wet jeans. Our family photos hung across the length of the upstairs hall. I stopped in front of the photo of my second wedding.

There hadn't been any photos of my first wedding. There *had* been a photographer, but none of the photos were ever developed. The groom, Dr. Richard Bruce of New South Wales, Australia, was my photography professor at Arkansas State, the man who photographed me nude with his Leica MP and showed me how beautiful I could be. He was the first man I had ever truly loved, who said I was the first person he ever truly loved, too. He never showed up at the church. Two handsome young Arkansas state troopers were waiting in the church parking lot to arrest him for bigamy. I never thought I'd see that bastard again, until he showed up at Michi Mori's kiddie-porn trial and took the stand as a witness for the defense.

Mom slipped up behind me, silent as a ghost, and put her

arm around my shoulder. She was still so tall, she made me feel like a little girl. I barely came up to her chin. We looked at the picture of me in my second wedding gown and Reed Lyons in his powder-blue tuxedo. Mom wore a lemon-yellow dress with an enormous hat. She looked like she had stepped off the set of *Steel Magnolias*. The wedding ceremony was held in Overton Park, the reception at Brooks Museum, just around the corner from the Shell, where they found Cole Ritter's body yesterday morning.

I asked her, "Do you know what a caul is?"

"No."

"It's the amniotic sack. Sometimes a baby is born inside it." I looked it up in my dad's old Webster's dictionary that morning.

"Oh, that." She smiled and hugged me. "I still have a piece of yours in your baby book. The nurse said it was good luck. Do you want to see it?"

"Not really."

"Why do you ask?" I could hear the anxious, unspoken question in her voice—was I pregnant? I was happy to let her keep thinking that, rather than tell her I'd been seeing ghosts again.

She squeezed my shoulder and said, "Have you tried talking to Reed recently?"

"We talked Thursday night."

"Maybe you two can patch things up. Reed is a good man, you know, and he loves you. And he makes good money. You ought to know by now how important money is, especially if . . ."

"Reed is stalking me," I said before she could finish. "He hired someone to follow me around." I twisted out of her grasp, went in my old bedroom and slammed the door. It really was just like old times again.

22

DINNER WAS SOLEMN, AS WERE all Thanksgiving dinners at the Pastor home. Dad was well into his fifth Wild Turkey by the time the rolls were ready. Mom stared out the window the whole time we ate. I often wondered why they seemed so put out by my habitual holiday tardiness, as if any amount of turkey and dressing could ever make this day what it used to be and could never be again.

After the pie, I went out on the front porch to smoke. Dad followed me, drink in hand. The yard still showed a few patches of white where the snow hadn't quite melted. The porch swing's plastic cover smelled like a school bus.

Dad stood in the dark, the ice cubes in his glass tinkling, saying nothing, while I smoked and flicked my ashes over the rail into the azaleas. I was seriously considering driving home tonight. Whatever it was, they either needed to tell me or stop acting like somebody was about announce they had cancer.

"So what's up?" I asked. It wasn't a casual, conversational question. It was a demand.

He sucked at his drink, drained the glass and spit out an ice cube. "It's your mother," he said. Breast cancer. I thought, *She's got breast cancer.* "She worries about you."

"Is that all?"

"That's her job. She worries about you, and I worry about her. That's my job. She's scared to death something is going to happen to you."

"Why?"

"Hell if I know. You know I don't worry about you. Anybody who can make it through Coast Guard rescue training can take care of herself. But a mother never really stops worrying. Your mother puts a lot of store in her faith in God. She believes her Gift of the Spirit is prophecy, but she just worries more than most. Can you blame her?"

"No." Other than her habit of saying grace over a meal, my mother had never struck me as being particularly religious. Then again I hadn't been to church with her in almost twenty years. Maybe things had changed. Maybe she had found Jesus, as old women often do.

"She just wants you to be happy," Dad said in the dark. He tinkled the cubes in his glass. "You're always . . ." I heard him try to take another drink, but all he had left were ice cubes. ". . . not very happy," he finished clumsily.

"She thinks being married is the road to happiness. That was her road, not mine." I didn't need her judging me. I didn't judge her. Most of the time, anyway. Someone drove by and I saw my father's face in the glare from the lights. He looked sad, resigned, staring into his empty glass.

"You think you know her pretty good, don't you?" he stated.

"She *is* my mother."

"What if I told you she had an affair?"

"I'd say you're lying." He didn't respond, just swirled the ice cubes in his glass. "When?" I asked.

He was quiet for a long time. "Jeez, it must be eighteen, nineteen years now. After you left the second time, I think."

I didn't know what to say.

"She confessed, of course," he continued. "Couldn't live with the guilt. She's still upset with me because I didn't ask for a divorce. She thinks I don't love her."

"Do you?"

"Of course I do. Jesus, I thought you were smarter than that." I couldn't imagine my mother with anyone other than my father. My father I could imagine with just about anybody you care to name.

"Did you tell her about your affairs?"

"Of course not."

"Why not?"

"Because I really do still love her."

"If you loved her, you'd tell her," I said. "You wouldn't sit there and let her think she's the bad guy."

"The *bad guy*!" he laughed. "How old are you again?"

"I'd tell, if it were me." I said. As a matter of fact, it was me, and I did tell. And just like my father, Reed hadn't asked for a divorce. I wondered if my father was also tormenting my mother with her sin, never letting her forget how she had betrayed him.

Dad said, "If you really love somebody, you shut your mouth and live with the guilt, even if it kills you. Sin is compounded by confession. Look that up in your Funk and Wagnalls. Confession may comfort the soul, but only because it forces other people to bear the burden of your guilt, and that's hardly fair to them. Ignorance is bliss, and half of communicating is knowing when to shut your cake hole."

"What a selfless martyr you've become," I said.

"If I didn't love your mother, do you think I'd have gone to so much trouble to hide what I've done?"

"What about me? You never seemed to care that I knew."

"That was an accident," he said. "I never meant for you to find out."

"My finding out didn't stop you."

"You didn't try to stop me either, did you? If you had asked . . ." His voice got louder. He was almost yelling.

"Would you have stopped?"

He thought about that for a minute. "Probably not. An apple a day keeps the doctor away, but too many apples will kill you. Monogamy isn't natural for a man."

"But it's fine for women? Is that what you're telling me, *Daddy*?"

"I never said that," he said, quiet again, in control once more. I could almost see him smiling. "If women were naturally monogamous, I wouldn't have been nearly so tempted. I've always preferred married women. The happier her marriage, the better she is in bed."

"What am I, your therapist?" I flicked my butt into the yard. "You should be paying me for this."

"How about I buy you a drink," he said.

"I think you should."

I followed him to the kitchen. Mom leaned against the sink, staring out into the dark backyard. As we entered, she jerked and picked up a dirty plate. Dad had bought her a brand-new Whirlpool dishwasher for their anniversary, but she only used it for pans and mixing bowls. She still washed all her tableware by hand.

Dad filled two crystal tumblers with ice and poured a stiff shot of Turkey into each, followed by a splash of 7-Up for mine. He drank his undiluted and strong enough to straighten your pubes. Even with the 7-Up, mine made me suck in my cheeks. While we sat at the kitchen table drinking our health, Mom stacked the last plate in the drying rack, wiped her hands on a dish towel, and disappeared into their bedroom.

Dad was pouring us another round when she returned. She had a manila folder pinched in her hand. She laid the folder on the table and rested her fingers on it. I looked at Dad and he shrugged.

"So how did your date go?" she asked pleasantly.

"It was OK," I lied. I had begun to dread what she had hidden in that folder. I imagined cut-out copies of dresses from wedding magazines. I couldn't go through that with her, see the disappointment on her face.

"What's his name again?"

"James St. Michael."

"And he's a pilot?"

"Yeah."

"Friday morning, before I went shopping, I stopped by the library," she said. "Your father designed that library." I nodded. I had spent many a Saturday afternoon there my junior and senior years of high school, throwing together last-minute term papers and research projects.

"I think it's his best design." She opened the folder, in which lay a single Xeroxed copy of the front page of the Memphis newspaper. She slid it across the table. On the right was a head-shot of a gorgeous young woman, mid-twenties, with short dirty-blond hair and supermodel cheekbones. She looked familiar, and now I knew where I'd seen her before. The headline read "FedEx Pilot's Wife Found Brutally Murdered." The caption under the photo read, 'Police say Ashley St. Michael's husband is not a suspect at this time.' Because the copy was reduced to fit on a single piece of paper, I couldn't read the story. I didn't need to. I knew now where I'd heard James St. Michael's name before, because I'd taken the crime-scene photos of his murdered wife.

"Jacqueline, please tell me you're not dating this man," my mother said in a trembling voice.

Sunday

23

MARY WAS MY DEAD GRANDMOTHER'S name, the woman I never met save in photographs and graveyards. Jacqueline was for Jackie Kennedy. If I'd been a boy, I would have been named Robert Enoch—Robert after the younger Kennedy brother, Enoch after my dentist grandfather. But my father wouldn't allow these bits of Democratic family trivia to be known, lest he offend some Republican and lose a contract. In 1966, the year of my birth, Democrats still ruled Arkansas government top to bottom, but it paid for a man like my father to avoid political conflict. He never voted.

My mother told me the tragic history of my name when I was nine. She thought Jackie Kennedy was the most beautiful woman in the world, not least because she had been married to the most beautiful and tragic hero in American history. When Jackie married Aristotle Onassis in October 1968, my mother felt personally betrayed. She tried to get people to start calling me by my first name, Mary, but by that time, I was little Jackie Pastor to the whole town.

Of course, Robert Kennedy had been assassinated in June 1968, so no matter what, I was doomed to bear an inauspicious name. It was enough to make a body superstitious.

When my brother Sean was born in December 1968, my mother picked the name Sean Wallace out of a Jonesboro phone book. My father agreed without telling her that he had always wanted to name his firstborn son after the original James Bond. At least Sean Connery never let my father down, except in *Highlander 2* and *The League of Extraordinary Gentlemen.*

Sunday morning, Mom sat on the edge of my bed and begged me to go to church with them. I hadn't brought any church clothes, but she said there were dresses in my closet I could wear. She opened the closet to show me clothes from high school and college, plus my old Coast Guard uniform. I wouldn't even get out of bed. I hadn't worn a dress in five years. My old dresses wouldn't fit. Two of me could fit inside some of them. I didn't particularly care to remember that fat fifteen-year-old girl. I still had nightmares in which I was two hundred pounds and sprouting a mall claw as big as a rhinoceros horn.

Mom and Dad dressed and left as though going to a funeral. I watched them back out of the driveway in Mom's Oldsmobile. I shuffled downstairs to the kitchen. Mom had left me half a pot of coffee, which I drank black and lukewarm. I sat at the table and flipped through the Sunday edition of the *Arkansas Democrat-Gazette.* The front page was all about Arkansas beating No. 1 LSU in triple overtime the previous Friday afternoon. That hadn't just been a game, it was a historic event, like the Athenian defeat of the Persians at Marathon. I no longer followed Arkansas football, but I still felt that familiar rush of tribal joy reading about their victory.

On page A7, I noticed a three paragraph mention of the Playhouse Killer's most recent victim—internationally famous playwright Cole Ritter, winner of the Pulitzer Prize, two Tony awards, and any number of European honors. There was little in the story that I didn't already know, save for the general level of astonishment that someone so famous should die in so "theatrical a manner." No pun intended on the part of the reporter, I'm sure. But this was bound to put our Playhouse Killer on the national and international stage. I hadn't thought of that.

I folded the paper and laid it on the kitchen counter. I called Adam on the telephone. When he answered, I said, "James St. Michael."

"What?" He sounded like I had woke *him* up for a change.

"What do you know about James St. Michael?"

"Other than he killed his wife?"

"Why isn't he in jail?"

"We're still building a case against him."

"Bullshit. It's been two years. What are you waiting for?"

"What's your interest in him?" he asked.

"Just wondering. I was going over some old photo files and I couldn't remember."

"You wake me up to ask me about some old case, when I haven't slept since Thursday night?"

"Sorry."

"Sorry, my ass. If you know something, tell me."

"I don't know anything," I said. "What do you know?"

"I know he was in large to some guys." He covered the phone with his hand and mumbled something to someone, then came back, "He needed money." He wasn't alone. I don't know why that surprised me.

"Drugs?"

"Gambling. Up to his neck. He had a good job, brand-new FedEx pilot straight out of the Air Force. Her family had money. She had a big insurance policy."

"Did he collect?"

"No. Last I heard, he was suing FedEx to get his job back."

"They fired him?"

"They didn't want a suspected murderer on the payroll. I don't blame them."

"But what if he didn't do it?"

"She was killed in their bedroom. No sign of a break-in. Doors and windows locked, house key in her purse. He had the only other key with him when we questioned him. She wasn't raped, but he beat the hell out of her, strangled her. You took the pictures, Jackie. You saw her. It was pure rage. A murder like that is personal, not some random act."

"So why haven't you arrested him?"

"He was working the night of the murder," Adam said. "We have witnesses who were with her while he was on a plane to San Diego."

"That's a pretty good alibi. So how do you figure he killed her?"

"Obviously he hired it done. He may have been in San Diego, but that doesn't mean his house key was with him. Sooner or later we'll find out who he hired, but we can't move on him until we do."

I lit my very last cigarette and opened the window above the sink. It looked cold outside, but with the window open it felt about sixty degrees and damp, like it might start pouring down rain any minute. The last of the snow had melted away.

"Where are you?" Adam asked.

"My parents' house."

"Are you clean?"

"Sure I'm clean. You think I'd use here?"

"You have before."

"I forgot I told you about that," I said. Though Adam never had my eye for details, he never forgot anything. "In the future

I'll try to remember not to tell you anything you can throw in my face."

"I'm not throwing it in your face. I'm just trying to keep you honest about yourself," he said.

I decided to change the subject. "I just saw something in the Little Rock paper about Cole Ritter."

"I was up until two last night talking to some newspaper from Paris."

"Don't you think it's a hell of a coincidence that the killer's last two victims were from Michi Mori's house?"

"You know me," Adam said. "I don't believe in coincidences."

"Michi's a suspect?"

"No."

"Why not?"

"Because Thursday evening he had a heart attack."

"No shit! Is he dead?"

"Not yet. Friday afternoon he was still in IC at Methodist Hospital."

"Maybe Michi killed Cole and that's what gave him the heart attack," I suggested.

"Cole rode with Michi in the ambulance to the hospital. He told the EMTs he was Michi's personal physician. Idiots believed him."

"So what happened?"

"About nine o'clock, Cole leaves the ER, tells the nurse he's going to get a cup of coffee and make a phone call. Security cameras pick him up exiting through the Union Avenue doors. That's the last anybody sees of him. He didn't call a cab. He didn't get on a bus. He didn't make a phone call. He didn't get a cup of coffee."

"Shit."

"Shit is right. I'm starting to wonder if we'll ever catch this guy. He doesn't fit the profile. What if all we think we know about serial killers is based on the stupid and unlucky ones we've caught? The good ones we never catch, so we have no idea who they are or what they're like."

"This guy's not a ghost, Adam." If he were a ghost, I'd have seen him by now. "He's just a guy. He'll fuck up and you'll be there to give him the chop. You just need some sleep."

"When are you coming back to Memphis?"

"I'm just putting on my shoes."

"Call me when you get in. I want to see this place where you're going to meetings," he said, and hung up. I felt sorry for him. It felt good to feel sorry for someone other than myself for a change.

I went upstairs and changed clothes, got my stuff together. I had to get out before my parents made it back from church. I'd be disappointing them by cutting out, but they were used to being disappointed. It was easier this way for everyone, no clumsy goodbyes, no making promises everybody knows you won't keep. As I was dressing, I found six hundred dollars lying on top of my suitcase—five hundred for the camera, and another hundred to tide me over, because that's the kind of guy my dad was. He knew I was planning to skip out on them. If I had hung around to thank him, he might've been embarrassed.

Before I left, I made one more phone call. I had Jenny's number in my cell phone. It rang a few times and then her voice mail picked up. I left a message for her to call if she had a minute. Before I got downstairs with my suitcase, she was ringing me back.

"I'm glad you called," she said.

"Why?"

"I was worried about you. Are you OK?"

"I wanted to apologize."

"For what?"

"For leaving like that."

"It's OK. We knew why you left."

"It wasn't him. It wasn't the guy from the bathroom. I screwed up."

"I heard what happened," she said. "I thought it might have been you, but I didn't know for sure."

"Thanks for not telling to the cops."

"What was I going to tell them?" She paused. "Are you sure you want to be telling me this?"

"Not really."

"I'm about to go into church," she said. Somebody said good morning to her.

"OK. Well, thanks again."

"Don't mention it."

I didn't hang up right away. There was another thing I needed to ask her, but I was afraid to ask it, because I already knew the answer. But I had to ask it. "Who is Ashley?"

"A friend of ours. She was killed Thanksgiving weekend a couple of years ago. We meet at Bosco's every year to drink to her memory."

"Why Bosco's?"

"That's the last place we saw her," Jenny said. "In fact, we're probably the last people who saw her . . ." Her voice caught and she cleared her throat. ". . . alive. Jesus, it doesn't get any easier to talk about this."

"Talk about what?"

"Please don't think I'm crazy, but the night Ashley was

killed, I knew something bad was going to happen. I begged her to let me drive her home, but she said she wanted to stop and say hi to somebody."

I felt my gut wind up in a knot. *She knew her murderer.*

"Did you tell the police that?"

"Of course."

"One more thing. Was her name Ashley St. Michael?"

"Oh my God!" Jenny was quiet for a long time. I heard the clock in the hall ticking, then it started to chime eleven o'clock. "Did you know her?" she asked in a whisper.

"No, but I saw her picture in your phone. And I met her husband."

"You know Jimmy?" She sounded very relieved about something. "God, I haven't seen him in what, more than a year? How's he doing?"

"That's hard to say. I don't know him that well. We only met last week." It was hard to believe it had only been a week.

"I'm glad he's getting out and seeing people again."

"Do you think he killed his wife?"

"Jesus, no! No way. No way in hell."

"How do you know?"

She cleared her throat and told somebody to go on inside. "Listen," she said in a low voice. "You know how rare it is to find that one person who is perfect for you in every way?"

"Sure. I see it all the time in movies."

"Most people never find it, or think it doesn't really exist except in books and movies, but Jim and Ashley had it. It was the real thing. You should have seen them together. It breaks my heart. It sounds corny as hell, but they were true soul mates. When Ashley died, I thought it would kill Jim. He wasn't the same person. He was a broken shell. Anybody could see that. And then the police started accusing him of her murder! God, there's no fucking justice in the world. I'm sorry, excuse me."

"It's OK," I said.

"Anyway, whoever killed Ashley killed Jim, too. Will you ask him to call me?"

"I will. Well, thanks. I'll let you go."

"I'm glad you called, Jackie," she said.

"So am I." What she had told me about James meant nothing. It just meant she believed in fairy tales. A therapist will tell you the kind of relationship James and Ashley St. Michael enjoyed almost never lasts. They are an aberration of the moment. The years pass and people change, they grow apart, or one grows away, leaving the other behind, bitter, hurt, and jealous. Perfect compatibility only exists in television commercials for dating websites. Compatibility isn't necessary to have a successful marriage. My parents were the perfect example. Forty-five years of quiet desperation, yet they were inseparable.

But clearly Ashley had met her murderer, sought him or her out.

"Wait a second," Jenny said before I hung up. "You mean to tell me you just met Jimmy last week, and then a couple days later you find my cell phone in a garbage can?"

Smart girl, that Jenny. For somebody who still believed in fairy tales, nothing got past her.

24

I LOADED UP THE CAR, then went back to the house to lock up. My parents kept a spare key in a fake rock in the azaleas. I locked the door and returned the key to its rock. That's the first place an experienced burglar looks before he goes through the trouble of kicking down your door. You might as well hang the key on a hook by the mailbox. My parents wouldn't survive in a place like Memphis. I backed my car out of the drive and drove away. But not back to Memphis, not yet.

I turned off Pyburn into the Masonic Cemetery and drove around the loop until I reached Pastor Corner. I parked and tossed my cell phone on the seat, because there were certain times and places where you don't want to be connected to the world.

My brother's grave was one of them.

It was a simple upright square of polished granite, set next to the unfinished stones that marked my parents' plots. I stood on my own empty grave, looking down at my brother's occupied one—Sean Wallace Pastor, Beloved Son. Dead at fifteen. Murdered.

The last time I saw him alive was the Saturday night after Thanksgiving. He'd gone over to a friend's house to watch

movies. I woke up in bed that night with him standing at
the door. I said, *You finally made it home* and he said, *Yeah.* I
said, *Did you get in trouble?* and he said, *No. Night,* I said, and
he said *Good night, Jack.* He always called me Jack. I rolled over
and glanced at the clock and went back to sleep. I woke up a
little after six the next morning with my father shaking me. He
told me to get dressed and come downstairs. When I told him
to leave me alone, he yelled at me to just fucking get up, which
is the only time in my life he ever swore. It scared the shit out
of me. I thought it was nuclear war. We used to worry about
the end of the world back in the day. I thought we were going
to make a run to the Ozarks, where Dad had a cabin in the
mountains. While I was getting dressed, I noticed the police
car in the driveway.

I went downstairs and there were two Pocahontas cops sitting on the couch looking miserable. I heard my mother in the
kitchen rattling coffee cups, making up a tray. My father was
still in his pajamas. He had a glass of straight bourbon in his
hand. "Your brother's been killed," he said without preamble.

"Here?" I shrieked, terrified, thinking someone had come
in the house while we were sleeping.

"Not here," my father said.

"Last night. Sometime before midnight. That's when we
found his body," one of the cops explained without looking
at me.

"But that's not possible."

"He was in an accident," the other cop said.

"No he wasn't!" I was screaming, I know, because my
mother ran into the room and crushed me to her breasts.

"He's not dead!" I jerked away and shoved her. She fell on
the couch with her long legs up in the air. My father tried to
grab my arms to keep me from hitting her. I kept screaming,

over and over, "He can't be dead. He can't be. He can't." One
of the cops got me in a bear hug and lifted me off the ground.
Mom was screaming and running around the room punching
herself in the head. I nailed the cop in the nuts three times
before he crumpled to the floor. It was a small town and my
dad was rich, so they didn't arrest me.

I was having a common reaction to grief. That's what they
said when I told them my brother wasn't dead, that he couldn't
be dead, because I had seen him and talked to him at 2:45 in
the morning, three hours after the police found his body. Nobody believed me, of course. I was being hysterical. Just like a
girl.

My parents didn't believe me either, but then they'd never
believed me or Sean when we told them our grandfather's
ghost lived in the attic, or about the old man who stayed out by
the elm tree in the front yard, or the Indians in the woods, or
the dead kid on the playground at school. By the time I was
twelve I stopped telling anyone what I saw. The only person
who ever believed me was Sean, because he saw them, too.

When Sean was killed, his ghost didn't stay in the attic
with Grandpa. After saying good night to me for the last time,
he moved on, and I hated him for that. I wanted him to hang
around and haunt me. I used to go up to the attic and beg him
to let me see him just one more time. There really was no justice in the world.

His grave was immaculate. My mother came every week for
twenty-four years to place new flowers over him. The grounds-
keepers kept the leaves raked and the grass mowed, trimmed
and edged. There was nothing to do but stand and stare at the
stone and the grave that wasn't even a mound anymore. There
wouldn't be any new Pastors born in Pocahontas, nor any old

ones planted in Pastor Corner after my parents died. Sean was the last male of the old family line. There probably wouldn't have been any more Pastors even if he had lived, but that was no consolation.

I took a rainbow bumper sticker and tube of superglue out of my pocket. For twenty-four years, on the anniversary of Sean's death, I came here and put a rainbow sticker on his gravestone. And then someone would come along behind me and peel it off. For a long time I thought it was my mother. We never talked about it. It might not be her. It might be anybody in that town. But it was probably her.

At first the police said Sean had been hit by a car, run over while crossing the highway. Hit-and-run—that's what they told us. That's what we said at the funeral. No one could say what he was doing out there, crossing the highway in the dark, miles from anything. They were investigating but they had no leads. At school, people were saying differently. They said somebody had killed Sean on purpose. Somebody I knew. Nobody would talk to me about it. Certain people began to avoid me, including my old boyfriend. So I hung around, acting normal, acting like nothing in the world was wrong, and all the while I listened to them, every word I could eavesdrop and overhear. Eventually, I learned that a girl I knew was dating a senior named Zack who knew something.

One day in April, I cornered her in the bathroom and shoved her head down the toilet until she told me what I wanted to know. She was a little pug-nosed cheerleader thing. She found out she liked breathing better than keeping secrets and being popular.

My father had Sean's body exhumed and examined by a coroner in Little Rock. Turns out he had been beaten to death and his body dragged behind a car to disguise his injuries. The local county coroner had missed these pertinent details because his son, Zack Taylor, had been the driver of the car.

During pretrial, Zack's father said it had been a normal, everyday fight between two teenage boys that ended tragically when one of them fell and struck his head on a rock. This was the delta, endless fields of mud and damned few rocks bigger than a marble. The Little Rock autopsy said Sean had been beaten with blunt objects while his hands were bound above his head. The coroner saw evidence of left- and right-handed blows from at least three different objects. Under interrogation, Zack named his accomplices. With his friends Wayne English and Dakota DeSpain, Zack strung Sean up and beat him to death, then tied him to the back of his truck, dragged him down County Road 405, and left his body in a ditch beside Highway 67.

At the trial, the defense tried to justify what the boys had done. They put a sophomore named Dan English on the stand. Dan was Sean's best friend and the younger brother of Wayne. Sean had gone to Dan's house that Saturday night to watch movies and play pool in their basement. Dan English was a big kid and a burgeoning golden god on the Pocahontas High School swim team, but on the stand he looked small, pale and frightened, like he hadn't slept in a month.

The defense attorney asked Dan if Sean Pastor drugged him and performed "various disgusting homosexual acts" against his will. The killers claimed they had come home to find my brother raping Dan, and in their rage, they had beaten Sean to death with pool sticks.

Dan English fell apart on the stand and denied the drugging story. Obviously this wasn't what he had been coached to say. The defense attorney tried to end the questioning, but

Dan kept going, hysterical and furious, pounding the rail with his fist. "Wayne and them took us out to the farm and they hung Sean from a tree. They beat him with fence posts and baseball bats and made me watch. I loved Sean. I died that day! I died!"

He wasn't the only one.

The only reason they hadn't killed Dan was because his older brother was there. They beat the hell out of Dan for being a fag, but they didn't go so far as to kill him. If I had been there, they wouldn't have killed Sean, either. The thing was, I should have been with those boys that night. I was going steady with Dakota DeSpain, but that weekend I was having my period, so I stayed home. I didn't want to hang out with Wayne and Zack and that crowd, but that's what Dakota always wanted to do if he couldn't screw me.

If I had been there, I could have stopped it. They'd have had to kill me, too. Sean died because I was on my menses. My brother would still be alive today if I hadn't stayed home, and maybe I would still be alive, too.

The judge ordered the jury to disregard Dan English's emotional testimony. Strangely enough, they disregarded the judge's instructions. Wayne English got twenty-five years, reduced to five on appeal, but Zack and Dakota were only sentenced to two years apiece. Zack's father, the county coroner, didn't even lose his job for trying to cover up my brother's murder. County coroner was an elected official, after all, just like the sheriff, and there were still a lot of people in that town who thought Sean Pastor got what he deserved. Dan English went on to Southern Cal on a swim scholarship, and in his third year hung himself from a diving board.

That's why I come home every Thanksgiving weekend, with the hope of seeing his ghost just one more time, so I could tell him I'm sorry, so I could tell him goodbye. I stood by his grave, waiting, probably not more than ten minutes. It had become a ritual, as pointless as any other, but I kept it religiously. I didn't cry anymore and Sean never showed, not even a prickle of cold on the back of my neck. I superglued the rainbow sticker to Sean's headstone, got in my car, and drove the fuck back to Memphis. Let Mom try to peel that one off.

Monday

25

ADAM WAS THE FIRST TO call me, about nine o'clock, leaving a message on my voice mail. He didn't have anything new on the killer, just an interesting detail. Cole Ritter's first publicly produced play had debuted at the Overton Park Shell in June 1966. About two minutes later, he called back and left another message. He said, "Ashley St. Michael was a professional photographer. You're buying a camera from her husband. I don't believe in coincidences, Jackie." And he hung up again.

About eleven o'clock, James called and left a message. He wanted to meet tonight. He didn't say why, but he didn't need to say why. It had become painfully obvious that he had sold his wife's camera because he needed money. And now he needed that last five hundred a lot worse than I did, which meant he was probably still in deep to the same guys as when Ashley was murdered. Maybe they'd killed her to send him a message. But that was too easy, and I didn't believe in easy any more than Adam believed in coincidences.

I woke up to the rain again, a good steady soaking rain sheeting down the bay window in the bedroom. I rolled off the couch, crawled into bed, and slept until twelve, woke up, crawled back to the couch, and ate cold pizza out of the box. Deiter called and left a message. He sounded excited. He said *fock* a lot. He said to come over right away. So I dressed, grabbed the Leica, and drove over.

I followed him inside and to the back of his shop, where he had my pictures printed out and thumbtacked to the walls. He had cleaned up the place enough to get close to the photos on the wall without standing on a pile of dirty underwear. While I examined the prints, he opened a beer and a package of Twinkies. He offered me a Twinkie, but I took his beer.

"Is this all?"

"Is this all? What the fock do you mean is this all. There's your Playhouse Killer," Deiter said as he pointed at the photos on the wall.

In three out of the dozen a person could be seen hiding behind a piece of scenery. But that's all it was—a person. Deiter had pulled out enough detail to show that our backstage slinker had short dark hair and thick eyebrows. But that could be anybody. Hell, you could even mistake it for me on a bad day, and I didn't have very many good ones.

"I'm not a miracle worker." Deiter was hurt and angry. "I did what I could. I got you a face out of this shit. Maybe the killer looks like Gumby, I don't know."

I was sorry. This really was the first solid piece of evidence we had. I told Deiter this and made him jolly again. I liked him jolly. But I knew if I showed these pictures to Adam, he'd say the same thing. It was pretty much useless as evidence, except as a sort of balm of Gilead. But Deiter had done his best. I couldn't ask for more. Actually, I could. I had hundreds of pictures taken of the Playhouse Killer's victims and their murder scenes. I didn't want to bring them all to Deiter, so I asked him to show me how to manipulate the photos to bring out more detail. If the killer was in the habit of watching the police process his murder scenes, I might find his face in one of those older pictures, maybe one good enough to show Adam.

Deiter plugged the Leica into his computer. He scrolled down until he found the pictures of Cole Ritter's murder scene and opened one I had taken of the construction. "Here's a good trick," he said and inverted the colors, basically changing the photo into its own negative on the screen. The effect was surreal. The construction site turned into an alien moonscape in which each block of shattered white concrete became a patch of nearly featureless black, while darker areas leapt out in strange, disturbing brilliance.

"Fock, there he is." He pointed at the ghostly figure of a man standing behind some trees at the back of the amphitheater.

"There who is?"

"Your killer."

I leaned over his shoulder for a closer look and got a good noseful of Deiter's unwashed body. He reverted the image to its original colors, and now that I knew a man was hiding there, I could easily see him among the trees. But there was something dark and bulky covering his face. "That's just a cameraman from the news," I said. "He's holding a video camera."

"Is that not rather small for a news camera?" Deiter asked.

Maybe so. Still, it made more sense that it was a cameraman. There were news people crawling all over the place trying to get a picture or a comment. The killer would have to be one frosty SOB to stand there in full view, filming the scene of his own crime while we worked it. Of course, he had apparently been ballsy enough to watch us at the Orpheum, hiding in the scenery not twenty feet from dozens of cops.

Deiter opened the other photos of the site, and in each, our voyeur's face was partially obscured by his video camera. So all we really had were a few more ill-defined photos virtually useless for making a positive identification. The question was, why hadn't I seen him when I was taking the pictures? I'd been looking right at him through the viewfinder.

Deiter seemed to read my mind. "This is no ghost, Jackie. I've seen pictures of ghosts and I tell you this is a man. The camera does not lie. Only the photographer lies."

26

M ONDAY AFTRERNOON TRAFFIC WAS MASSIVE and sluggish, with a gray drizzle coming down, bury-ing the top of the Clark Tower in thick cloud. I could smell the greasy fumes coming from the KFC down the street. I sat at the stop sign for about five minutes waiting to turn right on Poplar until this POS powder-blue Camaro stopped traffic to let me out. I waved my thanks and drove west, then north on Perkins, headed for home. The stack of photos Deiter had printed out lay on the seat next to me. Every once in a while, I'd look down at them, at the hidden face of the man who had been murdering gay men across Memphis virtually unhindered for four years now. I knew I was going to have to show the photos to Adam. Eventually. I didn't know how I was going to do it. The more I thought about it, the more I thought the best thing would be just to drop them in his lap. Let him decide what they were worth.

I bottomed out turning into the parking lot behind my apartment and slid to a stop in the spot nearest the door. As I reached across the console for the camera and pictures, a pale blue Camaro eased into the lot behind me and stopped with its ass hanging out in the street. The fenders were beat all to hell, patched with rust and gray primer, and the hood was a darker shade of blue than the rest of the car, but the tires shined new and black and the windows were tinted dark as welder's glass. It was the same car that had let me out on Poplar over by Deiter's place.

When the driver saw me, he tried to back out but he had to stop because of cross traffic. I ran up to his car, grabbed the passenger-side door handle and tried to open it, but it was locked. I couldn't see the driver because of the tinting. I screamed, "Tell that motherfucker Reed if he has me followed again, I'll kill him! You hear me? *Entiendes?*" I kicked the side door, adding another dent. I looked around for a rock or brick and spotted a quart bottle of Miller half full of piss sitting on the curb. As I reached for it, dude backed his car out into traffic, tires squalling on the wet pavement, horn blaring. He T-boned a late model Toyota, spinning it 180 degrees into oncoming traffic. I ran back to my car and grabbed the Leica off the front seat, then followed him out into the stalled traffic, snapping away while he shook the cobwebs out behind the wheel. He finally came to his senses before I could get around in front of his car. He put it in drive and floored it, wheels smoking. I zoomed in on his license plate as he sped away. The old lady in the Toyota fell out of her bent car screaming, streamers of gray hair plastered to her face, blood pouring from her nose.

I walked back to my car and grabbed the killer photos off the front seat. It was just like Reed to have me followed, but I had the bastard this time. That old lady would sue his sorry ass for every dime he had. Other people had stopped and walked her over to the curb, gave her a handkerchief to cap the flow of blood from her crimped schnoz. I gave her a business card for the slimiest lawyer I knew and took a full set of photos of her wreck and injuries, which progressively worsened while she waited for the ambulance and her head filled with dreams of avarice and an easy retirement.

I wondered what idiot my soon-to-be ex-husband had sent to follow me. From the look of the car, I guessed one of the illegals he hired to mow lawns and keep up his vacant properties. I hoped so, anyway. I hoped Reed would get nailed for a few immigration violations as well as liability for the reckless driving of his employee. I heard a pack of sirens coming from the other side of the overpass. It wasn't long before Adam's unmarked cruiser rolled up, followed by a traffic cop and a fire truck. He climbed out of his car as though aching in every bone. "What are you doing here?" I asked.

"I heard the call on the radio and recognized the address. You know I don't believe in coincidences."

I described the accident to Adam and the traffic cop. The latter seemed inclined to assign at least part of the responsibility to me, since I had threatened the driver with a bottle of piss. I showed them the pictures I had taken. He left to run the plates and report the hit-and-run.

"You're not going to believe this," I said to Adam. Now seemed as good a time as any.

"Try me."

"I've got pictures of the Playhouse Killer."

"Bullshit." I let him dangle for a few seconds without saying a thing. I just held the bundle of 8x10 glossies to my chest. "You'd better not be bullshitting me, Jackie."

"I'm not kidding. I've got the pictures right here." I put them in his hands.

He flipped through them, frowning. "I don't believe it."

"I told you. Of course, you can't see his face very clearly."

"I'll want the original image files."

"Of course."

"Why didn't you tell me before now?"

"I only found out just now," I lied.

I invited him inside. An ambulance drove up as we climbed the stairs. Mrs. Kim stuck her head into the hall, looked at us and slammed her door. We entered my apartment.

"This is a nice place," Adam said. He walked around, staring up at the ceilings while he pretended not to be scoping the place for drug paraphernalia. "Better than it looks from the outside. Did you go to a meeting yesterday?"

"Yep."

"Sorry I had to skip out on you. This case is eating every free minute." It was the first time I could remember that he didn't question me about my activities in more detail. Maybe he believed me because he had checked—as my sponsor, all it took was one phone call to find out if I had been going. Or maybe he believed me because I didn't have to lie about it.

I turned on my laptop and plugged in my Leica. Adam examined the photo printouts I had spread on the kitchen table. I offered him a drink, but all I had was beer and tap water. "They got sodas and stuff downstairs," I suggested.

"I'm OK." He flicked the pictures aside. "These are useless. You can't see the guy's face at all."

I lit a cigarette and offered him one, and to my surprise he took it. He lit up and sat back in the cheap creaking dinette chair, blew a cloud of gray smoke into the air over his head. God he was good-looking. I wondered if he had a girlfriend. He'd never talked about anybody romantically.

"Think about what these photos mean." I leaned over the table and laid my hands on top of the pictures. "Our boy was there, watching us the whole time. Maybe watching us every time, for all we know."

"He's got balls," Adam agreed. Then he asked me for a beer. He was falling apart in front of me. This case, especially the last week of it, was killing him. He was weakening to temptation before my very eyes, and I was the source of that temptation. But I wasn't going to say no to him.

I grabbed a beer from the fridge and opened it. He pulled two prints out of the stack, one from the Orpheum and one from the Shell, laid them side by side and studied them while he sipped his beer. "If these two are even the same guy."

"It would be a hell of a coincidence," I said. I opened my photo files from the serial killer's previous murders.

The first file I pulled up was the Simon twins folder. I clicked through the images without seeing anything unusual. Next I tried the Richard Buntyn scene from the Playhouse, where the killer had earned his infamous moniker. I opened each file and inverted the colors the way Deiter had shown me, hoping I would get a glimpse of the killer hiding backstage like he had at the Orpheum. But there was nothing there. Just cops and more cops, Adam looking a good deal younger than he did now, though it had only been two years ago.

That left the Jim Krews murder—the killer's first, as far as we knew. It had been four years ago. This killing had always seemed the most personal, the most tragic. The Simon twins had been younger, but something about the scenes I had photographed that day in midtown suggested a brutality unrivaled by any of his subsequent murders. Maybe he thought the same thing and had spent the last four years trying to recapture the magic of that first murder.

27

One May morning four years ago, Jim Krews's parents had come home from vacation in Europe to find their son's partially eaten corpse spitted, whole hog, over a brick barbecue pit in their backyard, warm coals still glowing beneath him. His killer had carved off his penis and portions of his buttocks. These relics were nowhere to be found and the investigators on the scene assumed they had been eaten, maybe with fava beans and a nice bottle of Chianti. I had several photos of the picnic table and the words scrawled across it, in barbecue sauce—*For I have sworn thee fair, and thought thee bright, who art as black as hell, as dark as night.*

Cause of death was blunt-force trauma. He'd been beaten to death with a brick. During the autopsy, Dr. Wiley found a decorative glass unicorn in the victim's rectum. He was a poetry major at Rhodes College, the campus not far from his home. After the barbecue-sauce poetry was identified by a brand-new homicide detective as a quote from Shakespeare's Sonnet CXLVII, they briefly took the victim's Shakespeare professor into custody. That new detective had been Adam McPeake.

Then the Warren Academy auditorium burned down and in the ruins they found two seniors, Roger and Loeb Simon, twin brothers, and both noted homosexuals. They were naked and cooked in their own juices inside an antique iron bathtub that was part of the set for a production of Thornton Wilder's *Our Town*. They had been trussed up with twine and left in the tub with a heavy piece of carpet covering them while the auditorium burned down around them.

Because all three victims were young homosexual men, the police began to suspect the killings might be related. But as there were no similar murders for almost a year after the Simon boys, the possibility of a serial killer faded as a working theory. All other trails led to dead ends and the investigation stalled.

That ended on a Tuesday morning a little over two years ago. On the Monday night before Thanksgiving, the body of an art historian named Richard Buntyn was discovered on the stage at Playhouse on the Square. My photos of the scene showed a naked man stuffed headfirst into a wine barrel. Imagine everyone's surprise when the body was removed and a severed pig head floated to the top. Adam McPeake immediately recognized the scene as a staging of the death of the Duke of Clarence from Shakespeare's *Richard III*, in which the Duke is stabbed and drowned in a malmsey-butt. Dr. Wiley later determined the victim had been raped with a butcher knife.

Adam was the first to connect the dots between the Buntyn, Krews and Simon murders. The Simons, he observed, had been trussed up and baked in a pie, like the characters Chiron and Demetrius in *Titus Adronicus*, again Shakespeare. But Adam's most remarkable detective coup came when he identified the Krews backyard as the same place where Tennessee Williams's first (now lost) play *Cairo, Shanghai, Bombay!* was performed. That's something you won't learn from the Chamber of Commerce. The glass unicorn discovered in the victim's rectum pointed to Williams's *The Glass Menagerie*. That the victim had been cannibalized suggested *Suddenly, Last Summer*, also Tennessee Williams, in which Sebastian, a frustrated young homosexual, is killed and eaten while on vacation in Europe.

Because of the pig's head, the police suspected the killer might be a local butcher or pig farmer. Under normal circumstances, a pig's head isn't particularly easy to get hold of, but this was Memphis, where you can pick up a pig head for a song at the barbecue festival. Krews had been barbecued, pointing to someone into the competitive barbecue scene. That all four victims were known homosexuals suggested hate as a motive. They thought he might be a repressed homosexual with religious delusions. The FBI sent in a profiler who suggested a white male, late twenties or early thirties, who had held a variety of menial jobs, socially inept and pathologically shy, a creature of the social shadows, a wallflower who probably grew up with a domineering father figure who sexually abused him. His victims likely were people he encountered on a daily basis, thus the extremely personal nature of the crimes. But they never found a solid connection between the four victims other than the theatrical nature of their deaths. They shared no mutual friends or relatives. With the Buntyn crime referred to as the Murder at the Playhouse by the press, it wasn't long before a local theater critic dubbed him the Playhouse Killer. He became Memphis's most famous serial murderer since George Howard Putt. The police were certain he would strike again, sooner rather than later, now that he had captured the media's attention.

They were wrong. Two years went by without a murder. Billet began to suspect the killer had either moved away, died, or been imprisoned for an unrelated crime, but the media never let the story go. Every time a young man turned up dead, whether a cracker white boy from Germantown or a gang banger from North Memphis, they wanted to know if it was the work of the Playhouse Killer.

Two years passed with no official victims. There was, however, one unsolved murder that Adam argued also belonged to our killer. The victim was a transsexual named Patsy (Patrick) Concorde, her body found raped with a cedar branch on the Monday night before Thanksgiving on the corner of Walker and Neptune. The killer tied her to the bumper of her own car and dragged her down Neptune Street. He torched the Mustang and left the body unposed beside it. Adam was certain it belonged to the Playhouse Killer, despite the lack of an obvious connection to a play. Through a local antiquarian, he learned that the old Dionysian Theatre once stood at the corner of Walker and Neptune, but it burned down in 1928. In the Greek play *Hippolytus*, by Euripedes, young Hippolytus rejects the advances of his stepmother and is dragged to his death behind his own horses (Mustangs) after Poseidon (Neptune) frightens them. And finally, *Hippolytus* was first performed at the Dionysian Festival in Athens in 428 BC.

Chief Billet told Adam it was too big of a stretch to connect the murder to the Playhouse Killer. Patsy Concorde's death had all the hallmarks of a traditional hate crime. He argued that the anniversary of the Buntyn murder was merely a coincidence. I agreed with Billet. The theater references were too obscure and depended on the killer possessing an encyclopedic knowledge of local history. But Adam stuck to his theory, mostly because the killer had already proven that he knew more than most about Memphis theater lore. He argued that the killer was interrupted before he could pose the body in its proper theatrical scene, otherwise there would have been little doubt.

Now it looked like Adam might have been right. Last Monday was the one-year anniversary of Patrick Concorde's murder, and the second anniversary of Richard Buntyn's slaying. The Simon and Krews murders all happened on Mondays as well. It looked like the killer was even more cunning than we thought. And now he was really getting busy.

The photos of the Krews murder scene were distressingly repetitive. It was my first job of this type and I was trying to impress the boss with the quantity of my work. There was one angle I kept returning to—I don't know why. It was a portrait of the victim. Jim Krews had been found skewered on a rotisserie above an outdoor barbecue pit, facing the sky with his arms and legs curled up against his body. I had taken numerous photos of his profile against the far fence and the green trees beyond it.

In one of the photos I noticed something I'd never seen before—the top half of a head sticking up over the fence. All I could see were the eyes and a crop of short black hair, but even these were blurry. I remembered how they had found the body while the coals under it were still warm, plates on the picnic table, ice in the plastic picnic cup of fizzing Diet Coke sitting on the brick wall of the barbecue pit. The killer had almost been caught sitting down to his dinner. The cops made a thorough search of the area, but apparently not thorough enough, because here he was peeking over the fence. The best part of that day for him was probably watching us process his handiwork. Maybe that was the thrill he had been trying to recapture ever since.

Someone knocked on the door. It was the traffic cop. He'd

run the plates on the hit-and-run. They'd come back stolen, which pretty much figured. Reed wasn't that stupid after all.

Adam thanked him and started to close the door when I asked, "Who do the tags belong to?" The traffic cop told us the name. Adam closed the door, turned to me and leaned against the door.

"That's a hell of a big coincidence," I said. "Almost as big as this." I turned my laptop around, showing him a photo of the back of the smashed-up Camaro. I pointed to the bottom right corner of the rear window, where a faded rainbow apple sticker was peeling from the glass.

28

Adam drove, even though he shouldn't have. He'd had a beer while still on the clock, and now he was driving a police vehicle with alcohol in his system. Not enough to get a DUI, but you only needed enough to register on a breathalyzer if you were on duty. If anything happened, the department would cover it up as a matter of course. But he was still technically on probation for cocaine abuse, which was how he became my NA sponsor. If somebody wanted to make a stink about it, they could. Somebody like Wiley, for instance.

"Rape kit came back on Ritter," Adam said as he wove through traffic. He was doing about ninety down Union even though the other drivers weren't exactly falling over themselves to get out of his way.

"Yeah?" I said through clenched teeth. "Not even a week. What got into Wiley?"

"He thinks he's gonna solve this one himself."

I grabbed the dash as he slammed on the brakes to avoid hitting a school bus. As we whipped by, I saw the terrified faces of about twenty kids staring down at us.

"Jesus, be careful."

Adam leaned across me, flipped off the bus driver and kept going. "Turns out Ritter wasn't raped."

"That's interesting."

"Damn. Wiley couldn't wait to tell the chief about it and make me look bad." He barely slowed down to take the left turn onto Belvedere, whipping across oncoming traffic. I saw cars piling up sideways to avoid us.

"Wiley thinks Ritter's is a copycat murder?"

"Wouldn't you?" Adam asked. We slid to a stop about a hundred yards north of Michi's house. Adam slammed the door so hard I thought the glass would cave. He figured Wiley was right.

But if Wiley was right, whose picture had I taken? Who was the guy with the video camera hiding in the trees near the Shell?

I joined Adam on the sidewalk and we started toward Michi's house—just a couple of regular people out for a stroll in the pouring rain. I had my Leica in its case under my jacket and Deiter's ghost-hunter ball cap pulled down low over my eyes. Adam wore jeans, a black polo, and a Memphis Grizzlies windbreaker.

You couldn't see Michi's house until you were right up on it because of the neighbor's hedge. The limbs of the sycamore trees dangled as though already weary of winter and rain, the water dripping off their twig ends and pattering the brim of my cap. Adam paused at the end of the hedge and pointed at a shard of red reflector plastic lying in Michi's driveway. He was wearing his class ring, East High class of '91, with a ruby for his birthstone.

"Don't you think we ought to call in the cavalry on this one?" I asked.

"First I want to see if anybody's home."

We walked down the hedge bordering Michi's property. The neighbor's backyard was surrounded by a high brick fence topped with iron. I climbed up on Adam's shoulders for a scout. The yard was shaded and landscaped, with about two hundred variegated hostas growing under the trees. They also had a big doghouse in one corner. I didn't see a dog, but I didn't particularly want to be climbing over the fence when White Fang came busting out.

The side hedge ended at the fence and there was a narrow, overhung path lined with stepping stones running along the foot of the wall. We crept through and squatted, staring up at Michi's brooding brown mansion, streamers of rain dancing among the fairy ironwork and lightning rods. Adam sat back on his heels. "Jesus. That's one big fucking house. Where'd Michi get his money?"

"His wife." She was old Memphis money, cotton baroness, in control of her own fortune before she was thirty. She and Michi met at the theater. She left him after he was castrated, but for whatever reason they never divorced. Maybe she still loved the old perv. When she died of breast cancer, she left her entire fortune to him.

"Some people have all the luck," Adam said.

The garage in back was an old carriage house, the kind of place that people in this neighborhood remodeled and rented out to hip young liberal-arts majors. It was detached from the mansion, sitting about twenty feet back. We couldn't see the doors. There were several cars parked along one side of the driveway. We used these as a screen to make our way around back.

As we squatted behind the fender of the last car, I could see Michi's kitchen window at the far corner of the house. It was dark. All the windows on the bottom floor were dark. We'd have to cross a fair amount of open space to reach the garage. Anybody could be sitting in one of those windows watching us and we'd never see them. The garage door was open and inside it sat the powder-blue Camaro with the caved-in rear end and the faded rainbow apple sticker in the window. The driver had removed the stolen license plate.

The same car had been parked in Michi's driveway a week ago Sunday when I came to sell him the photos of the Simon twins. As soon as I saw that rainbow sticker in the picture of my fleeing hit-and-run stalker, I knew it was one coincidence too many. String enough coincidences together and you'll find a conspiracy, Adam always said.

"Let's call in backup," I suggested. He stared up at the house and fiddled with his class ring as though it bothered him. "We can't let this guy slip by us."

"If he's smart, he won't even be here."

"He's smart."

"Let's go talk to Michi."

"I thought Michi was in ICU."

"He was released this morning," Adam said.

"What about his heart attack?"

He shook his head. "Panic attack. They sent him home with a scrip for Xanax."

We crept back along the line of parked cars and paused for a minute in the shelter of the hedge path. Adam looked back at the house, quietly casing it. He said, "If the killer is one of Michi's boys, maybe we can get an ID without telling him what we're looking for. He probably just ditched the car here because he's familiar with the place. We don't want to spook the others if we don't have to. One of them might tip the guy off."

We circled the hedge and walked up Michi's driveway. Being a cop was an easy enough role to slip into again. It was like riding a bicycle. The only part I didn't like was not having somebody to cover the back door, in case our boy bolted. No way he would hang around once he spotted us.

At least the porch was out of the rain. Adam rang the doorbell and we waited. We waited a long time, ringing the doorbell every minute or so. I tried to see in through the porch windows. Nobody answered the door.

"I'm gonna kick it in," Adam said.

He rang the doorbell again, keeping his finger on the button for a long time. I put my ear to the door and listened to it ring again and again, somewhere deep within the house. Finally, I heard someone swearing as he approached the door. I didn't recognize the voice.

The door popped open violently. A big linebackerish boy of about nineteen filled the doorway with his naked white chest and telephone pole thighs. He wore backwards sweatpants and was barefoot. The veins standing out on his neck were as thick as my thumb. "What the fuck!" he yelled.

Adam showed him a badge. The veins shrank and his face went white. He swallowed and looked from Adam to me and back again. "Yes sir?"

"Can we talk to Michi?" I asked.

"You know Michi-san?"

"We're old friends." The boy looked doubtful, but the badge in Adam's hand didn't give him much choice. "I'm his photographer." I stepped in front of Adam. "Can you find him for us? It's really important."

He stepped back, but only far enough to let us into the hall. Adam closed the door. I took off my cap and hung it on the hall tree, then kicked off my shoes like I was at home. The boy relaxed a little, seeing that I knew the house rules. There were eight pairs of men's shoes under the hall tree—tennis shoes, loafers, work boots.

"Who'd you say you were?"

"Jackie Lyons. Tell him it's Jackie."

"Y'all wait here, OK?" He headed off to find the old man.

I sat in the slipper chair by the door. Adam dragged his brogans across the Persian rug, drying them off. "This place gives me the creeps," he said.

"You OK?"

"Yeah. I just wish I hadn't drank that beer." He smacked his lips and grimaced. "You shouldn't have given it to me."

"I thought I was being a friend."

He shrugged and sighed, then wandered down the hall. He looked into a room, then stepped inside and turned on the light. "Jackie?" he said. The way he said my name hit like a cold finger on the back of my neck in the dark.

He stood in a dining room beside a big oval mahogany table polished so you could see the reflection of the ceiling fourteen feet overhead. The far wall was a huge window streaked with rain. The wall to the right had built-in cabinets, panes of glass in the doors, glass shelves, mirrors in the back to double the recessed lights. Hundreds of thousands of dollars' worth of antique china, Japanese pottery, silver, gold and crystal crowded the shelves. The opposite wall was covered with two medieval tapestries.

Only there should have been three tapestries.

29

Y OU REALIZE WE CAN'T USE anything we see here to get a warrant." I stood beside Adam looking up at the huge blank space on the wall. He stooped and picked up a chunk of plaster lying on the floor at the edge of the Persian rug.

"The killer must have ripped it down and used it to wrap Cole Ritter," he said. He pointed out a pair of ragged holes high up the wall near the ceiling.

"That kid told us to wait in the entry hall. He doesn't even live here. He can't grant us legal entry. We have to wait until Michi sees us."

Adam continued to poke around the room. He opened a drawer in the china cabinet and picked up a sword, a perfect mate to the one we'd found skewering Cole Ritter's body like a cocktail weenie. "This cabinet was open, wasn't it?" Adam asked me.

"The sword was just laying there in plain sight." He wouldn't listen to me and now I was going to have to lie for him.

"Excuse me!" a man said as he walked by me. He was an older guy, balding, wearing a white knee-length kimono. "Do you have a warrant?"

Adam laid the sword back in the drawer and turned. The man stopped as though he'd hit a wall. "Adam!"

"Hi, Dave," Adam said.

Dave Straw, theater manager from the Orpheum, backed up until he bumped into me. He jerked a step forward and whipped around with a vicious glare. "*Excuse me*," he snarled, then turned back to Adam. "What are y'all doing here?"

"What are *you* doing here, Dave?"

"I'm an old friend." Dave was trying to maintain control of the situation. I was close enough to see the hairs on his arms and the back of his neck stand up, prickled with goose bumps and popping sweat.

Adam smiled the smile of an old friend and rested an elbow on the tall back of one of the dining-room chairs. "We're looking for the owner of a blue Camaro with a rainbow sticker on the back window."

Dave ran his hands down the front of his kimono. His legs were so white they were blue, and completely hairless as though waxed.

"He doesn't live here."

"The car's parked in the garage."

"It is?"

"It had your tag on it about an hour ago, when it was involved in a traffic accident." Adam ran his hand across the top of the chair. The room smelled like Old English furniture polish. I wondered if anyone had ever eaten a meal on the table. "That would be the tag you reported stolen Friday."

"It's not my car," Dave said.

"I realize that. I saw your car in the driveway." His eyes flickered across mine.

"Where's Michi-san?" I asked.

Dave didn't like that question. If he only answered one line of questioning at a time, he probably could have kept his lies straight. "Still in bed. He's been there since he came home from the hospital."

"Did you bring him home?"

Dave nodded and looked pleadingly at Adam. "Let's go talk to him," Adam said.

It took a minute for the message to get to Dave's feet. Adam gave me a wink. He was one damn good cop. If I'd had a partner like him back in the day, I might still be a cop myself.

We followed Dave upstairs. He took the back stairs by the kitchen, which were steep enough that I could see right up his kimono from behind. He was wearing plaid boxers, something of a disappointment. I had expected nothing less than panties.

I had never been in the upper floors of Michi's house. The halls were narrower than those downstairs and painted a soothing pastel green with simple white trim and crown molding. It almost looked normal—almost, because nothing in Michi's house was normal. There was a lingering foul smell that no amount of potpourri or Ralph Lauren cologne could completely mask. It was similar to the smell downstairs, only sharper, and without the respectability given by the overlying odors of antique furniture and carpets. The rank was more pungent here, closer to the black heart of Michi's lair. I had smelled it before, in the back rooms of cheap porn shops where they showed dollar-a-minute movies in little booths with sticky floors and doors that wouldn't lock. Where men sought anonymous sex with faceless men kneeling on the other side of glory holes gnawed through the walls. Half the men I arrested in those places didn't call themselves gay or even bisexual. It was the debasement they sought, to give in to the darkness of their own souls, or to reaffirm their own deep self-loathing. Or maybe it was the cheap thrill, or the danger, or the unencumbered, un-emotional physical release.

And it wasn't just the layer upon layer of rotting semen caked in the floor cracks that gave those places their smell. It was the rawness of the exposed human psyche, like an abscessed tooth or a gangrenous wound. It was hellish and dark and fly-specked, and in those places people ceased to be human and became mere receptacles, disposable objects to be used and thrown away.

This was Michi Mori's inner sanctum, his unholy of unholies. Its pastel green normalcy, its vacuumed beige carpetness, belied the unfathomable debaucheries celebrated behind its paneled white doors. All the doors were closed, like in a hotel, and the quiet was profound. Dave stopped at the third door on the left. He tapped the hollow wood with the knuckle of this middle finger, then turned the knob and opened the door. "Michi-san?" he whispered as he leaned inside.

The lamp by the bed was on and the covers were pulled back. The place looked like any normal person's bedroom, like my parents' bedroom, neither overtly masculine nor covertly feminine. It was clean and tidy, no clothes on the floor, no drawers half open. I wondered where Michi kept the photos I'd sold him. The bed was empty. "Maybe he's in the bathroom." Dave crossed to another door and stopped with his ear close to the wood. After a few seconds, he said "Michi-san?" and tried the handle. The bathroom was dark. He flicked on the light. "He's not here."

As we exited the bedroom, two boys came out of another room down the hall. Neither looked older than twenty, both extremely good-looking, naked with shaved pubes and dicks like sausages hanging in a German shopkeeper's window. One of them had a folded towel and a bar of green soap. Neither seemed the least bit surprised or ashamed.

"Keith, have you seen Michi-san?" Dave asked.

"Not since this morning."

"He said he needed something from the wine cellar," the other boy said.

"When was this?" Adam asked. "What time?"

The two looked at one another and shrugged. "I don't know. Maybe around ten?" Keith offered

"It was before ten, wasn't it?" the other said.

"I don't think so."

"He was in the kitchen."

"Isn't he in his room now?" Keith asked.

"No," Dave said.

"God, I hope he hasn't fallen down those stairs!" They ran by us.

We followed, down the stairs and past Michi's kitchen, which was dark except for the light over the stove. By this time, we'd lost sight of the boys, but the swinging door marked their trail. I had just started down the cellar stairs, Adam close behind me, when a shrill scream came from below, cut short by a noise like a bowling ball dropped on a concrete floor.

We found Keith lying beside an enormous pool of dark, glossy blood, two streaks showing where his feet slipped. He lay on his side holding the back of his head. There was too much blood for it all to be his. His friend had slid barefoot through the pool and now knelt beside him.

We were in a cellar easily half the size of the house. The roof was supported by thick, ancient wooden beams that ran in parallel lines into the gloom. The floor was painted concrete, the walls concrete brick and lined with wine racks. There were wine barrels stacked up under the wooden stairs. Four light fixtures hung over an empty corner near the barrels, where someone had built a wooden platform about six inches off the floor, like a simple stage. A couple of old couches and chairs stood before it, crushed cigarette butts littering the floor around them.

The pool of blood ran from the stage across the floor and collected at the foot of the stairs. An antique desk sat at the center of the stage, and on it stood a chemistry set like something out of an old Frankenstein movie. A Bunsen burner hissed under a round beaker boiling with some dark liquid. A huge, leather-bound book lay open on the corner of the desk, its pages soaked red with blood. Sitting atop the spine of the book, with his mouth forced open in a hideous O of surprise by a gleaming silver speculum, lay Michi's severed head.

30

THE POLICE FOUND MICHI'S BODY scattered all over the cellar. For once, I let Wiley's boys take the pictures. Adam found me upstairs in the kitchen with Dave Straw. Dave sat at the Skovby kitchen table in his vomit-flecked silk kimono, hands cuffed behind his back. I looked out the window and watched the cops wandering around the backyard in the rain, kicking at the hostas under the elm trees. One of Dr. Wiley's techs passed in the hall with a white plastic bucket. He dropped it as he descended the stairs to the cellar.

Adam spread my photo printouts from the Orpheum and the Jim Krews murder scene on the table. Dave turned his head away rather than look at them. "I didn't know them, Adam."

"Who owns the blue Camaro?"

"There are so many boys. I can't keep track of them all."

"Have you run the VIN number?" I asked.

"It's been ground off." Adam sat across from Dave and said, "A little while ago you knew him. You said he doesn't live here."

"Did I?"

"Yes, you did."

"It's Endo's car," I said. Dave's head snapped around, confirming my guess. I opened the fridge, took a Heineken from the door and unscrewed the cap.

"Who is Endo?" Adam's question was directed at me. He wanted to know what else I knew, and how long I had known, but I had only then figured it out. Ever since last Monday night at the Orpheum, I thought the killer was Dave. When Adam introduced us, his hands were wet because he had just washed them. Then, when they uncovered the body, he excused himself and probably slipped backstage to watch from behind the scenery. Then the plates from the Camaro came back with his name. He was involved in the theater, and I guessed he was secretly gay. It all seemed to fit together.

I said, "Noboyuki Endo. Michi's grandson."

Dave sank forward until his forehead touched the table. For an older man, he was surprisingly limber. "You and Endo?"

"Once," Dave said to the table. "Just once."

"You've known all along, haven't you?" Adam asked him, but I wondered if the question wasn't for me, too.

Dave shook his head. "Just since Monday."

"That boy on the stage of the Orpheum with a pipe up his ass was a message to you, wasn't it? A message from Endo."

"How did you know?"

"That scene downstairs is from Marlowe's *Doctor Faustus*," I said.

Adam stared hard at me. "I don't get it."

"Faustus makes a bargain with Lucifer. For twenty-four years he would have the demon Mephistopheles to teach him magic." I took a long pull of beer to give myself time to put it together in my head, all the little ends and pieces coming together, each one leading to the next revelation. The beer seemed to help. "Endo's birthday was last Friday."

I took another pull, whirled it in my mouth for a second,

then swallowed. "He's twenty-eight. He came to live with Michi when he was four after his mother killed herself—twenty-four years ago."

"And from that you deduced it was Endo?"

"It was just a wild ass guess. Dave confirmed it, and now I think it's pretty obvious Endo chose to stage *Faustus* to celebrate the end of twenty-four years with his sorcerer."

"So what's your deal with Endo, Dave? How did y'all hook up?" Adam asked.

"Endo's a master carpenter. Every theater in town wants him for their productions, and not just because his grandfather is Michi Mori. But Endo doesn't like building things. He thinks he's an actor. I saw him do Othello once, only it was Laurence Fishburne as Othello. People thought he was joking because he's so good at impersonations. He can do just about any actor you name. He had every line memorized, every inflection, voice and poise and timing perfect, but none of it was real. He was just parroting another actor's performance.

"So I felt sorry for him, you know. Even though he makes it hard because he's such a prick. He hated us, said we were a bunch of vampires leeching off his grandfather. Like he wasn't doing the same thing. Can I have a cigarette?"

"I'm out," I said.

"Look in the drawer by the stove." I found an open pack of Michi's Winstons under a brochure for Maui. I shook one out, lit it and hung it in the corner of Dave's mouth. He nodded his thank-you and took a long shuddering drag and blew the smoke out through his nose.

"When Endo was a kid, he was cute, in a creepy way. One minute he's standing in the doorway staring at you with those huge black eyes of his, then you'd turn around and he'd be gone, just like that."

The cigarette seemed to help. Some of his color came back and he stopped sweating. He tilted his head to keep the smoke out of his eye. "Endo built that stage in the cellar. When he was a kid, he used to put on shows for Michi's guests. It was cute, you know, but God, he was so serious, and he'd get *sooooo* pissed when people laughed at him, he could hardly move. One time, I think he was about sixteen, he did the tomorrow and tomorrow scene from that Scottish play, and after it was over, Michi told him he'd never be an actor but he was a superb carpenter, because he had turned the cellar into this incredible castle dungeon set. Michi got him his first job at Theatre Memphis. He majored in theater but never got a part in any of the college productions, none that I ever heard about. After he graduated, he became master carpenter at the McCoy."

"The McCoy's at Rhodes College," Adam said to me. "That must be where he met Jim Krews."

"It's a black-box theater. They hardly ever need a carpenter," Dave said. "He wasn't there long, anyway. Once word got out, directors started hiring him for productions all over town. He's worked pretty much everywhere. He even did some set work for that Johnny Cash movie."

Adam pulled out a chair and sat across the table from Dave. "So let me make sure I understand. Endo worked for you at the Orpheum. Anything else?"

"We had sex *one* time, if you can call it that," Dave said. He sat up in the chair and flexed his hands in the cuffs. "Just once. He wanted me to humiliate him, piss on him, that kind of thing. I wouldn't do it. He hasn't left me alone since. Keeps calling my house. I'm married, Adam, you know that. I got kids in junior high."

Adam nodded sympathetically. Dave's marriage was over now. There was no way he could get through this without being outed. His marriage was important enough to him not to make a call about Endo, but not important enough to give up the closeted lifestyle.

"Tell us about Monday night. The theater was closed. What were you doing on the stage?"

"Checking the ghost light."

I almost dropped my beer.

"We leave a light on stage when there's no one in the theater. It's an old tradition, so the ghosts can put on their own productions. It's really so anybody wandering around the stage in the dark doesn't fall off. It had gone out, a safety hazard. I was going to check on it when I stumbled over Chris's body."

"So Endo turned off the light, knowing you'd come down to check on it and stumble over his little production. But why kill Hendricks? And what was he trying to say by staging *Edward the Second*?"

"Endo hates fags," Dave said.

"That doesn't make any sense. Endo is gay," I said. I took the smoldering cigarette butt from his mouth before it scorched him. His lips were so tacky some of the skin came off stuck to the butt. I dropped it in the sink.

Shaking with fear and emotional exhaustion, Dave said, "I don't know what Endo is. Whatever he is, they don't have a name for it. He wanted me, but he hates homosexuals, especially his own homosexuality. That's the only reason he killed Chris and left him there for me to find. I guess he wanted to show me he could do it."

"You knew him well enough to know he was the killer." Adam's voice was strained.

"I told you before, I only figured it out after he killed Chris. And even then, I didn't know for sure." His lips were trembling, but I couldn't tell if it was grief or terror. I doubted whether he knew himself

"You might have made a phone call, just the same," Adam said. "If you had, two people might still be alive."

"Don't you think I know that?" Dave cried. "If I had talked after last Monday, he would have known it was me. You think I want him coming over to my house, fucking with my kids, my wife?"

"We could have provided protection."

Dave laughed, not a little hysterically, and way too long for my comfort. I thought someone was going to have to slap him, like in the movies. "You can't stop Endo!"

"Lay off the histrionics, Dave." Adam stood up. I thought he was going to do it, but Adam was too good a cop for that.

"You didn't even know where to start looking until he decided he was ready to be caught!" Dave shouted.

"Ready to be caught? What's that supposed to mean?"

"It means what it means, Adam. Jesus Christ! Endo killed Michi. He's done with this shit, all this theater, all this life. He's ready to close the curtain." Dave laughed that half-crazy giggle that sounded like he almost couldn't stop this time. Not without help.

I reached across the table and backhanded him across the face. Luckily I had taken off my wedding ring. He stopped laughing and stared at me, just as surprised as the hysterical woman in the old movie. He tongued the blood on his lip.

Somebody had to do it. I could do it because I wasn't a good cop. I wasn't a cop at all.

31

IT WAS GOING TO TAKE hours to interview everyone and while we were there, more of Michi's *boizu* kept showing up. News of the murder hadn't made it on TV yet, but they were finding out somehow. The cops held them all for questioning, lining them up in the hall downstairs. Several stood there crying in each other's arms, but I couldn't tell if it was over the loss of their sugar daddy, fear of being outed or genuine grief at the death of that demented old Japanese pervert.

Adam was desperate to learn Endo's current address. One of the cops found his car tags stuffed into the garbage can behind the garage. His Camaro was registered to a Wayne Endo at Michi's address. Other than Dave, nobody in the house would admit to knowing him. It was going to take all night to get any information. Meanwhile Billet and Wiley showed up to wave their egos around and make things infinitely worse.

I asked Adam for a ride home. He couldn't leave yet, of course, but I was so tired I didn't care. He wanted to call me a cab and put me up at a hotel, but I didn't want a hotel, I just wanted to go back to my apartment. Most of all, I didn't want to be around when he found the photos I'd sold Michi. They were tearing the house apart, looking for anything that might lead them to Endo. Only four people in the world knew where those photos came from, and one of them was dead. I knew Adam wouldn't charge me or even tell Chief Billet, but I also knew I'd probably lose him forever. Today would probably be the last day of our friendship and he didn't even know it yet. I was already grieving.

We were in the dining room. Adam watched them finger-print the sword he'd found earlier, while one of Wiley's techs vacuumed the rug. They weren't going to discover Endo's where-abouts in the carpet. They didn't need any more fingerprints, either. Collecting trace evidence was useless at this point, but they were following procedure because procedure was all they had. Sometimes that's all you have to keep the snakes out of your brain—chickenshit routine. We'd stepped over the edge of known territory in Michi's cellar today. We were all flying on autopilot.

It was the silent efficiency of the murder that had every-body freaked, even Adam. Michi had been savagely greased, his body dismembered and scattered like Easter eggs in the cellar of a house full of people, and as far as we could tell, no one had heard a thing. Not one cry, not one meaty thunk of cleaver through flesh. How did Endo kill that shrill old eu-nuch, who'd scream like a baby if he chipped a nail, without anyone hearing or seeing? That a man could die that way didn't jibe with the normal order of the universe.

No one had seen Endo at the house that morning. They'd seen his car. They'd assumed he was lurking around some-where, spying through the peepholes he'd drilled in nearly every wall and floor in the house. They were like mouse holes—everywhere you looked you'd find another one. Some had been stopped up with chewing gum or covered with pic-tures or lamps. But there was always another one close by, smaller and better hidden. In all the times I'd been in Michi's house, I had never noticed them. It creeped me out wondering how many of my visits Endo had secretly watched, how much he knew about me and what he might do with that information, if anything.

Adam watched the tech dusting the handles on the china cabinet. "I don't think it's a good idea for you to go home today," he said without looking at me.

"Why not?"

"Because Endo's still out there. Until we find him, I'd rather put you up in a hotel. How's the Peabody sound? Billet will sign for it."

"Endo doesn't want me," I said, trying to convince myself more than anything. "He kills fags. That's his deal." I had kept the pack of stale Winstons I'd found in Michi's kitchen. I lit one and blew smoke at a spy hole in the ceiling above my head. It was no bigger than a BB. "He'd be stupid to stay in Memphis now. Besides, what could he possibly want from me?"

"I don't know. And I don't like not knowing. It doesn't make sense that he was following you today. That's what worries me."

"I'll lock the doors. Anybody who tries to come in will get a face full of baseball bat." I was frosty. I was hard as nails standing there flicking ashes on the rug, dual cool, brassing it out, even though my guts were rolling around like a nest of fornicating rattlesnakes.

"Do you still have your piece?"

"Hell, no. Got rid of that after the accident." I touched the old scar on my cheek where the bullet had gone through. I hadn't sold it for moral reasons, though—I needed the money.

Adam left off watching the techs sweep the room and walked me to the door. Several uniformed cops were standing on the front porch dicking the dog and watching it rain. They shut up as soon as we stepped outside. Someone was coming up the driveway through the rain, walking slowly and looking at all the cop cars. He stopped about halfway up. Adam nodded and the cops along the porch rail unbuttoned their holsters.

He shouted, "Come on up." Everybody was ready to give chase. I think they were looking forward to it. The guy in the driveway looked back the way he had come. "Don't try to run!" Adam ordered.

The guy walked slowly toward us, his hands in the air. He was a she and she was a postal worker in a gray rain suit with a sack of mail on her back. "What the hell, people?" she said as he neared the porch.

"Sorry," Adam said. The cops made room for her on the steps and she came up, shaking off the rain. Adam held out his hand. "Any mail for Michi Mori?"

"I can't give you his mail," the postal worker said.

"This is a police investigation. There's been a crime here."

"And the mail don't leave my hand except under the direct order of a postal inspector." She brushed by him, walked up to the mailbox hanging from the wall by the door, and stuffed in a handful of mail. She turned and glared at Adam. "What you do with it now is your business. I got my route."

She left, vanishing into the rain. The cops on the porch stared at Adam, snickering and elbowing each other. Somebody said, "Sheee-yit." He ignored them and removed the mail from the mailbox, shuffled through the letters, then pulled one out and tossed it to me.

It was a bill from a property-management company, addressed to Wayne Endo.

32

I RODE WITH ADAM. HE barely spoke on the way, but I could see the anticipation written on his sweaty face. He bit his lips and swore at the people driving too slowly. We drove without flashers or siren so we wouldn't alert Endo to our arrival. There were two squad cars behind us, and five more converging on Endo's apartment as we turned off Central onto Airways Boulevard and headed south. I tapped the bill from the property-management company against the dash, nearly as impatient as Adam.

Endo's place was a little one-room hellhole at the corner of Airways and Fairbanks, across the street from the Mississippi Lounge. I'd driven by the place a hundred times and never seen it—four apartments, two up and two down, with boarded windows and gang symbols spray painted on the bricks. It looked derelict, but people still lived there. Some of them were outside, standing on the balcony as we parked by the curb. Endo lived in the bottom apartment on the far end. The door was open. A cop stepped out and lit a cigarette, then dropped it when he saw Adam.

"Y'all were supposed to wait the fuck outside," Adam barked.

"Door was open, Sergeant. We was afraid the locals would get inside. A couple of boys was nosing around. They booked it when we pulled up."

"Anybody in there?"

"There's no there there," the cop said like some kind of mystic.

Adam stared at him for a moment, then entered. I switched on my Leica and followed him.

Endo's apartment was a single room about six feet by six feet, walls painted sky blue, red carpet twined with golden arabesques. A ticket booth with bulletproof glass stood out from the wall just across from the door. A hand-lettered sign hung crookedly in the window. It read, "Closed Monday."

"See what I mean?" the cop said behind me.

Gold curtains at the back of the booth might have hidden a door. Other than the door we entered, there were no other exits. A pair of paintings hung on the left wall. One was David's *The Death of Marat*, the other was of the same scene showing the dead man hanging out of his bathtub, but from a different angle, with a woman in a blue-striped dress standing in a corner by the window.

The right wall held a different pair of paintings: one a crude clown, the other a simplistic portrait of an overweight man with startled eyes, painted in four flat colors—mauve, white, yellow and black. The signature was J. W. Gacy.

"Do you hear that?" Adam said. I heard music playing, something operatic, but distant and tinny. It was coming from behind the clown painting. As I touched my ear to the wall, my head brushed the picture frame. It tilted and a hidden door swung open about the width of a hand. The music grew louder.

Adam and the other cop drew their pieces. I stepped back

to give them room. Adam kicked the door open and entered low, covering the room while the other cop followed him. They turned immediately to their left and disappeared.

Endo had torn out all the interior walls, leaving an open, warehouse space, like an artist's studio. He had painted the remaining walls black. The windows were boarded from the outside, the glass painted as black as the walls. Bare lightbulbs hung from wires stapled to the naked rafters. The floor was swept clean, but there was a raw smell of sawdust, paint and mineral spirits to go with the stacked scraps of lumber and pyramids of empty paint cans in the corners. The back door was nailed shut and braced with two-by-fours.

He had built a low stage behind the box office, like the one in Michi's basement. On it stood a small table and atop that sat an old Monkees record player from which the music came, scratchy and weak through the tiny mono speaker. I turned off the record player and looked at the faded RCA Victor Red Seal label—Puccini's opera *Turandot*. The song was "Nessun Dorma"—"None Shall Sleep."

"He must have been here within the last twenty minutes," Adam said. He sent the cop outside to get statements from the neighbors, find out if anyone had seen Endo leave. In this neighborhood, people made it a habit not to see anything. I started shooting pictures. I wondered if Endo had killed any of his victims here. It seemed like the perfect place, a nice, cozy, private little corner of hell for him to build his fantasy world.

The three large metal cabinets against one wall drew our attention. Adam opened the first one and found Endo's carpentry tools, boxes of nails and screws, more cans of paint, paintbrushes and paint thinner, rolls of plastic sheeting and folded drop cloths spattered with paint. The next one held hundreds of videotapes in black plastic boxes. On the bottom shelf

were a video camera and a couple of Nikons, one of them missing its lens. Everything was covered with a thin layer of dust.

The third cabinet contained Endo's shrine to himself. It
looked like a theatrical makeup table. It was wired with a bank
of lightbulbs at the back surrounding a large mirror. The lights
came on by themselves, and an open laptop on the makeup
table flickered to life, playing film of Endo on his stage silently
pantomiming a scene. He was naked and covered in green
paint. He stopped frequently to touch himself.

Adam opened all the drawers. In the first one we found a
scrapbook. The book contained hundreds of loose newspaper
clippings, mostly reviews of various plays around town, going
back almost ten years. I guessed these were productions he had
worked on. Among the clippings of reviews were several stories about Michi Mori—fundraisers, art openings, that sort of
thing.

Toward the back, I found the article about the Richard
Buntyn murder in which Endo was first called the Playhouse
Killer. I also found several stories about the Simon twins, then
the Krews murder, and finally a small article identifying Patsy
Concorde's body near Elmwood Cemetery.

"You were right," I said to Adam and showed him the clip-
ping.

He barely looked at it. "Look at this. This drawer was
locked." He pried it open, finding a butcher knife and an old
bottle of Williams Pride barbecue sauce. At the bottom of the
deep drawer lay a loud yellow sports coat, neatly folded.

"I think you'll find that coat belonged to Chris Hendricks."
I had seen him wearing it the day he died.

"Trophies?" Adam asked. A menu from the Blue Monkey
fell out.

"Maybe."

I leaned over and shot a picture of the inside of the drawer. There was an old house key lying at the bottom, but something at the back caught my eye. I reached inside and pulled out a human skull. It was missing the lower jaw and several upper teeth, and there was a small hole over the left eye.

"Who do you suppose this belonged to?"

Adam took the skull and returned everything to the drawer. "We probably shouldn't touch anything else until Wiley gets here," he said. I resumed shooting photographs.

I walked slowly around the room. Something seemed out of place, or perhaps missing. It looked like Endo had been living here for years, building his sets, putting on his one-man productions. Other than the hint of trophies in that drawer, this didn't seem like the lair of a ruthless serial killer. I don't know what I had expected. The place was meticulously organized, every tool in its place, every videotape labeled and arranged by date. No human remains rotted in the bathtub, no lampshades decorated with human fingernails. No empty pizza boxes, no dirty towels or piles of underwear. There were no towels or underwear at all, or any lamps or lampshades or bathtubs, or even a kitchen or a bathroom.

"Where did he sleep?" I asked.

Adam looked at me, then sketched a quick turn around.

"Endo doesn't live here," Adam said, his shoulders slumping.

33

V AN HELSING AND I DIDN'T know yet where Dracula hid the coffin. We had only found his workshop. With Michi's money, Endo could afford dozens of apartments, spread out all over the city. It might take weeks to track them all down.

Adam secured the scene and waited for Wiley and his forensic team to arrive. He asked a female cop to drive me home. Her name was Cyntheria Waters. I said goodbye to Adam and tried not to let it show that it might be the last time he would see me as a friend. Wiley was bound to find the photos I sold to Michi. He may have been an ass, but he was a thorough ass. I'd be lucky to get away without having charges filed against me by the DA.

Officer Waters and I ran through the rain to her car. She let me sit in the front seat so I wouldn't look like a perp. It had been a long time since I sat in the front of a squad car. Her cruiser still had that new-cop-car smell.

"Where to?" she asked. I gave her my address. She looked at me like I was an actual human being, not a washed-out junkie. It felt kind of good, but I knew it wouldn't last. I was her friend for the moment because I was Adam's friend.

"Adam, that is, Sergeant McPeake said you used to be a cop." She pulled out and headed east.

"Yeah." As we drove away, the last car in the line parked along the curb flicked on its headlights. I watched it make a U-turn behind us.

"Glad you got out?"

"Sometimes." She stopped for traffic, then turned north. The car—a black Nissan Murano—followed. As we neared the fairgrounds, I watched the Murano make a left turn onto Cooper. Waters glanced at me, then eyeballed the rearview mirror. I didn't tell her what I had seen.

"Are you doing all right?" she asked in a sisterly voice.

"Everything is essence." I opened the camera case and took out the Leica, remembering that I still owed James five hundred bucks for it. The camera was on, even though I had turned it off after finishing up at Endo's workshop. There was a message on the screen—Memory Card Is Full, Do You Want to Switch to Internal Memory? I clicked yes and a second message appeared—Internal Memory Is Full. I turned the thing off.

"Can I see?" Waters asked.

"See what?"

"Your pictures."

I looked at her for the first time. I mean really looked. I was surprised by how young she was, even though I'd been about her age when I joined the force. Mid-twenties, good skin the color of expensive dark chocolate, short-cropped curly hair, small in the chest but big in the caboose. If she was taller than me, it wasn't by much.

"Why do you want to see it?" I already knew the answer. Everybody is a rubbernecker, even the best ones. People can't help it.

"I've never . . ." she began, then realized how rookie she sounded. She wasn't a rookie. She may have looked soft, but I could see the nails in her eyes.

"I'll show you when we get to my place."

"Thanks." She smiled and drove on.

Waters sat behind the wheel while the engine idled and rain slid in wrinkled sheets down the windshield. She scrolled through the tiny LCD images of Michi Mori's remains, the pooled blood, the spatters on the wall and ceiling, his dismembered parts scattered like garbage in an empty lot. Every once in a while, her breath would catch and she would call on Jesus in a small voice.

"That's pretty intense."

She started on Endo's workshop, clicking through quickly, only stopping once to examine the photo of the skull. She was close enough for me to smell her deodorant, something that was supposed to smell like a tropical breeze or morning rain. Her nails were buffed and there was an apple in the cup holder. She was trying to take care of herself, not rot behind the wheel like some cops.

"I guess you get used to it, huh?" she asked.

"If you do, you end up just as bad as they are."

"What happened here?" She showed me a blank black image on the camera.

"I don't know."

She passed the camera back to me. Her hand was steady but she didn't look me in the eye. The last photo at Endo's apartment was followed by about two hundred blank images that had eaten up the space on the memory card. I turned the camera off and tucked it back inside its leather case.

"I'd better go," I said, and opened the door.

"You gonna be OK?" she asked before I could close it.

"Sure. Why?"

"I heard that old man was a friend of yours."

My back was already soaked and I could feel the cold rain running down my thighs. "Just a perv I busted once, a long time ago."

"Oh," she said, and turned her head away, already moving on. Smart. I wished I could do that.

The stairs were slick from people going in and out of the rain—a lawsuit waiting to happen. A garbage can in the corner was overflowing, something inside moving around, scratching. I hadn't checked my mail since I moved in, so I opened my box and found a single letter inside addressed to me. The return address was from Reed's new office in Collierville. I tore it open:

Dear Bitch,

I think the hardest thing for me to come to terms with was the realization that after I worked so hard and so long to suppress my perfectly natural male desire to sleep with as many women as would have me, and instead devoted myself to the ideal of monogamy for your sake, it should be you who broke our sacred covenant before God. While I suffered and denied myself like a fucking monk sitting in the snow waiting for you to get in the fucking mood for our once a month, you'd been out there fucking all my friends all along, doing God knows what with them and leaving me alone on my side of the bed while another man's tadpoles wriggled through the swamp of your rotting uterus. I thank God every day now that you are barren. I thank God I'm not stuck raising a child not of my blood. When I think of all the women I could have had and all the

a perp's forehead. The batteries were dead, of course, but I took it anyway. I pulled on a windbreaker and a hat, stuffed James's money in one pocket, cell phone in the other, stepped out into the hall and locked the door behind me. The hall was dark and silent, but the garbage can at the bottom of the stairs was still rustling with rats.

Mrs. Kim sat on a folding metal chair in the residents' private laundry room, reading a Korean newspaper while the washing machine rattled against the wall behind her. She jumped as I stumbled out of the elevator, as though she expected to see a ghost. It had stopped about a foot above floor level. I had to pry the accordion cage door open to escape. Mrs. Kim returned to her paper with no expression on her face at all.

The Laundromat smelled like bleach and scorched rubber, the floors gritty with unswept laundry detergent. Somebody's Converse tennis shoes were bumping around inside one of the dryers. I stood at the front window and looked at the rain running down the glass. It was already pitch dark out. The tae kwon do school was just letting out. A couple of girls passed still wearing their white uniforms and black belts, plastic grocery bags protecting their hair.

I watched the traffic pass for a while, then walked down to the mercado to buy some batteries. Mynor looked up and smiled as I entered. He was watching a Mexican soap opera behind the counter.

"What're you watching?"

"*Pecados Ajenos*," he said. "It means *The Sins of Others*."

"Good?"

"It's OK. I like this actress, Catherine Siachoque." He pointed her out on the screen. She looked about my age, but a hell of a lot better-looking.

"She's gorgeous."

"She's the killer. She's very good, though."

There was nobody in the store and the Tejano music was turned down low for once. It looked like Walter had already gone home, taking his empty gin bottle with him. On a hunch, I asked Mynor, "Have you seen a young Japanese man hanging around?"

"I don't know how to tell a Japanese man." Mynor shrugged. "Mrs. Kim's husband was around earlier, but he's Korean."

I realized I hadn't seen Endo since the trial, when he was twelve years old. All I had were the pictures I'd taken and his face was never clear. I tried to describe him. "He's Asian, of course, about twenty-eight, dark complexion, with short black hair that stands straight up, thick eyebrows."

"That sounds like my brother-in-law," Mynor said.

"Just do me a favor. If anybody like that comes in and asks about me, call the cops, tell them you've seen someone fitting the description of Noboyuki Endo."

"The Playhouse Killer?"

"You've heard?"

"*Sí*, it was on the five o'clock news." He sat up on his stool and searched the aisles with his eyes. "Why would the killer come here?"

Why, indeed. I walked to the door and looked out into the mist. Each streetlight was surrounded by a golden halo. Cars were stopped at the red light in front of the store, but none of them looked familiar to me. "He probably won't. But if he does . . ."

"Mrs. Jackie, are you in trouble?"

I lit a cigarette and blew the smoke against the glass doors. "I'm just waiting for the bus. I'm going to see a friend."

34

THE NUMBER 53 BUS WAS empty. I rode it down to White Station and got off in front of a titty bar that used to be one of the best places in the city to bust pervs. They were the only joint in town that had real live women under glass, put your money in the machine, pick up the telephone, and watch the curtain go up. That was back when we had a DA who promised the city's Baptists he'd close all the adult shops in town. He lasted about two years, the shops were still there, but now the internet had done what the cops and the Jesus Nazis couldn't—destroy their business model.

I boarded the number 43 and sat down next to a couple of Mexican women dressed in hospital scrubs. Several more sat at the back of the bus talking in Spanish. The two women I sat behind didn't talk. One of them kept crossing herself and glancing at the grisly half-body apparition floating above the seat behind the driver. I smiled at her fear.

All of the living passengers left the bus together at Walnut Grove. The dead guy behind the driver didn't pay attention to any of us. He was alone on his own trip to God knows where. I got off in front of St. Louis Catholic School. I still had a good half mile walk ahead of me through the rain and mist of November, but I had my flashlight to keep me company.

Shady Grove was a quiet, affluent East Memphis neighborhood. The south side of the street was populated by enormous houses and circle driveways shaded by towering oaks and elms, the north side lined with smaller houses and lawns, though still upscale enough to keep riffraff like me away. The first block down, I startled a wealthy black woman in a London Fog coat out walking her schnauzer in the rain. The dog wore a little matching gray coat and seemed almost as frightened as its owner. I nodded politely as I passed and she smiled like she was about to pee herself.

A late-model white El Dorado cruised slowly by and disappeared over the next hill. I couldn't see the driver through the window, but I noted the plate number, just in case. The street was especially dark between the streetlamps, each one farther apart than I remembered, the orange light of the sodium vapor lamp shining down in a narrow cone swirling with mist, with enormous gaps of woodsy nothing between. The smell of the wet leaves rotting under the trees was oppressive. Just the sort of place for an early-morning jogger to find my body tomorrow. My phone started buzzing in my pocket.

"We got a lead on Endo," Adam said.

"Great." I let out a big sigh. They hadn't found the pictures yet.

"We got a call from a car-rental place a little while ago. They're missing a black Nissan Murano, rented to Cole Ritter. They didn't make the connection until Michi's murder hit the news tonight."

"I've seen a Murano," I said. "It was parked outside Endo's apartment."

"No shit?"

"Followed us down Airways, then turned west on Cooper."

"Jesus, Jack." He called me Jack, just like Sean used to. "You're good when you're straight. I wish I had your head for detail."

"Thanks." It was good to hear, even if he was patronizing me.

"Do me a favor and make sure your door is locked," he said.

"Why?"

"Endo knows where you live."

I thought about that for a minute. Endo knew the building but not the apartment, and if he went asking about me, Mrs. Kim wouldn't speak to him and Mynor would call it in. I had made sure of that. At the same time, coming out here on this quiet residential street after dark, with nothing more than a flashlight, was monumentally stupid. Adam would have had a stroke if he knew.

"Door's triple-locked," I said. "Besides, if it was Endo in the Murano, he saw me riding in a cop car. He probably thinks I have police protection."

"You do have police protection. Waters is sitting outside your apartment. If she sees that Murano, she'll call in the cavalry. Just promise me you won't open the door unless it's me."

"Promise." There was a car coming toward me, the beam of its headlights bouncing in the drizzle. "Gotta go. The pizza guy is here." I hung up. The car sped up and swerved toward the curb, slid to a stop beside me. Fear like a cold finger touched the base of my skull. It was the same white El Dorado that passed a few minutes before. As the driver rolled down his window, I poked the beam of my flashlight in his eyes.

He threw up a hand to block the light. He was an older guy,

early sixties, sporting a combed-back black pompadour, slightly graying at the temples. He reminded me of Rex Morgan, MD, for some reason. "Can I help you?" he asked.

"Probably not."

"Please turn off your light." I did, then started walking. I wanted to get under one of the streetlamps. He followed beside me in his car. "I don't think I've seen you around here before." He gave me a forced smile.

"You looking for a party?" I asked. His smiled changed to a thoughtful frown. "Just kidding. I'm here to visit a friend."

"Really? And who would that be?"

"That's not really any of your business, is it?"

"Actually, it is my business. We have a Neighborhood Watch in this neighborhood," he said, smiling again with those wonderful white caps of his. "I'm watch captain for this street."

"Bully for you." I said. He looked like a dentist. I could smell a dentist a mile away. "Isn't this the neighborhood where a woman was brutally murdered in her own bedroom?" I flashed the light in his eyes again. "I guess somebody took that night off, huh?"

"Our watch group was formed *after* the unfortunate incident."

"I'm going to visit a friend," I said. "If you don't believe me, call the cops. Otherwise, leave me the fuck alone, OK?"

"I'll be watching you," he said.

"Do I look like I give a shit?" He rolled up his window and drove away. He was lucky I didn't bust the caps in his face. But having that swinging dick around was better than being out here alone. I probably should have sweetened up to him and begged a ride, even if it was only another block to James's house. I was starting to get a little vertigo from the tension.

James's house sat back from the road amid the trees, across

the street from a Presbyterian church, its half-circle driveway hidden behind a tall privet hedge that bordered the sidewalk. The front door stood open, a warm yellow light spilling out onto the driveway. It must be nice to live in a neighborhood where you didn't have to lock the door. It reminded me of my parents' house in Pocahontas. I didn't think there were still places like that in Memphis.

I clicked on my flashlight and searched the shrubs and flower beds to either side of the door, looking for fake rocks. No one could see me from the street, not even Dr. Rex Morgan if he passed. A nice cozy little place for a murder.

At either end of the driveway stood these raised brick flowerbeds with a Victorian-style lamppost in each, variegated ivy twirling up the posts and nearly engulfing the unlit glass-paned lamps. I searched around the posts and the brick borders and found nothing there either. I checked under the door mat but from the looks of it, James regularly swept and washed his front steps. He also cleaned and mulched his flower beds in the fall, raked out the dead leaves, covered his outside faucets with insulated caps to keep them from freezing, all the solid, responsible homeowner crap Reed always paid Mexicans to take care of.

The mist turned into a downpour while I was digging through his flower beds.

The house had a detached garage. The door was closed. The garage backed up to the neighbor's hedge, with trees from the neighbor's yard hanging over the roof. I walked behind the garage and found a couple of rotting, leaf-choked flower boxes barely hanging from the wall below the windows. It looked like James had never been back here. There was a boy's bike rusting against the wall, a pair of lawn chairs lying folded up in the leaves. I shined my flashlight through the dusty garage windows and saw a blue Dodge Neon parked beside some kind of car hidden beneath a canvas shroud. By its low profile and outline I guessed something European and sporty. I scraped the leaves from one flower box and found a plastic frog about the size of a baseball half-buried in the damp, black humus. It was hollow with a rubber plug in the bottom, the kind of garden ornament made for hiding a door key, like the fake rock that my parents kept in their flower bed. This one was empty.

I took it with me, climbed the steps and pushed the doorbell with the butt of my flashlight. The hall behind the door looked like it went straight through to the back of the house, with a chandelier above the entrance and hardwood floors that gleamed like a bowling lane. James stepped around a corner holding the sports page.

"Jesus, you're soaked." He looked past me at the empty driveway. "How did you get here?"

"Bus." I held out the plastic frog for him to see. The rain had already washed most of the mud away.

"What's that?"

"A key frog. I found it in the flower box behind the garage." His face puckered with a confused frown. "My guess is the person who murdered your wife found a key in this. That's how he got inside your house, and that's how he locked the door behind him when he left."

35

I PUT THE KEY FROG in a gallon plastic bag and set it on the kitchen table. James handed me a flowery dish towel from a drawer.

"How long have you known?" he asked. He opened the fridge and grabbed a can of Dr Pepper. He didn't offer me one. Other than a few sodas, the fridge was empty. Not even any moldy mystery meat.

When he closed the door, there was this little old lady standing in the corner between the fridge and the wall. She wore a print dress with a couple of inches of lace, a fat string of pearls, black gloves and black block-heeled old-lady shoes, which meant she'd been buried after Labor Day. With her bold swoop of thick white hair and narrow, almost-Chinese eyes, she looked vaguely familiar for some reason. She stared sadly at James, like she wanted to take him into her frail arms and comfort him.

"I've known about it for a couple of days. Why didn't you tell me?" I tossed my hat in the sink and rubbed my hair with the dish towel. As short as my hair was, it wouldn't take long to dry, but my jeans were cold and wet and stuck to my legs.

"It's not something you talk about on a first date, is it? How your wife was murdered and the police think you did it, but hey! How 'bout them Tigers?" He took a long swallow of his soda, then turned to face me. "Why didn't you say something before now?"

"I had to think about it. I was a little shocked. I'm sorry."

"Don't apologize. I should be apologizing to you." He downed the rest of the can and crumpled it in his fist, just like a normal guy would, except he was buttoned so tight he couldn't even drink a beer. It had to be a soda. "What would you have said if I told you?"

"Did you kill your wife, James?"

"Of course not." He said it softly and deliberately.

"Then why shouldn't I believe you?"

"The police don't."

"They don't believe anybody," I said. I pointed at the frog on the table. "They'll believe you now, though."

"What does an empty key frog prove?"

"How soon after you moved in was your wife murdered?" My teeth began to chatter with the cold coming off the old woman. James didn't seem to feel her at all. I wondered how normal people could go through their lives completely unaware of the death all around us.

"I don't know. A year?"

"Did you change the locks after you moved in?"

"We didn't need to. The woman who lived here had passed away." She smiled and tugged at one of her gloves. She was beginning to fade, the fruit pattern of the wallpaper behind her showing through her face. "We bought the house in the estate sale. Actually, Ashley's parents bought it."

"The old lady must have left a key in the frog and Ashley's murderer found it."

"But how?"

"Because he looked for it," I said. "That's how I found it."

"But there's no way to prove there was ever a key in it."

"You act like you don't want this to be true."

"You've no idea," he said, his voice trembling. "You have no fucking idea at all. It wasn't enough that Ashley was murdered. Because the cops can't figure out who did it, they blame me. But they can't arrest me because there's no evidence. The night she was murdered, I was on a plane to San Diego. So it pisses them off, because they think I've outsmarted them, and if there's one thing a cop hates, it's losing."

"Have they lost, James?"

"What's that supposed to mean?"

"It's just a question. It was a funny thing for you to say, so I asked."

"They're not looking for the real murderer because they think I did it. Meanwhile, he's still out there. Maybe he's killed somebody else. Who knows? The cops don't know. They don't care. The only thing they care about is pinning this on me. You show them that frog, it won't make any difference at all."

"Then tell me something that will make a difference," I suggested. The old lady continued to fade, taking her cold with her. "Something else the cops missed."

James leaned against the counter with his hands behind his back. There was a toaster with a mirror finish behind him and I could see him fiddling with his wedding ring in the reflection. He hadn't taken off the ring this time, even though he knew I was coming over. "When I got home and found her . . ." He didn't say *body*. "Ashley's car was parked in the driveway, but she always parked in the garage."

"So maybe she didn't that one time. Maybe she was in a hurry."

"Ashley drove a 1959 Fiat Pininfarina Cabriolet convertible that her father refurbished and gave to her when she graduated from college. She loved that car, never left it outside overnight. God, I remember once . . ." He stopped himself, looked away, and pressed his upper lip down into his lower lip to keep it still. While I waited for him to collect, I watched the old lady disappear. All that was left of her was a perfumy smell, floral and old-timey. It made me think of my grandfather's bedroom off the back of the house. He used to keep my grandmother's old, yellowish perfume bottle on his desk. Sean and I would sneak in just to smell it and gag at one another. It didn't matter to us that we were letting a last reminder of his departed wife escape into the air, never to be recovered.

James was having a hard time pulling himself together. His grief was as fresh and real as any I had seen. He'd have to be a hell of an actor to fake it. To spare him, I finally said, "You know what I think?"

He pushed his wrist across his nose and shook his head no. "I'm freezing. Do you have something I can wear?"

James led me back to his bedroom, down a long straight hall lined with photographs of him and his wife and their families. There were also photos Ashley had taken, truly artsy stuff like you see in a gallery, mostly black-and-whites, the kind of photos I had never taken and probably never could take. I didn't have the eye for this kind of thing. Ashley seemed to like old people with authentic-looking faces, craggy noses, beetling brows, collapsed toothless mouths, moonscapes of pores and forests of hair, hands knobby with arthritis and wormy with veins. My photos of the dead were vacation snaps by comparison, awkward frames made all the more horrible by their bland symmetry. No wonder Michi had loved them. The only work of mine that compared to Ashley's pictures were the black-

and-white photos of Endo I had accidentally taken with the Leica.

Ashley St. Michael's Leica.

James opened a dresser drawer that still contained an assortment of colorful women's sweaters, neatly stacked and folded. "These were Ashley's," he muttered, almost to himself. His fingers lingered over a red sweater with a white snowflake pattern around the collar. He looked up at me, eyes rimmed with red. "I'm not sure I'd be very comfortable seeing you in this."

"How about a shirt and some old sweatpants of yours?" He nodded and tossed a pair of jeans and a Carolina Panthers sweatshirt on the bed.

"I'll wait in the den," he said, and left.

I didn't remember much about the rest of the house but I remembered this bedroom. It was strange being here again. He hadn't moved any of the furniture since the night of his wife's murder. There was a new bedspread, but it was the same bed, the same matching pair of dressers, the same pants tree and avocado-green winged armchair in the corner by the closet door. I shucked out of my wet pants and shirt and pulled on his jeans. They were too big but I managed with a belt. The sweatshirt came down to the middle of my thighs. I pushed the sleeves up to my elbows, sat on the foot of his bed and stared at the floor where her body had lain. He had put in new carpet.

I could see her as plain as if she was still lying there. Maybe she was. She was facedown, head toward the closet, one foot partially under the bed. The first cops on the scene believed she had been posed, but they couldn't say why exactly. A hunch, they said. She was dressed to go out, and now I knew she had. She had photographed a society event, then had drinks with Jenny and her friends at Bosco's.

She hadn't been raped or otherwise molested, but she had been in a hell of a fight. She had bruises on her forearms, thighs, chest, back and face, but no tissue or blood under her fingernails. Cause of death was strangulation. The murder weapon—a pair of running shoes tied together by the shoestrings—was still wrapped around her throat.

36

I found James in the den holding the sports page, looking at it but not reading. Maybe he was seeing the life he might have led had things worked out differently, the children he would never have playing on the floor around his chair as he tugged his pipe and rattled his newspaper, the very image of the father he always thought he would be. Maybe these were *his* ghosts. He wasn't even aware of me until I touched his shoulder. "I thought you were going to change," he said as he turned in his chair. I was back in my wet clothes, shivering again.

"Can you take me home?" I asked.

"Sure." He set his paper on the end table and stood up. "What's wrong?"

"Something I need to check."

I was glad he didn't ask what, because I wasn't ready to explain yet. I couldn't stop shaking.

"You want to borrow a coat?"

"Please."

He took a jacket from the closet in the hall. Ashley's coats were still in the closet beside his own. He gave me one of his and I followed him outside. He opened the garage door with a remote control on his key ring. Another remote unlocked the doors of the Neon. The drive-out tag was still taped to the inside of the back window. It wasn't even a new Neon, maybe a 2001, if that. "What happened to your Lexus?"

"Sold it." He didn't offer to explain and I didn't ask.

I stood outside the garage in a steady drizzle while he opened the passenger door for me, ever the gentleman. I didn't get in. The other car, buried beneath its funereal shroud, seemed to lean to one side. "Are you coming?" James asked.

I asked, "Is that her Fiat?" He nodded that it was. "Can I see it?"

He stared at me for a moment, then closed the car door and joined me in the rain. He wasn't wearing a hat, his hair was dripping in his eyes.

"Why do you want to see her car?"

"I'm curious about something."

He turned and watched the long limbs of the shaggy hedge dancing in the rain. A black Mercury drove by and stopped at the corner, then went on. The rain hissed in the trees and clanged like random off-key bells in the gutters of the garage.

"Why are you doing this to me?" James asked without looking at me.

"Do you ever take her car out and drive it?"

"No." He shoved his hands in his pockets, stiffened his back and stuck his chin out. "I haven't moved it since I parked it in the garage the next day. I haven't even looked at it."

"If you want to wait in the car, I won't take a minute. I just need to check something."

Finally he nodded, but he didn't move, only jingled the keys in his pocket and blinked up at the descending rain. The sky was brighter now than when I arrived. The clouds had lowered and turned a sickly shade of brown from the glow of the city lights.

"I'll just get the key."

A few minutes later, he returned from the house wearing the same Memphis Tigers cap I had first seen him wearing that morning at the restaurant. He laid a single worn silver key in my palm.

I peeled back the dusty cover from the Fiat. It had once been a sweet ride, but now there were cobwebs in the grille and dirtdobber nests cemented to its crumbling convertible roof. One tire had gone flat, accounting for the list I noticed earlier. The dust on the windows made it impossible to see inside. The luggage compartment was as tiny, empty and dusty as the rest of the car, but on the carpet underneath the dust I found a couple of small dark brown stains that might have been grease spots. Judging by the care with which the car had been restored, I doubted I was looking at grease spots.

I closed the trunk and climbed into James's car. He backed it onto Shady Grove without once looking at me. "Did the cops sweep the car for evidence?" I asked.

"Not that I know of. Like I said, they didn't think it was important." He drove for a while with his knuckles turning white on the wheel. "Did you find what you were looking for?" he finally asked. He tried to be casual, but the tension in his voice was enough to stretch a tennis racket.

"Maybe. I won't know for sure until it's been tested." I pulled a damp pack of cigarettes from my back pocket. "Mind if I smoke?"

"Yes. So what do you think?"

I laid the pack on the seat between us, next to the hide-a-key frog in its gallon plastic baggie. "I think you didn't murder your wife."

"You'd be the only one."

"Not the only one," I said, remembering what Jenny had told me. "But I think I can convince some people who matter. I think I can clear you and then maybe you can get your life back."

"You have to convince me first," James said. "Tell me how I didn't do it."

"How you didn't do it is obvious enough—you were on a plane a thousand miles away. Also, why would you leave her body in a way that points suspicion right back at you. Most guys would have at least kicked down the door to make it look like a robbery. I believe the car in the driveway and the missing spare key point to an outsider." I looked at the key to Ashley's Fiat resting in the palm of my hand, the wards worn smooth from use. In the last few days, especially the last hour in her old house, I felt like I'd come to know her, even though what I knew about her was insignificant, not even enough to form a good theory. There were so many details I didn't know that could change everything, but for the moment my hunch felt right.

"I think she was murdered somewhere else and brought back to your house in the trunk of her own car. I found drops of blood on the carpet. The killer took her into the house, staged her body, then locked the door behind him as he left, maybe to divert suspicion to you. Maybe he knew you and wanted to frame you out of revenge, or maybe he just wanted to throw the cops a bone, knowing that once they got an idea, they'd never let it go. But to do that, he couldn't lock the door with her key. Your wife's keys had to be inside the locked house to make the mystery work. So he went looking for a spare key, just like I did, and he found one."

"How did he know we didn't know about the spare key in the flower box?"

"It was half buried. You couldn't see it."

"So why did he keep it?"

He had me there. That part didn't make sense. "I don't know, but I don't think it wrecks the theory. Maybe he keeps it as a memento. Maybe he doesn't know you have an alibi a thousand miles wide. Or maybe he knows cops well enough to know they always go for the easy answer. In most cases, the simplest explanation is the husband did it. Most female murder victims are killed by husbands or boyfriends, so that's who the cops look at first. Stranger killings are rare, except in a botched robbery or rape. But since this was neither, they're going to fall back on you as the most likely killer, even if they can't explain how you did it. Can you blame them?"

"Oh, I don't blame them," James sneered.

"They're just doing their jobs," I said.

As he turned west on Summer Avenue, a patch of street light swooped across his face and I saw the tears coming down. He pushed the back of his hand across his nose and looked away to hide them.

37

Waters's patrol car was still by the back door as we pulled into the parking lot, but now her blue lights were flashing through the rain. James looked at me, his eyebrows forming a question, which I answered with a shrug. Maybe Adam had finally found those pictures at Michi's house and told Waters to bring me in. James parked by the garbage Dumpster and I got out. Even if I was about to go down, at least I would clear James of the murder charge. The nobility of my mission gave me the courage, for once, to face whatever disaster was headed my way.

The rain had really begun to pick up and the whole of the sky from the south to the west was alive with lightning, but the storm was still too far away to hear any thunder. Waters was writing something on a clipboard propped against the steering wheel. An Asian man with short black hair sat in the backseat with his hands cuffed behind his back and the front of his dirty white T-shirt speckled with blood. His face was completely calm, betraying no emotion whatsoever.

I knocked on the glass with my knuckle. Waters looked up and rolled down her window. "Didn't you hear me banging on your door?"

"That's not Endo," I said.

"What?"

I pointed at the man in the back seat. "That's Mr. Kim. He lives here." Mr. Kim smiled and gave me a small bow with just his head. His lips and teeth were red with blood. James came up and held an umbrella over me. "Noboyuki Endo is Japanese. Mr. Kim is Korean."

Waters stared at me for a moment with her pen still pressed to the clipboard. "Do you think I'm stupid or something?" she said. "The Mexican guy who runs the mercado called in a domestic disturbance. I run upstairs to find this old fucker beating the holy hell out of his wife. I bust him in the face to make him let go of her. Now she doesn't want to press charges. That's what these bitches always do. They just want you to pull the old man off, but try to take him downtown and they act like he hung the fucking moon. Did you know this son of a bitch is a preacher?"

Mr. Kim said something in Korean that didn't sound like a prayer. Then he spat blood on the back of the seat. Waters glared at him in the mirror and continued, "I was just about to call Adam because I couldn't get you to come to your door. He said you were supposed to stay put with the door locked. I'm just waiting on somebody to take over my babysitting job so I can drive this bastard down to 201 Poplar."

"I don't need a babysitter. My friend here is going to stay with me tonight."

Her eyes flickered over James, taking him in, appraising him in one glance. "You sure?" Her frown said she didn't like what she saw.

"I'll be fine."

"What's your name?" she asked James. He told her. "Are you on television?"

"He gets that a lot." I took his arm and started for the door. "We're going inside now."

"Adam said for me to wait here," Waters called after us.

"Suit yourself."

"What was that all about?" James asked when we were on the stairs.

"It's complicated," I said.

I paused at my door, listening. I heard a woman crying somewhere, just like before, only this time I was fairly sure it was Mrs. Kim two doors down. I unlocked the door and James followed me inside. I turned on the kitchen light.

"Your heat's working," he observed. He shrugged out of his jacket and hung it on the back of a chair. I locked the door and tossed my keys on the table. He stuck his umbrella in the sink and opened a cabinet like he lived there.

"I don't have any cups or glasses. If you want something to drink, there's a market downstairs."

"Beer?"

"I won't argue with that."

"I'll be back."

I grabbed my laptop from under the couch and set it up on the table. My clothes were still wet but the apartment was warm enough and I was no longer shivering. While the computer booted up, I turned on Ashley's Leica—my Leica, I reminded myself, even though I still hadn't paid James the last five hundred.

I plugged the camera into my laptop and scrolled through the almost two hundred blank black images that had eaten up most of the space on the camera's memory card. I opened one and used the photo software to adjust the light levels the way Deiter had shown me. This image caused my heart to hammer in my chest. I recognized it, because I had just been there. It was a photo of James's kitchen. The next one was the hall. The next one the bedroom, as though the photographer were snapping photos every few feet. But the bedroom was empty. The photos continued, wandering through the house, back to the same rooms again and again. I stopped looking at them after the first twenty and scrolled to the end.

The last photo was different. It was my apartment, looking into the bedroom from the kitchen, the bedroom lit up by a flash of lightning. I had stopped even trying to figure out how these pictures came to be on the camera. The question in my mind now was why. What was it trying to show me?

I opened a second folder on my computer's hard drive, sorted the subfolders by date, and scrolled down to the folder titled Playhouse. It contained the photographs I had taken of the Richard Buntyn murder scene at Playhouse on the Square. After working that scene and collecting my money from Chief Billet, I had left, bought a deck of scag and was stoned out of my skull when Adam called me later the same afternoon to photograph the Ashley St. Michael murder.

I had forgotten both murders happened on the same day. I clicked through the photographs of James's bedroom from two years ago. Ashley lay on her stomach, right foot partially under the bed, right hand extended toward the closet, left hand under her body. Her face was turned to the left. She was wearing black heels, jeans and a green sweater. The heel of her left shoe was broken off. There was blood on her upper lip and the bottom of her nose, which had been broken in the struggle. A pair of Nike running shoes, laces knotted together, were wrapped around her throat and lay side by side at the base of her skull.

From my seat at the kitchen table I could see the lightning flashing in the sky outside my bedroom window. They were still only distant flickers, not the brilliant stabs of light that illuminated the night like day when a storm is right above your head. The only sound was the gentle unbroken roar of the rain hammering on the roof. I could see the floor of my bedroom where on two consecutive mornings last week I found my own running shoes lying with their shoestrings tied together. I could almost feel her there, watching me, willing me to put it all together. I stopped breathing, waiting for her to appear.

Maybe ghosts don't cast shadows. Not real shadows, anyway. Shadows on the mind. I breathed again and wondered where James had gone with that beer.

38

I OPENED THE LEICA'S INTERNAL memory folder. Dozens of thumbnail images filled the screen, photos Ashley had taken that had never been erased. I clicked the first one on the list.

It was a party scene. I recognized several people, local business leaders and their spouses and dates at a fundraising dinner for the Boys and Girls Club. The next photo was a different party but the same people. Michi Mori posing with the mayor. Michi wore a red and white tuxedo and had his cane. He looked like a peppermint candy. The mayor had his arm around Michi's shoulder, dwarfing him. His attention was directed off camera at someone else.

More photos of parties, openings, debuts, tennis tournaments, golf tournaments, fundraisers and gallery showings. The cream of Memphis society, presidents and vice presidents of industry and commerce, wealthy inheritors of old cotton money, graying politicians and their young wives, basketball players and tennis stars, authors, actors and directors, hot new artists and rappers, plus the tired old superstars who wouldn't go away. Ashley St. Michael had freelanced as an entertainment photographer for just about every publication in the city.

I found a photo taken at the governor's mansion in Nashville and spotted Cole Ritter in the background standing next to a tall, Arab-looking art dealer named Richard Buntyn. Richard was sipping red wine from a plastic cocktail glass and the gold watch on his hairy wrist, big as a can of snuff, caught the light of the flash. Just behind Buntyn and Cole stood their future murderer—Noboyuki Endo, leering out from the shadow of a Tennessee state flag.

I knew it was Endo, even though I hadn't seen him since he was a kid. Although the photograph couldn't have been more than four years old, he still had the same cruel yet vacant wedge-shaped face, eyes just a little too far apart, like the face of a cow, and two thick dark eyebrows that almost met over his nose. It was like he hadn't aged at all.

The door banged open and I jumped to my feet, sending my chair skittering into the kitchen cabinets. James almost dropped his bag of beer and nachos. I had forgotten to lock the door when he left. "Jesus, you scared the hell out of me," he said as he recovered the bag from around his knees.

"You scared the hell out of *me*."

"That cop was still sitting out there when I went down, but she's gone now. Are you OK?"

"It's nothing. A friend ordered police protection for me." I pulled the chair back to the table and sat down. My hands were shaking, my fingers already trying to curl around a needle. I could almost smell the hot metallic reek of a spoon full of boiling dope. I rubbed my tracks, as though I could rub them out, erase them, make the sudden ache go away. They'd heal eventually, if I could just let them heal, if I could quit picking at the scab of my addiction.

He set the bag on the counter and unpacked a twelve pack

of Bud and a six-pack of Michelob, a big bag of tortilla chips and a jar of salsa. Almost like he planned to stay for a few days.

"Why do you need police protection?"

"They think maybe the Playhouse Killer is after me."

He walked to the door and locked it. "Why would they think that?"

"He followed me here this morning."

"Really?" He reached into the bag and pulled out a pack of Marlboros. Good man, I thought. He tossed them to me. "What does he want with you?"

"I wish I knew," I said. While he put the beer in the fridge and opened the salsa, I clicked on the next photo and peeled the wrapper off the smokes. I still had almost a full pack of generics, but I'd take free Marlboros over generics any day. I blew the smoke out through my nose. "I don't think he's following me anymore. If he's smart, and I don't think this guy is stupid, he'll be a thousand miles away by now."

The next image was hazy and gray. It had been taken in low light with a fast shutter. It took me a minute to realize what I was looking at. It was the backstage of the Playhouse on the Square. The only light source was the ghost light, stage front. The rest was shades of black. I bumped up the light levels and the scene jumped out. Endo was working Richard Buntyn's body headfirst into a malmsey-butt. The next three photos were variations on the same theme as he struggled with the body's dead weight, but in the last photo in the series, Endo was looking back at the camera.

"What are you looking at?" James asked. He unscrewed the cap off a bottle of Michelob and handed it to me. I set it on the table without drinking.

The next photo was clear enough. It was Endo from about

two feet away, reaching for the camera. "That's the Playhouse Killer. Noboyuki Endo."

"You were that close to him?"

"I didn't take these photos." The words barely made it past my lips. Endo had killed Ashley St. Michael. I clicked on the next picture.

A black Reebok basketball shoe consumed most of the frame, but there were recognizable things in the background, a dresser drawer, and something else, blurry, maybe hair. Blond hair.

I clicked the next picture. We peered into James's bedroom from high up in a corner. I could tell it was shot from the closet, because I had taken a couple of photos from that angle myself. In the picture, Endo was leaning over her body, arranging the running shoes on her back.

James backed into the corner between the refrigerator and the couch. "Where did you get that?" he asked in a voice moaning and hollow with grief.

"Your wife took some of these photos before she died," I explained. "These are from the camera's internal memory. It looks like she photographed the killer before he caught her." It also looked like someone else photographed Endo arranging her body. Question was, who?

He slid to the floor, his mind in shock. *Buddy, you have no idea. Wait until I tell you she's still here, still inside this camera, trying to take a picture of the freak who murdered her.* Although I could see James was becoming overwhelmed, I still had too many questions. Questions that needed answers. "Why did Ashley go to the Playhouse? The building was supposed to be closed."

"Monday night, she met some friends at Bosco's after photographing a party at Donovan Enterprises." His words sounded practiced, almost robotic, as though he had recited them over and over searching for the same answers I sought. "She left alone about ten o'clock." His story confirmed what Jenny had told me.

I tried to fill in those blanks, outlining the storyboard of her last moments. "Bosco's is behind Playhouse on the Square. Richard Buntyn's Explorer was found in the parking lot outside. She had taken Buntyn's picture before. She probably didn't think anything about walking up to him to say hello. She told her friends she was going to say hello to a friend before heading home. Instead, she found Endo in the Playhouse doing his thing. She took some pictures." It occurred to me then how incredibly brave this woman had been, but her bravery hadn't saved her. It had cost her everything. She should have run, but she didn't know what she was up against. "Then Endo spotted her. Maybe he heard the shutter. My guess is he murdered her inside the theater."

James was shaking now, worse than I ever had, even in my worst withdrawals. He looked like he would fly apart. So much must have rushed through his mind—anger, hate, fear, remorse. Guilt. The inescapable guilt of not being there to protect her, drawn away by his meaningless job as a glorified overpaid delivery boy. "So why didn't she call the cops? She had her cell phone!" he cried in anguish. He'd probably asked himself that question a thousand times, and there never was a good answer.

And here I was, dissecting the murder of the woman he obviously still loved more than life itself, because I had to know. I couldn't let her go now, and I couldn't go to him and comfort him in his hour of despair. I had to fit the pieces together. It was an addiction worse than smack, and I was made a monster by my need. I had used heroin to dull that need, make it recede into the brown fuzzy edges of existence, so I wouldn't lie there torturing myself with the faces of the ghosts whose murders I couldn't solve.

"By the time she knew what was happening, she may not have had a chance to call the cops." My words not only made her last moments hopeless, they made them inevitable.

"Christ," he whispered. Death came at her too fast to avoid. She had screamed and nobody but her killer heard it. She had struggled bravely and lost bravely. She never had a chance.

"After that, Endo drove her home," I finished.

James struggled to his feet. He stared at the blank television. His chest rose and fell in shuddering gasps. He took a couple of steps, staggered and caught himself on the arm of the couch. I knew something was about to pop. He lurched another step and froze, a look of panic on his face.

I pointed to the bathroom. He dove for it and slammed the door behind him. I waited for the inevitable noises but it was several minutes before they came. Then they wouldn't stop.

39

IT WAS BEGINNING TO THUNDER outside, a distant rumbling like an old man talking to himself in the next room. I drank my beer and scrolled through the photos of Endo's victims. Adam rang while James was still in the bathroom. I'd been dreading this call, but I answered. "I can't believe you're with him, Jack." He called me by Sean's pet name again. That didn't make this any easier.

"With who?"

"James St. Michael. I know you're with him. Waters ran his plates."

"You can send Waters away. I don't need protection," I said.

"He killed his own wife!" He sounded utterly exasperated. He must have thought I had a death wish, fraternizing with a wife killer and blowing off protection from a serial murderer. At least he hadn't found the photos yet.

I said, "He didn't kill his wife." I couldn't do anything about Endo, but I was ready to walk through fire to clear James.

"You sound so fucking sure."

"I am sure."

"Why?"

"Because I just found a photo of the killer standing over

Ashley St. Michael's body. It was Endo. Endo killed Ashley
St. Michael." He didn't respond. Silence. It was like the call
had dropped. Finally, I said, "Hello?"

"I heard you," Adam said. "Where did you find the photo?"

I told him about the pictures in the Leica's internal memory. He was quiet again for a long time.

"Ashley was with friends at Bosco's that night, the same
night Richard Buntyn was killed. Bosco's is behind the Playhouse on the Square. My guess is while she was leaving, she
spotted Buntyn's car in the parking lot. Since she was a society
photographer, she probably knew the guy. He was big in art
circles, right?"

"Yeah," he said. I wondered if Endo was out there, maybe
driving by at this very moment, looking up at me. I backed
into the shadow by my bed, just in case.

"Or maybe she knew Endo. He's in some of the other photos
I found on her camera. There's one with Endo, Richard Buntyn and Cole Ritter at the governor's mansion, if you can believe it. So maybe she sees the backstage door open, she pops
in to see what's up, say hello, whatever, but when she gets
there, she finds Endo doing his thing with Buntyn's body. She
worked a big party earlier that evening, so maybe her camera's
memory card was full, because she used the internal memory
to shoot the photos. She gets three or four shots before Endo
hears the camera's shutter. He chases her down, they fight, and
eventually he strangles her with whatever is handy, puts her in
the trunk of her own car and drives her home. He sets up her
body in the bedroom to make it look like somebody strangled
her with her own shoes, then he gets the bright idea to lock
the doors and make it look like the husband did it."

Adam chuckled. "Bullshit, Jackie. How did he lock the
door? Her keys were on the bed, inside the locked house." That

was the puzzle he had been trying to solve, and I finally had the answer.

"He found a spare key outside."

"Outside, where?"

"In the flower box behind the garage."

"Shit," he swore. I couldn't tell whether he believed me or not. It was still pretty flimsy, evidence-wise, but it provided reasonable doubt. Not enough to convince a cop, but certainly enough for a jury. "How do you know that?"

"Because I found the key holder," I said. "It's a fake frog. It was hidden in the flower box, but there's no key in it. Why hide a keyholder if there's no key?"

Adam didn't answer. The bathroom was quiet, too, not even any running water. I sat on the edge of the bed and felt for my baseball bat. It wasn't under the covers where I had left it.

Finally, Adam asked, "Who took the photo of Endo standing over the body?"

I didn't have a logical answer to that question. Pictures had a way of showing up in the Leica's memory all of their own accord. I couldn't tell him what I really believed. "This camera's kind of touchy. Sometimes it takes photos by itself."

"Or maybe her husband took the photo," Adam offered.

"From San Diego?"

"OK. His alibi is airtight. That's why he's still walking around. You've done some good work and surprised me a couple of times. Now let me tell you a story maybe you don't know. James and Ashley St. Michael were the hot new thing in town. Ashley had a free pass to every society event. She was gorgeous, and as you know, James is no slouch. He's a Goddamn Adonis, right?" I didn't need Adam to tell me that.

"Half the golf widows in town were plotting to get him in the sack. They tried and failed, numerous times. I have their depositions on file. He seemed utterly devoted to his wife, beyond reproach, too monogamous if you ask me. His story was just too good to be true. People were started to think he was gay. In any case, this whole time he's losing his shirt at the casinos and private poker games, playing against people who can afford to lose in one night what he makes in a year. Ashley's people are rich as the pope, and she had taken out a fat life insurance policy, but he can't get at that money if he kills her. Somewhere along the line, James meets Endo. Maybe he hires Endo to whack his wife so he can collect the life insurance . . ."

"Only he never collected it," I interrupted.

Adam didn't break stride. ". . . or maybe he and Endo become lovers, and maybe after a couple of times together he drops Endo like nobody's business and Endo decides to get back at him, kill his wife and frame him for it. After what he did to Dave, you have to admit it fits his pattern."

"Then that clears James," I said.

"No it doesn't. How did Endo know about that spare key, unless James told him about it? He wouldn't plot her murder and risk everything on the chance he might find a spare key."

"I found the empty key frog because I was looking for it. A lot of people keep a spare key outside."

"And people change the locks when they move into a new house."

"They bought the house in an estate sale."

"I know that." He sounded tired, frustrated with the investigation, exasperated with me because I wouldn't stop arguing with him. If Endo got away now, Adam would be blamed for it, not Billet, and certainly not Wiley. And here I was, wasting his time when he should have been tracking down the killer. He went on, "All I'm saying is Endo is the link. We never connected him before because none of his victims had an obvious relationship with one another. He was the only common point in all their lives. And their deaths."

The bathroom door opened. James stepped out and leaned against the doorjamb. He pressed a wet towel to his forehead. He looked into the bedroom and saw me talking on the phone, then staggered to the couch and sank into the ratty cushions.

"I don't think Endo is a typical serial killer," Adam continued. "He knew all his victims. That's why we couldn't pin him down. He doesn't fit the profile. He killed them to punish them, for whatever reason. My guess is he felt betrayed."

"Any sign of him yet?" Adam still hadn't mentioned the photos I'd sold to Michi. I hoped they would never find them.

Fat chance of that. Who was I kidding? It was only a matter of time. To build the case against Endo, they would tear Michi's house apart, brick by brick, just to make sure there weren't any bodies hidden in the walls. My pictures would show up eventually, and that would be that.

"Nobody has seen the Murano since you spotted it this afternoon."

"It may not have been the same one."

"That would've been a hell of a coincidence," Adam said. "I don't believe in coincidences. I don't believe Ashley St. Michael just happened to stop by the Playhouse the night Richard Buntyn was killed. I don't believe Endo just happened to find that spare key outside her house. There's something bigger going on here, something we can't see because we're too close to it. Which is why you've got to drop this guy, Jackie. James St. Michael stinks. His story stinks. I don't want him there with you."

I lowered my voice to keep from screaming into the phone. "*You don't want him here?* Who the fuck are you to tell me what you don't want? If you're so worried about who I'm seeing, why don't you just ask me out yourself?"

"First of all, I'm your NA sponsor. It wouldn't be right for us . . ."

"That's bullshit."

He interrupted me. "Second, I'm gay."

Now it was my turn to sit there with my chin in my lap. I'd always assumed Adam was straight, a good heterosexual boy of the standard cop mold. A little uptight, sure, married to his job, definitely, but that wasn't exactly unusual for a cop, especially one moving up so quickly through the ranks. He never talked about his personal life, people he was dating, anything. I never suspected it was because he was gay.

"I thought you knew," he said when I didn't answer.

"I didn't."

"Does it make a difference?"

"No. Well, it does, of course, but not like that." How could it? I was floored by his revelation, still off balance by the suddenness of it, and still angry at him for trying to direct my personal life.

"I wish you would trust me on this guy, Jackie," he said.

"You're wrong, Adam."

"How can you be so sure?"

"James is a decent guy."

"Jackie, you've never been right about a man in your whole life," he said. The bastard was right. That's why it hurt so much.

"I thought I was right about you," I said, and hung up.

40

I TURNED THE RINGER OFF and dropped the phone on the bed. I didn't want to talk to Adam if he called back, and he would call back. Any minute now. He always called back when I hung up on him.

James was lying on the couch with his arm over his eyes. I checked the front door to make sure it was locked. James sat up and looked at me over the back of the couch. "That didn't sound good," he said.

"Sorry. You weren't supposed to hear."

"I tried not to listen. You should have closed your door. But I appreciate what you're doing." He rubbed his face with both hands, going from his chin up and over the top of his head, like a swimmer getting out of the pool. His eyes were puffy and dim in the light.

"It's nothing," I said.

"You have funny ideas about nothing. It didn't sound like nothing."

I changed the subject. "Are you all right now?" His face looked like a clay mask in the glow of the laptop.

"I'll be OK . . ." He choked it off before it started again.

"You need a fresh beer." I got him a can of Budweiser from the fridge.

He took a small sip. "Your friend, the cop," he said. "He doesn't like me being here."

"Screw him."

"Did you tell him about the picture you found?"

I shrugged and flicked cigarette ash on the floor between my legs. James carefully stood his beer on the arm of the couch, like a man defusing a bomb. A droplet of dew ran down the side of the can and sank into the other stains in the fabric. "I hate cops," he muttered. "They're bastards. Every last one."

"Adam's not a bastard," I said, wondering, *Why am I defending him?* Adam *was* being a bastard about James. "He's my friend. He's worried about me."

"Is that all?" James asked.

"What's that supposed to mean?"

He wouldn't look at me now. He traced another drop of dew down the side of his beer can. "He's a guy. Maybe he has personal reasons for not wanting me here."

That pissed me off, even though it shouldn't have. I'd practically accused Adam of the same thing. It didn't change how I felt now. "First of all, Adam's my NA sponsor, so that's not going to happen because it would be a violation of trust. Second, he's gay. So don't go second-guessing other people's motives if you don't know the first fucking thing about them, OK?"

He picked up his beer and held it to his mouth without drinking. "Sorry," he said. He took a long swig, his throat rising and falling like a piece of machinery. He socked that can away like a regular frat boy, crumpled the empty in his hand. He wiped his mouth with his sleeve. "It's just that every time I turn around, some cop is trying to screw up my life."

"Cops see it all," I said. "They don't always get it right."

"Yeah, but when they get it wrong, innocent people die with a needle in their arm."

"Why do you think so many cops end up alcoholics, drug addicts, divorced?" I was describing myself.

He shrugged, sullen. All he could see was his own point of view, and I couldn't blame him. One thing you don't want in your life is some cop who's married to the idea that you broke the law. It really won't matter if you're innocent or guilty, he's going to find a way to bring you down. All the same, I could understand Adam's concern, and deep down I still harbored a niggling doubt about James. How did Endo find that key, unless he already knew about it?

"Maybe I can help you see the situation from a cop's point of view," I offered.

"I really don't care to see their point of view," he said.

"Just sit still and listen for a minute. Like I said before, when a woman is killed, cops automatically look at the husband or boyfriend. That's a fact of life. Also, you're up to your ass in debt . . ."

"How . . ." he started to say, then realized how stupid that question would sound.

I continued, ". . . up to your ass in debt. Your wife had a big insurance policy and her folks had money. That's motive."

"I never tried to collect on her policy."

"Because the insurance company wouldn't pay as long as you were a suspect."

"I didn't want to collect."

"You couldn't collect, whether you wanted to or not. Cops don't care about your noble intentions. All they see is the insurance policy and how much you stand to collect."

"OK," he said, calming down a little. "I can see that. I never thought of it that way. But it's not gambling debt."

"What then?"

"Stocks. I was in deep, day trading, borrowing money to cover my losses."

"Borrowing from who?"

"Leg breakers. The banks wouldn't talk to me anymore."

"If you needed money, why not sell the house?"

"The house belongs to Ashley's parents. They bought it for us as a wedding present, but the title is still in their name. They're very controlling people, especially her dad. We had to stay married for ten years before they would give us the house outright. After the . . ." He paused again and his eyes watered up. "After Ashley died, they let me keep living there for her sake, until I was actually convicted. Innocent until proven guilty. They're Democrats."

"How generous of them," I said.

"They don't talk to me anymore. We talk through their lawyer. After I lost my job, I needed every penny to pay the lawyers and keep the gorillas off my back. The other day I got a margin call, so I sold Ashley's cameras. I had no choice. I sold my Lexus a couple of days ago."

"So you defintely had motive. Means is obvious enough—you were her husband." I had to stop myself. Here he was helping me to dig his own grave, yet for some reason I still trusted him.

I continued, tried to be more diplomatic, and failed. "All that's left is opportunity, and that's the sticky part. You have a perfect alibi."

"Exactly," he said without moving his lips. They were flat gash across his face.

"But that doesn't mean you weren't involved. You could have hired it out." Then, because I still had that niggling doubt, I said, "Wayne Endo," to see how he would react.

He didn't, except to say, "What?" That eased my mind a bit. Either he didn't know Endo or he was a damned good actor. Damn good. The best ones always are. Not even Perry Mason can shake them.

"Did you ever know or meet a man named Wayne Endo?" I asked.

"Not that I remember."

"Never talked to him in a chat room online?"

"I don't do that kind of thing."

"Never picked him up in a bar anywhere?"

"You mean like a gay bar?"

I didn't say anything.

"I was married!"

"Lots of gay men are married. You wouldn't be the first."

He just shook his head. This was a pointless line of inquiry, anyway. Adam was wrong about James and I knew it. I took a drag and blew the smoke at the computer screen, then clicked to the next image in the camera file. It was a picture of me, naked, asleep in bed with my brother's baseball bat clutched between my legs. I had kicked off the covers. The angle was low and foreshortened, as though the camera had been sitting on the nightstand when the photo was shot.

I closed the image, but left the computer on. "Endo isn't your typical serial killer," I said. "He may not even *be* a serial killer. He murders people he thinks have betrayed him, or to send messages to people who have betrayed him."

"What's that got to do with me?"

I probably shouldn't have told him. If he did have something to do with his wife's murder, all I was doing was giving him the opportunity to cover his tracks. But I didn't think he was guilty. Maybe I didn't want to think he was guilty. "Maybe you met Endo. Maybe you had a brief affair. Maybe he fixated on you and when you didn't return his affections, he killed your wife and tried to frame you for it."

"But that's not what happened."

"What really happened doesn't matter," I tried to explain. This wasn't some show on television. Justice might not prevail in the end. "All that matters is what the DA *thinks* happened, and what he can convince a jury to believe about you. Which is more plausible? That you had a gay affair that went bad and your lover murdered your wife? Or your wife just happened to be in the perfect place at the perfect time to catch the Playhouse Killer in the act, that he killed her, staged her body, found a hidden and unknown key that allowed him to frame you, then accidentally took a photo of himself standing over the body of his victim?" Just as I finished, a tremendous crack of thunder broke right over our heads, putting an exclamation point on my conclusion.

James said nothing, but his eyes had that drawn look of panic, as though for the first time he could see how thin the line was keeping him from death row. If Endo was captured, the cops, maybe even Adam, would paint the same scenario and Endo would plead to it to buy himself a reduced sentence. That's all it would take to put James St. Michael on a gurney.

He had never faced that reality. Like most people, he assumed truth would win out, and justice would be served in the end. Meanwhile, he'd blamed the cops.

I almost told him about Sean. Maybe if he knew that I understood what it was like to lose someone, he could unload some of that grief. But I would have sounded like a Narcotics Anonymous counselor. *Hello, my name is Jackie, and I'm still grieving my brother's murder.*

Truth was, I really couldn't know what James had been through, just like he couldn't know what I'd been through.

You can talk about it, but nobody can share those dark watches of the night with you. James had been dealing with this the best he could for two years, but the cops wouldn't let him move on. They wouldn't let him bury his wife.

I reached across and took his crumpled beer can, tossed it in the trash in the dark. I couldn't even see the garbage pail, but Zen-like I swished it, nothing but net. The thunder was pretty much constant now, but still distant, except for that one crack.

"You want another beer?"

"Please." I sucked the foam off the top before handing it to him. He thanked me and set it on the arm of the couch without taking a drink. I stood in the door with the cold blowing out around my legs. James was staring sightlessly into the bedroom, one side of his face lit up by the light from the refrigerator. The other side was so dark I couldn't see it.

"I didn't kill my wife," he said, turning to me. "I loved Ashley. I still love her."

"I believe you."

"I wish I could believe you do."

"I wish you could, too." He sat with his chin resting on the back of the couch. His hair was softer than it looked, but his cheeks were rough. He needed a shave. "If I thought for one second you had murdered your wife, do you honestly think I would kiss you?" I leaned forward in the chair and kissed him on the mouth. He kissed me back, but only a little. Ashley was still there inside him, the memory of her, holding him back. I could feel her. I could almost see her. He was the only thing holding her in this world, but if he let her go, they'd both be lost.

I kissed him again and this time he put his hand on the back of my head, and now he clove to me with a terrible desperation, like a drowning or starving man. I don't know if I was merely standing in for his lost wife, if he even knew who he was kissing. It didn't matter. I could hardly breathe but it didn't feel like I needed to breathe. I was starving, too. Two starved children devouring each other. I felt the wet on my cheeks from his tears and he let me go just enough to breathe, and rested his forehead against mine.

"I've spent the last two years wondering whether I'd ever prove my innocence," he said.

"Nobody's innocent," I said, and kissed him lightly on the cheek. "We're just not all guilty. Can you stay here tonight?"

He nodded.

41

His mouth tasted cool and earthy, like water from a mountain stream, like snow and the wind and the melting sunlight, with just a hint of beer. Mine felt like a bayou full of rotting gar and lovesick bullfrogs. I couldn't remember if I had brushed my teeth that morning. I hadn't eaten all day. I was living on cigarettes and beer.

I took his hand and pulled him to the bedroom door so he could see the bed against the wall. It was easy enough to spot it in the strobes of lightning outside the window. I put a hand on his chest and kissed him again, briefly, just with the lips, and said, "Give me a minute." I let my hand drift down his chest, over the rippling muscles of his belly, just so he had no doubts what I intended. Then I took the two steps back into the bathroom and closed the door.

I gazed in the mirror for a moment and hardly recognized myself. My face was so pale my eyebrows looked like someone had drawn them with Magic Marker. My eyes were tiny beneath them, squinting suspiciously at the person in the mirror. I pulled down my jeans and panties, then shucked off my shirt and bra and tossed them in the shower.

I faced my naked self in the mirror once more. At least

with tits I looked more like me, or the me I expected. My vision remained about twenty-one years old, back in the day when married photography professors asked me to stay after class and model for them. But my ribs, God, my ribs. I looked like a medical specimen. The smack had eaten away at me all these years. It was going to take awhile before I stopped looking like a junkie. *Thank God for darkness as well as light. I hope I wake up before he does.* I opened the medicine cabinet, leaving the mirror tilted against the wall so I wouldn't have to look at myself again.

I loaded up my toothbrush and set about trying to scrub eight years of cigarette tar from my teeth. I heard James say, "Hey!"

I stopped for a minute and listened, but all I heard over the running faucet was the approaching storm, an almost continuous grumble of thunder. I turned off the light and opened the door.

James was lying on the bed with his shirt off, but still wearing his jeans. He lay almost against the wall, his face hidden in the shadow thrown by the headboard from the red streetlight outside the window. The light turned green. I suddenly felt ridiculously awkward, standing naked before him in that ghastly glow.

My laptop was still on, its screen shining off the refrigerator door in the next room. My camera rested beside it on the kitchen table, still plugged into the computer. Each flicker of lightning made the camera lens wink like a dark and knowing eye, with a weird purplish dot of light glowing deep within the lens.

Something moved in the corner by the fridge. I froze with my hand on the doorknob. Another flicker of lightning showed nothing there, but I noticed that the drawer next to the refrigerator was open. I hadn't opened it. Nothing but silverware in there. Maybe James had.

In the next flash I saw a butcher knife floating before me, about chest high with the handle toward me. There was nothing there, nothing holding it, just the knife with the blade ground down and sharp enough to split a hare. I let go of the door and tried to say something but nothing came out of my throat but air.

A disembodied voice, like the voice of some thousand year old crone, spoke out of the darkness in a thin crackling falsetto. "Is this a dagger I see before me, the handle toward my hand?" The knife floated between me and my laptop and I finally saw the hand and body, like a clot of darkness, featureless, almost shapeless, crouching with the knife held up like an offering.

I finally found my voice. "Who are you?" Just a little hysterical.

"Life's but a walking shadow," it answered.

I turned, shouting for James, and something struck me a terrific blow across the small of my back. Before I could think, it struck me across the back of the legs. I stumbled and sprawled on the bed on top of James, grabbing his arm to keep from sliding off, because my legs no longer worked. He didn't try to grab me or hold me up. He didn't even look at me.

I couldn't move. The muscles of my back and legs were tight as car springs. I tried to lift my head but it felt as though my neck wasn't made to bend that way. My face was almost on top of my cell phone. Adam was calling. I tried to push the talk button with my nose, but something grabbed my leg and rolled me over, lifted me stiffly by one elbow and dropped me next to James on the bed, so that we lay side by side. But by that time, I blacked out.

42

I WOKE IN A FLASH of intense light, blinked, waiting for the crack of thunder that never came. He was leaning over me, the glow of the Leica's LCD screen lighting up his featureless black mask of a face. The green traffic light showed the rest of him well enough to see that he wore black gloves, a black shirt and pants that looked like pajamas or some kind of karate gi and a black hood that completely covered his face except for a slit across the eyes. There was something wrong about his eyes, the way they stood out. By the sound of the storm, I couldn't have been unconscious more than a few minutes. Either that or I'd slept through the whole thing.

When he saw I was awake, he dropped the camera to his side and pulled off his hood. I tried to move but he had tied my knees together with one of my bras. I guessed it was another bra binding my wrists. My brother's baseball bat lay on the dresser against the mirror. One end was dark with blood that wasn't mine. The dresser drawers were pulled out, my clothes spilled all over the floor, hanging from the knobs. At least I could move a little. Unconsciousness had loosened the rebellion of cramps paralyzing my back from the blow of the baseball bat. James's elbow dug into a soft spot below my ribs.

I turned my head to look at him. The mattress under his head was soaked through, the back of his skull a soft mass of wet hair. I watched his chest for a moment. It wasn't moving. The light outside turned yellow, then red.

I turned away. Endo squatted at the end of the bed now, peering at me over the wad of sheets and blankets. His face was completely black with stage makeup. In the red light, the black didn't show up at all. His eyes seemed huge and disembodied, floating in space until a strobe of lightning showed the rest of his frizzy head. He rested the Leica on my knees. I wasn't as afraid he would rape me as what he might do to James' body.

"Did you know that ninja techniques of stealth were first mastered by puppeteers in medieval Japanese Bunraku theater?" he asked in his cracking falsetto. It sounded like it hurt to talk that way. He cleared his throat. "Two years ago I was in a production of *Waiting for Godot* at the Germantown Community Theatre. I was the tree. It was my job to move around the stage without being noticed. The actors would get up and walk around, and when they went back to the tree, it would be in a different place on the stage."

"Is that how you got into my apartment?"

"No, your landlord let me in. I told him I was an old friend. He was most accomodating." He rose and walked to the window, peered up at the flickering brown sky. "This is gonna be some show," he said. The light turned green again and he stepped back into the shadow by the dresser. I heard him opening drawers, but with his back turned, I couldn't see him. He was a ghost, his falsetto floating out of the darkness, "Sorry to tie you up like that. I saw what you did to that dyke behind Bosco's and I didn't want you jumping to conclusions about me." So it was Endo who followed me into the women's bathroom that night. I wondered how long he had been stalking me.

"Walter wouldn't have let you in," I said.

"You're right. The man was downright rude. Tried to wallop me up side the head with a bottle of gin, but his heart wasn't in it. I think he was afraid of spilling the gin. He loved it more than his own life."

"What did you do to Walter?"

"I didn't touch him. If you must blame someone, blame Newton. Blame gravity. Blame God. It makes no difference."

"Where is he?" I asked, trying not to sound angry. I tried to pretend this was a normal conversation, but Endo made normal conversation impossible.

"Look for him yourself," he giggled and closed his eyes. "If you do not find him within the month, you shall nose him around the elevator." He sat on the end of the bed in almost exactly the same place where the ghost of Ashley St. Michael perched, looking at me with almost exactly the same featureless black face, until he smiled and reached across to rub James's leg.

I worked myself around until I could pull my knees up and ease the strain on my back. My neck was resting on my cell phone. It was vibrating with an incoming call. I hoped this was Adam calling back. If he called and I didn't answer, he would either send a patrol unit over or check on me himself. Now I wished I had listened to him. He'd been wrong about James, but not Endo. I thought Endo would be somewhere over the Caribbean by now, yet here he sat on the end of my bed with a smile on his blackened face so pleasant you'd think we were talking about baseball or the weather. He gave James's leg one last shake and stood up.

I aimed both feet at his nuts and connected so hard it shoved the whole bed against the wall with a loud bang. Other than a brief stagger to regain his balance, it didn't seem to phase him. "You have strong legs," he said. "But you can't hurt me. Do you know, I haven't slept since I was four years old? They tell me I used to sleep, but not anymore. It's like I'm not even human. Tee hee hee!" His operatic little giggle made me cold all over. I landed a solid two-footed kick, hard enough to knock his balls out through the top of his head. He shouldn't even be breathing. It was like I had kicked a corpse.

He knelt beside the bed and dragged out my suitcases, opened them, closed them and pushed them back under the bed. "What are you looking for?" I asked.

He glanced around the room as though mentally checking off a list. "You know what."

"Honestly, I don't."

He left the room. I heard him banging around in the kitchen, dragging pots and pans out of the cabinets, opening drawers. In the dim light of my laptop, I saw him toss the couch cushions aside, then tip over the entire couch. He used his butcher knife to rip up the upholstery. Without looking at James, I tried to roll over so I could get my legs off the bed and at least stand up. I wanted to break a window and shout for help, but I couldn't roll over without falling off the bed.

Endo returned, stopping in the doorway with hands on hips staring around the room. "I searched the whole house. It wasn't there."

"What house? What wasn't there?"

He smiled at me. "Like you don't know."

"I honestly don't."

"Even if you did, you wouldn't tell me. *But ve haf vays ov making you talk.*"

He pulled a small black bag from his pocket and sat on the end of the bed. He opened the bag, removed a smack junkie's rig—hypodermic needle, bent spoon, stub of a votary candle, and worn Zippo, which he flicked open, holding the blue flame up to his face." My grandfather must have sent the box to you before he murdered Cole."

"Michi murdered Cole?"

Endo held the votive candle to the wavering blue flame. "Do you remember the day you sold Michi the photos of those Simon boys?" he asked. He had been watching me that day, probably though one of his spy holes. I remembered him dashing past the kitchen door, just before I left. "Michi hadn't bought me a birthday present yet, so I begged him to get me a copy of your full collection of Playhouse Killer photos." His eyes shone as he spoke the name given to him by the media, and I recalled the scrapbook of theater reviews we'd found in his apartment. He was his own biggest fan.

"Cole Ritter came in just as I asked Michi for those pictures and he started laughing. *Why Wayne*, he says, *are you our little ole Playhouse Killah?* Michi looked at me. I saw it come together like a puzzle in his fat little eyes. Cole thought it was hilarious. He couldn't stop laughing because Michi never suspected a thing. Michi's cane had a sword in it. He stuck it through Cole's heart because he wouldn't stop laughing. So I helped my grandfather cover it up, made the murder look like one of mine. We had to hurry or I would have staged it better."

Endo was lying, of course. I said, "Cole rode with Michi to the hospital."

He shrugged and changed his story without missing a line. It was just another narrative to him, one just as good, just as real to his fantasy world mind as the next. "Michi caught me tearing his bedroom apart searching for the pictures. Only at that moment did he realize who I was and what I had become, right under his nose. He drew that sword from his cane and told me to me to get out of his *hay-ouse*. So I did. I wasn't ready to kill him, anyway. I didn't think he would turn me in, but I had to have those pictures, see? After I left, he had his little heart attack, or acted like he did. I was still in the garage when the ambulance showed up. I thought he might tell Cole about me on the way to the hospital, so I called Cole and told him I wanted to give him the whole story. I figured he'd want to hear it from me before he called the cops, because the great Cole Ritter always has to know everything first. The man never wrote an original thing in his life—it was all gossip. Michi told me all about Cole Ritter. Gossip was the only thing the great Cole Ritter was ever any good at.

"Cole agreed to meet me, but first I had to take him home so he could get his little tape recorder because he was going to write a play about me, he said. We sat in Michi's dining room drinking his wine until about two in the morning. I told him everything and when I was finished, he said he wanted to me to blow him. So I did. And when he was done and sitting there smoking his smug little cigarette, I took a sword out of the drawer in the china cabinet and stabbed that dirty little arras rat through the spleen. It was his own fault. He should have seen me coming because that's how he would have written our scene."

Endo closed the Zippo and picked up the camera. "It's not important now," he said. He took a photo of me. When the camera clicked, he frowned and turned it around to look at the lens. "What's wrong with the flash?"

"It doesn't have a flash," I said.

"It was working a minute ago." It was like he didn't hear me, or couldn't hear me. I was just another object to him, a subject, already a corpse in his mind, to be manipulated, posed, and photographed. He bashed the Leica against the bed post. "I don't like the way this thing looks at me," he snarled. He flung it through the door into the kitchen. I heard it smash against the wall and tried not to let the pain of losing it show on my face.

Instead, I tried to engage him, to buy myself some time, time for Adam to ride in and save the day. "Do you like to take pictures, Wayne?" I used his name, the name he preferred to bring us together on a more personal level. I asked him about himself, about what he liked to do, to bring him out of his fantasy world and into the moment. This is what they taught us to do in hostage negotiation training.

It worked. "Oh yes," he said, warming immediately to the subject. "It's one of the few pleasures I allow myself. But I find I prefer video. Still photos are too limiting, don't you think? You can't get the true feel for a scene unless you're actually there. Video is better for that. I wish I had brought my camera, but I hadn't really planned to kill you. I have nothing against you, Jackie. You're a wonderful photographer. All I want is my package."

"All your pictures are on my laptop. Every picture I've ever taken. I photographed every scene you created, all your best work."

"Even Michi's?" he asked, suddenly excited, like a child at his birthday. "Nothing in his life became him like the leaving it." He paused, smiling at me, his teeth floating in the darkness like the grin of the Cheshire Cat. "That's from *Macbeth*, you know."

"You can have them all. Take the laptop. Anything you want."

"I've never been with a woman before." He edged up the bed until he was sitting beside me. He took off his gloves and laid his hand on my left breast. His hand was hot from the gloves, or maybe from the fever consuming him. He was sweating through the black paint on his face. It started to run down his cheeks. "Sometimes I've wondered what it would be like to be with a woman."

"You could try it," I offered. I was fishing for anything to stall him. Even that.

"You're a beautiful woman. Anybody can see that. Truly, truly desirable. But this . . ." He tweaked my nipple. "It's just meat to me."

"What could it hurt to try? You never know. You might like it."

"I'm not really atttracted to women. I tried to go straight once." He circled my areola with his finger, teasing it hard despite my revulsion. "I gave up the gay life and accepted Jesus H. Christ as my Lord and Savior. I signed up for this Christian camp run by Pastor T. Roy Howard, where they promise to cast out the demon of homosexuality. My roommate was this good-looking little black boy from Memphis, about sixteen years old. They actually put us in the same dorm room together, if you can believe that, locked us in every night. His mama sent him to camp so his older brother wouldn't kill him. They didn't want no down-low brother in the family making them look bad in front of the black community, you see, so they sent him off to exorcise the demon of *homosecksha-lity*. You may have seen his people on television last week, pulling out their hair and flopping around on the sidewalk over their dead baby boy, that very same down-low brother they couldn't bear to have in their house—Chris Hendricks, of Hendricks Brothers Funeral Home."

Trying to keep him talking, I asked. "The cure didn't work for you?"

"Good God, no," he drawled, and in a flash of lightning I recognized his resemblance to Michi. He had the same tired eyes, worn out from seeing too much, and the same soft face and lips, or would have if he were about fifty years older and a hundred pounds fatter. I wondered if Michi looked like Endo when he was a young man, newly-married to his wealthy, white, lesbian wife. Endo even sounded like the old pervert. He had adopted Michi's Mississippi twang.

"That Christian camp was a Goddamn NAMBLA convention. It was a flop house for closeted preachers with a Socratic penchant for young boys. The counselors were supposed to be reformed faggots, but they had set themselves up with an unending stream of easy ass-boys, all in the name of the Lord. People were actually paying them thousands of dollars a week to bugger their sons. I remember this one session—Get the Low Down on Christ—honestly, they didn't even try to hide what they were doing. They even called their ministry 'Servicing the Lord.' So after about three days of trying to resist, what with that Hendricks boy crawling into my bed every night begging me to fuck him, I finally gave in. I stayed there about a week until I got tired of him and them and the whole damn thing. A man can get tired of just about anything."

"Why don't you untie my hands?" I asked. He ignored me again, lost in his monologue on a dark stage of his own creation.

"Michi was a saint compared to those Christians. At least he had to keep up appearances for the neighbors. This camp was about twelve miles back in the woods near Greer's Ferry Lake. The shit that went on out there would curl your hair. But I really did want to go straight, see, so I checked myself out. They didn't want to let me go because Michi was paying a lot of money for me to stay there and they said I wasn't cured yet. They were worried about the state of my immortal soul and the demons of homosexuality. So I showed them some

videos I had secretly taken of Dr. Howard baptizing . . . you
understand . . . baptizing in his seminary fluid three white boys
under the age of sixteen. They said I was cured and could go
home, even drove me to the bus station in Little Rock and left
me there without my camera or any of my luggage."

I tried to calculate where Adam would be at that moment
if he took off after the last phone call. If he left Endo's apartment, he'd drive up Airways to East Parkway and then east on
Summer. It was almost a straight shot. He'd be here any minute. If he was coming. I had to believe he was coming.

Endo crossed his legs, took his hand from my breast and
rested it on his knee. "I wanted to meet a nice girl just like
you, maybe even get married," he sighed melodramatically and
hummed a few bars of "Going to the Chapel." "Michi said he
would support us. He said he would buy us a house anywhere
we wanted. I think he was just trying to get rid of me. Then
one Friday afternoon I saw the woman of my dreams at the
Save-a-Lot. I followed her home. I couldn't figure her out, you
know? All my life I've been attracted to men no matter what I
did or thought, and then suddenly this girl comes along, this
magical, beautiful girl, long red hair and a face like an angel.
She had me properly confounded. About six o'clock she comes
out of her apartment all dressed up for a night on the town and
gets in her car and I follow her to the Blue Monkey and go inside and I can't believe this beautiful girl could be alone on a
Friday night standing at a bar all by herself and nobody talking
to her, so I know she is my miracle girl. I talk to her. She smiles
at me. She touches my hand and I buy her a drink, she buys me
a drink and then we move to a booth and before you know it
we're kissing. Me, kissing a girl! She tasted like a lollipop. She
was touching me but she wouldn't let me touch her because she
said she was shy, so I say let's go somewhere private. I take her

to my favorite spot out at Elmwood Cemetery. It's this secluded hole among the cedars and the graves, back away from the main road, hardly anybody knows it's there but I used to go when I was a kid to beat off. We're sitting there on a headstone kissing and she goes down on me for a little while, then she bends over this gravestone and she says, I'm saving myself for when I get married but you can do me and next thing I know she's laying over the headstone like she's broken or something and I'm holding a piece of a cedar branch as big as your wrist with her hair all in it. So I give her a good rogering with that stick, the dirty slut . . ."

"You're talking about Patsy Concorde," I said.

"Patrick! He hadn't had the fucking operation yet!" Endo screamed. His face wasn't the same, it was like a mask of rage that he put on when I wasn't looking. "Bitch tried to trick me. When I pulled down his panties and that thing flopped out I just lost it. I don't know. I don't know. She was so beautiful, I would have waited, I would have gone to the operation with her and shared all that if she had only just told me the truth instead of playing all shy and shit like she's some innocent little virgin cunt."

"So you killed her," I said. It was a stupid thing to say. I don't know why I said it. He pissed me off.

But he laughed. Threw back his head and laughed the fakest, coldest laugh I'd ever heard. "Killed her? Hell no, I didn't kill her. She was already dead. She never was alive, never real. She was an actor on the stage of life, for life is theater, honey. None of this is real. I'm not real. You're not real. He's not real. They're not real. I am he is you are we is she are he and we are all together. Nothing we do means anything, all that matters is how well we play our scenes. Tomorrow they'll play the same scenes again with different actors. So I didn't

kill anyone. I merely followed the script. All the world's indeed a stage and we are merely players. . . ." He paused, frowning and confused. "No, that's not it. The meter is all wrong.
I've got it mixed up. Line!"

Someone knocked on the door. Endo clapped his hand
over my mouth before I could scream. I tried to drive a knee
into his stomach, but I couldn't get enough leverage to make it
hurt. I tried to bite his hand. He forced my legs down and
grabbed something off the floor. "Don't get your panties in a
wad," he whispered as he crammed a pair past my teeth, gag-
ging me. "This is all part of the show. I hope you like it."

He put his knee on my tit and crushed me into the bed
while he pulled on his gloves, then his hood. Somebody was
really hammering on the door. Endo leaned his full weight
onto me until the black spots started to close around. I heard a
distant crack, like a stick breaking, and felt something give in
my chest. Then he left me in the bed with the springs bouncing up and down, hardly able to breathe at all.

The door exploded in the next room. I rolled off the bed,
landed on my shoulder and felt my broken rib grind against itself. I sat up, trying to twist out of the bra binding my arms. I
choked on the panties in my mouth, almost vomited and fought
it back down. I knew if I vomited into my gag I would drown.
Adam's head appeared around the side of the doorframe, scoping the room. I tried to scream but I think the noise only made
him more careless. He entered at a crouch, pistol held low in
both hands. Endo drifted in silently behind him with the baseball bat. He smacked Adam once across the broadest part of
his back. Adam let out a surprised wuff of air, staggered and
dropped to one knee. His gun popped off, punching a hole
through a pane of glass above my head. Then Endo hit him on
the crown of the head so hard the bat broke at the logo. Dots of

Adam's blood stung my face. He lurched to his feet, spun and landed on his back with his legs already running, the heels of his black department-issue brogans hammering the floor like a drum line, his whole body convulsing. It seemed to go on forever. His gun came spinning out and slid under the bed so fast I heard it hit the wall.

Finally, he lay still, breathing shallow, his eyes swimming in his face, then one big breath, taking it all in, and then out and no more. I watched him die, helpless. My knight in shining armor. His eyes tight shut, like he didn't want to see it coming.

Endo stood in the doorway, hugging himself and holding the broken bat handle to his chest. He pulled off his hood and dropped it on the floor, dragged the sleeve of his black pajamas across his mouth, leaving behind a white swipe of bare skin like a clown's smile on his face. "This fell sergeant is strict in his arrest," he whispered. "Yet who would have thought he had such blood in him!"

I said something, I don't know what. The panties in my mouth swallowed my words. It didn't matter anyway. I couldn't hurt him with words or make him stop or even give him a moment's pause. There was nothing human in him to appeal to. A shrill and eerie whistle blew through the bullet hole in the window, like a teapot coming to boil, and a fine mist of rain drifted into the room. The air grew bitter cold. The storm, so long in coming, arrived all at once. The rafters shook with thunder, the window rattled in its frame. The candle on the floor flickered and blew out.

"What's done cannot be undone," Endo said as he closed and locked the bedroom door.

43

H E WALKED SLOWLY AROUND ADAM'S body. "I wish
I had brought my video camera," he said. The storm
was really churning outside now, the rain slashing against the
window, misting the floor through the bullet hole. I lay over
on my side to ease my ribs and wait for death.

Endo unbuckled Adam's belt, unzipped his pants and
pulled them down to his ankles, then flipped his body over. I
turned my head and looked under the bed so I wouldn't have
to watch. It was too dark under the bed to see Adam's gun, not
that I could have reached it with my hands tied. I was glad for
the noise of the storm. I fixated on the most mundane thing
in the world—my empty suitcases. I imagined them full of
clothes. *When this is done I'll go on a trip. Where will I go? Some-
place warm, where the sun shines all day. It's so cold in Memphis
in November.*

Endo knelt beside me. "Are you crying?" he asked. He
pulled the panties from my mouth, then held an open beer to
my lips and I drank, thankful. He sat me up and leaned me
against the bed, but I kept my eyes averted. He sat on the floor
beside me with the candle, bag of white powder, spoon and
needle. He was naked, his pale flesh green in the traffic light,

his face black. He lit the candle and set it on the floor. "I have something here I know you'll like. This ain't no Nixon. This is the real goma, honey. This is red rum straight off the boat from Karachi, courtesy of the Taliban and the Goddamn CIA. I know a guy who brings it up the Mississippi River by barge."

He shook a fat deck of powder into the spoon and added a slosh of beer, then set it over the flame to cook. He leaned back, his shoulder resting against mine, like we were two old junkies sitting in an alley by a fire in a trash can. "I want you to understand I take no pleasure in killing you."

"Why not?" I tasted blood in my mouth. "Did it give you pleasure to kill Adam and James?

"They served their purposes. Everybody does. You have your purpose. He had his. They had theirs. Me? I'm an actor, but do you know how many lead roles there are for Japanese men? I tried to stage a production of *Ran*, which is *King Lear* set in medieval Japan, but I couldn't get backing for it, not even from my grandfather. Do you know why? They said there weren't enough Japanese actors in Memphis to fill out the cast. *It's fucking theater!* Use your fucking imagination! The actors don't have to be Japanese, just like you don't have to be a fucking moor to play Othello. Art is not a mirror held up to reality, but a hammer with which to shape it. Do you know who said that?"

I didn't answer. What was the point? Everything he said was scripted. His head was full of quotes, non sequiturs, nightmares and murder. I closed my eyes and rested my head against the side of the bed.

"Bertolt Brecht."

"Never heard of him."

"No, I didn't think you had. Otherwise you would have known I was doing Brecht's *Edward the Second*, not Marlowe's."

"What?" I opened my eyes and looked at him.

He twisted his comic mask into a sick smile and nodded. "My staging of *Edward the Second* was Brecht's version. I didn't expect anyone to realize that. *Who is dark, let him stay dark, who is unclean, let him stay unclean. Praise deficiency, praise cruelty, praise the darkness!* But I didn't want to correct you in front of your friends." He laughed and elbowed my broken rib. "Know what I mean?" I sucked air and sat up straight, feeling the bone push into my lung.

When I could breathe again, I asked, "Why are you doing this?"

"For the art of it, more than anything else."

"This isn't art, Wayne. Nobody but you will appreciate it."

"I'm the artist, honey. I'm the only one I have to please. But I also like the novelty of this. In Thespis's time, there was only one actor on the stage, plus the chorus. Aeschylus added a second actor and Sophocles a third. Phrynichus was the first to include female roles, but all the parts, male and female, god and demon, were played by men. Even in Shakespeare's time, all the parts were played by men. That's as it should be and the only way I've ever worked, until tonight."

"What about Ashley St. Michael?" I countered.

"What about her?"

"You killed her."

"No, that was James." He picked up the syringe and drew a full load into its chamber, then nudged the hot spoon off the candle flame, scorching a knuckle in the process.

"Bullshit," I said.

He winced and sucked his burned finger. "No, seriously. I've known them ever since they bought Martha Ritter's house. Ever heard of her? She was Cole Ritter's mother. I used to play at her house when I was kid, back behind the garage. It was a

great place to hide things." He giggled again, *tee hee*. "Cole
sold the house to James and Ashley after his mother died. I bet
James didn't tell you that. Anyway, because Ashley was a society photographer and my grandfather was Memphis society,
James and I saw each other about once a month and one thing
led to another, as they sometimes do."

"You're telling me you and James were lovers."

"He is so good-looking!" he cackled. "I did things for James
his wife wouldn't do. I told him things about myself I had never
told anybody. I confessed all the terrible things I had done
when I was young and confused. Then he got in trouble and
needed money, so he asked me to break into his house and
steal his wife's cameras so he could file an insurance claim. He
told me where to find the spare key in the flower box and everything. But when I got there, she was dead on the floor. He
had a camera set up in the closet to take my picture with her
body, but I saw the camera and took the memory card. That
ruined it for him because he couldn't collect her life insurance
until I was convicted. But like an idiot, I had told him of my
plan to stage *Richard the Third* at the Playhouse. So he was
waiting for me there and took my picture with the Duke of
Clarence. He's been blackmailing me ever since. Well, not
anymore," he finished with a soft laugh.

Endo scooted until he was sitting in front of me, stark naked with his black clown face, holding the syringe like a dart
he was about to throw for triple points. I turned my head so I
wouldn't have to look at him. I looked at James lying on my
bed with his mouth open and his eyes half closed like he was
waiting for something amazing to happen. I couldn't believe I
had been so wrong about him. I refused to believe it.

Endo continued, "Why do you think I tried to go straight?
Why do you think I waited two years to do *Edward the Second*?

When I found out the other day that James was trying to sell his dead wife's cameras, I put this production together to get back at him. I'm sorry I had to use you, but I needed somebody close to him. You go to war with the army you have, not the army you wish you had. This is the final act of the play. He won't blackmail me now."

I laughed, even though it hurt like Christ on the cross. Endo was lying again, of course. James was innocent. Endo fabricated the whole story. Truth was totally meaningless to him. But I wasn't ready to give up yet.

"James had no idea those photos were in the camera until tonight. If he was blackmailing you, he'd never have sold me the camera with the pictures still in it."

Endo laughed at me, that fake, falsetto cackle, sounding more like Michi than ever. "OK. You got me. But it makes a good story, doesn't it? That's what's important, a nice dramatic twist at the end. How am I doing, by the way? Convincing performance? Do you fear for your life?"

"Not really," I said. Not anymore, anyway. He was going to kill me. Nothing would change that. I wasn't about to make it easy for him.

"Good. I hope you're enjoying every moment of this. This is real theater, what theater should have always been. You probably think we're performing a tragedy, but this is Comedy with a capital C. If this were tragedy, some fault or flaw, some hubris would have led me to this point, but I've done nothing wrong. I grew up in the most ridiculous of circumstances. It's really quite funny."

He laughed harder and wiped his eyes with the heel of his palms, leaving two, upward-slanted teardrop eyes in his black face, completing his comedic mask. I saw nothing funny about it.

"My father was ruined in business and committed seppuku. My mother tried to follow him by holding me in her arms and jumping in front of a bullet train at Arihata Station. But the bullet hit her and missed me. *Why?* you ask."

I hadn't asked. I didn't care, but he was going to tell me anyway. It was part of the script he had written for himself. "Why did my mother follow an ancient Japanese tradition no longer kept by even the most traditional of Japanese women, especially since she was only half Japanese and could pass for white? What's more, why did I survive? If you can answer that, I defy you to believe in a just God. There is no such animal. So after mama killed herself, they mailed me off to America like a cheap plastic blow-up doll to be raised by my dear, demented old grandfather, Michi Mori, who hated me. He tried to give me away to anyone who feigned the slightest bit of interest in me, as though I were no more important to him than a stray cat who wandered through an open door into his kitchen. The happiest moment in my life was the day you took me away from him. I thought you'd come to save me. So why did you let them send me back?"

"I didn't know. I'm sorry."

"It's a little late for sorry, don't you think, Jacqueline? You knew what kind of monster Michi was. How could you send me back to him?"

"The charges against your grandfather were dropped," I said. Social Services returned custody of Endo to Michi. They never consulted with me about it. "I couldn't stop them." I hadn't even tried. What did I care about Endo? My life fell apart after that case, the department was riding my ass and I was using hard. Endo had been the last thing on my mind.

"I could have given you all the evidence you needed to put

Michi away forever, but no one would listen to me!" he shouted, and rammed his fist into the floor. "I have photographs of the boys who were funneled through Michi's house, traded or bought and sold for the personal use of senators, CEOs, Arab sheiks and mobsters, all kinds of famous people. Some of those boys even ended up in the White House. They'd kidnap kids from all over and bring them to Michi's house until buyers could be found. My grandfather used me like a steer. He'd send me down there to talk to the boys, calm them down and pretend everything would be ok as soon as we could find their parents. Then a white van would pull up, they'd take a few *boizu* to the airport and load them on a private plane and you'd never see them again."

I looked at him. In the red of the traffic light outside the window all I could see was the comedic smile painted on his face, but he wasn't smiling. It was the face of the Gacy clown hanging on the wall of his apartment. His dead black eyes glimmered with tears. "Are you serious, Endo?" I asked.

His façade cracked with yellow teeth. "Not!" he shrieked hysterically as he tied a nylon stocking around his left bicep. He pulled it tight with his teeth. "God, you are so easy. I made that up. Michi was a pervert but he was a decent one. He had no interest in little boys and he didn't trade them. That bit about kidnapping and the White House was something I read on the internet. Michi's only interest was himself. But isn't that enough to make him a monster? Did he have to bugger children and sell them into slavery before you people would try to stop him?"

"I did try to stop him."

"You're right," he agreed. "You did try. I owe you a debt of gratitude." He held up the syringe and squeezed a drop from its point, then stuck it in his arm and pushed about 5cc's into his vein. He undid the knot in the hose. I watched the muscles of his face relax, the smiling mask fall slack.

"That'll take the edge off," he sighed. He scooted his naked butt across the floor until he was behind me. I felt him push the stocking between my arm and back. Then he pulled my spit-soaked panties down over my face. I couldn't see until he tugged the leg hole around and uncovered my right eye. He said, "False face must hide what false face doth know. So this is comedy. But for you, it's tragedy. This will have to do for a tragic mask. Faceless, you can be whoever I want you to be. Tonight, you are Lady Macbeth."

"The cops are looking for you. We were at your apartment today," I said through my mask.

"Yes, I know. I saw you there."

"Someone probably heard that gun shot downstairs."

"In this storm?" The thunder was so loud, we were almost shouting.

"Killing me won't change anything."

"No, it won't change anything. But how am I going to set up the scene properly without Lady Macbeth? I have Banquo there on the floor. There lies Duncan on the bed—he was a goodly king. I myself will play the role of Macbeth." He twisted my arm around to get at a good vein. "Historically, Macbeth is the last play a theater will show before it goes bankrupt or burns down. The play is cursed. So let the police come. If it must be done, let it be done swiftly. *Macbeth* will be my last performance."

I barely felt the needle go into my arm. There had been so many there before it, what was one more? So what if Endo killed me? How many times had I tried to kill myself? How many more times had I been too scared to do it but hoped the junk would get me. Yet now, at the end of all things, I clung to my pathetic life, casting about for a bit of flotsam, all my rescuers floating facedown around me. But there I was, bobbing up again, trying one more time for a gulp of air.

"This isn't your style, Wayne. Lady Macbeth dies offstage by her own hand. She wasn't murdered. All the others were perfectly staged. They were works of art. You don't want to do me this way."

"Oh, but I do."

"Please don't. Please please don't."

"It's the only way."

He loosed the nylon and released his load into my arm, then broke the needle off and left it in my vein. He pulled me to my feet and shook me, then showed me the butcher knife. I don't know where he'd been hiding it. He stood me up in front of him as the drug found my brain and curled around it like a purring cat. He seemed to recede while his arms grew impossibly long. "Please don't," I repeated, though I was already starting not to care. "It's not too late."

"Nay, m'lady. I am in blood; stepp'd in so far that, should I wade no more, returning were as tedious as to go o'er."

I struggled with the demon throb of the drug dulling all the sharp feeling places. I fought to remain myself, clinging to the needle in my arm, which had begun to burn like a lit cigarette into my flesh. "But this isn't a theater. It's just an apartment over a store."

He smiled. His smile seemed to stretch across the thundering pillars of the sky. The tempest had come inside the room and was clashing over our very heads. "Oh, but it was a theater, once upon a time. They used to show gay porn in a little shop downstairs. My first boyfriend, Richard Buntyn, brought me here one night and let five of his friends rape me on stage.

I paid him back for that one with a red hot rod up his ass."

"But that wasn't Buntyn, that was Chris," I said thickly. The rain hissed on the roof, passing in waves like an avant-garde a cappella chorus whispering *wish-wish-wish-wish-wish*.

"Doesn't matter." He sliced up through the bra binding my arms and down through the ones wrapped around my legs. "But enough about me. This moment belongs to Lady Macbeth." I leaned back against the glass window and banged it with my head, hoping to break through and fall to the sidewalk below. I was so weak, I couldn't even do that. He jerked me away and dragged me to the center of the room.

"You must let the blood spurt upon your hands, m'lady, so the audience can see. Hold them close to your throat, like this." He took both of my wrists in one hand and pulled them up to my chest, then touched the edge of the butcher knife to my throat under my right ear.

The room vanished. We stood in an empty black box, in the center of a single spot of brutal red light. We were both naked, me with my tragic panties, he with his clown mask of blackened flesh. He lowered his head and began to speak, no longer in his weird castrato, but in a deep, roaring howl that merged with the storm, invoking the monster within the rattling cage of his own monstrous heart:

Come you spirits that tend on mortal thoughts, unsex me here, and fill me from the crown to the toe top-full of direst cruelty! Make thick my blood; stop up the access and passage to remorse, that no compunctious visitings of nature shake my fell purpose, nor keep peace between the effect and it!

The storm outside ceased, and I wondered if there ever had been a storm. I wondered if anything had ever happened before this moment, if I were not merely one of Endo's spirits conjured from his mind to act upon his stage, say my lines, and disappear.

Another voice, a woman's voice began to speak. I was frozen with horror, because she sounded like me. *Come to my woman's breasts, and take my milk for gall, you murdering ministers, wherever in your sightless substances you wait on nature's mischief! Come, thick night, and pall thee in the dunnest smoke of hell, that my keen knife see not the wound it makes, nor heaven peep through the blanket of the dark, to cry 'Hold, hold!'*

There was a flash of light from the kitchen. Endo glanced over his shoulder at the interuption and shouted "No cameras!" at our unruly audience of grim and silent critics. The theater drew back from around us like a curtain, but not completely. I could still smell the murderously sweet smoke of cooked heroin hanging in the air, feel the velvet black horsemen of the drug galloping through my veins and the rough wooden planks of the floor slick with blood beneath my naked feet. There were people surrounding us, an audience of grim, pale, disembodied faces. Seven white masks and three black masks and one little yellow one like an uncarved jack-o'-lantern. *The twelfth member of the jury is missing*, I thought, but I didn't know who or why. Something cold and hard touched my foot and I recoiled.

Another flash, then a thousand, like someone had turned on a strobe. Endo shoved me onto the bed and swung around, the knife gripped low against his thigh, the muscles of his naked legs trembling. "Shake not thy gory locks at me!" he bellowed through clenched teeth and charged from the bedroom.

I rolled off the bed and fell on Adam's pistol. I was losing myself in the rush of dusty cobwebs blowing through the attic of my skull. My fingers closed around the checkered grip of the pistol, and I tugged the mask from my face. Our audience of faceless faces moved closer, gathering into a chorus, whispering with the rain *List! List! O, list!*

Two came forward, light and black, day and night, and sang softly the conscience of the chorus into my numb ears, *Let no human pity stay thy hand. If thou didst ever love me . . .*

Revenge? I began to laugh. My laughter uncapped a well of blood in my chest. It stained my comic smile, spilled down my chin onto my naked breasts, and dripped to the floor between my trembling knees. The spirits withdrew, gravely silent once more, and disappeared into the reemerging walls of my bedroom. The room had gone utterly dark, even the traffic light outside the window. The storm had knocked out the electricity. I looked at the door. Flashes of lightning created the illusion of a series of still photographs:

Endo enters the bedroom, the Leica in his hands, his face a puzzled frown of concentration.

A woman stands before him, fiercely gripping the camera to her breast, frozen in a pose of frantic and impotent struggle to tear it from his grasp.

The camera flashes, the whole thing, like a ball of lightning birthed in their four hands by a magician's spell. His shadow leaps up on the wall behind him, huge, monstrous and armless.

Ashley turns, her face now a pale reflection of her life, horrible in its beauty, her mouth gaping.

Then there was darkness. The thunder paused, the storm quieted and the waters stilled as though Jesus had spoken— *Peace, be still*. I lifted the gun in my shaking fist and pulled the trigger, blindly. In the muzzle's flash, I saw the hilarious surprise on Endo's face. The bullet drove the camera's glass and metal guts into his chest.

He fell beside me and the storm resumed, redoubled in its fury, shaking the floor. I lay down beside Endo, he and I together. I drifted apart like a burning kite. It felt like hours and like no time at all. The storm bore down upon us in all its fury, but we were immune, watching from a distance. The rain misting through the bullet hole in the window made dew upon my cheeks and trickled into my eyes like tears going home, time in reverse.

A banshee siren began to wail. Endo opened his eyes one last time and looked up at the hail rattling like boney fingers against the window, a rictus smile on his bloodless, black kabuki face. "Air raid!" he sighed.

Another Monday

44

When shall we three meet again,
in thunder, lightning, or in rain?

When the hurlyburly's done,
when the battle's lost and won.
—MACBETH, ACT I, SCENE I

I HEARD WALGREENS BOUGHT WALTER'S old building and was going to tear it down. The mercado had already closed and as I drove by students were moving training
equipment out of the tae kwon do school. The For Rent sign
had been removed from the door of the empty bay, leaving its
rectangular ghost on the dusty glass. A coin-operated washing
machine sat on the sidewalk in front of the stripped-out Laundromat. In three hours I was supposed to be at a church in
Frayser taking photos of Mynor's daughter's wedding.

I pulled into the parking lot and entered by the open back
door, my shadow preceding me up the stairs. The air inside

was hot and reeked from the fresh turd sitting in the corner behind the door, buzzing with flies. All the mailboxes had their doors pried open and the floor was littered with old bits of junk mail and grocery-store ads.

My old apartment door was open, strips of crime-scene tape hanging around like old party streamers. The elevator at the end of the hall stood open, the elevator Walter had been so proud of, the one he died under, black and gutted by fire.

My apartment had been cleaned out. The door was still broken, the wood splintered around the dead bolt from Adam's kick. They hadn't even tried to clean up the blood in the bedroom. Homeless people had busted most of the window-panes. The floor crunched with bits of glass under my feet. The only thing left was the old wooden bed frame, still in its original position against the wall.

I had been clean for four months. I told myself I didn't want to be high again, but truthfully I was scared. Scared I would return to that stage Endo had constructed in his fevered brain. Whenever I used, all my ghosts came crowding around again— Adam, James, Ashley, Michi, Cole, laughing at me, always laughing. The only one who never appeared was the one I really wanted to see again, but like my brother he never showed his pale, transparent face. Like Sean, Endo moved on, I didn't know where, but I hoped it was hell, if hell would have him.

There was no longer any peace for me. No comfort, only pain. Which was how it had always been, only I was too blinded by need to see it. The need for heroin was still gnawing at my bones. It never went away. But I wasn't sick anymore, and the fear kept me clean.

Adam tried to save me that night. He'd been trying for years and he finally managed, the sorry bastard. He had to die tragically to do it.

But then again, it wasn't really tragic. It was comic. Ridiculous, like Endo. Endo was right. The only difference between comedy and tragedy was your point of view. The only difference was the mask you wore, and who was holding the knife. *Oftentimes to win us to our harm, the instruments of darkness tell us truths.* That's what old Bill Shakespeare had been trying to tell us in the play whose name we dared not mention. Bad things happen, but evil isn't just bad things.

I heard a crunch of glass behind me. Chief Billet stood in the doorway, a plain brown box clamped under one arm. He was smiling. Not patronizing. Just smiling like a man who had moved on with his life. He tugged at his suit collar with one gold-ringed pinky. Even with the windows broken out, it was hot in here. Hot for May.

"Once again you've managed to get on the bad side of this town," he said to me.

"What?"

"That Japanese boy took some very incriminating photographs of a few of Memphis' finest citizens."

"Why doesn't that surprise me?"

"A bunch of important people spent a nervous Christmas wondering what would come of this case." He switched the box to his hand. Nothing had come of the case. The killer was dead. There was no need to look for evidence.

"You did a fine job covering things up," I said.

"Thank you kindly." He fanned his face with his hand. "Can I buy you a drink?"

"You can buy me lunch."

Billet pushed back his plate of stripped-bare pork ribs and loosened his belt. He'd taken me to Cozy Corner, off North

Parkway near Jackson, a real nice part of town, almost as nice as my old place on Summer. As I slid into the booth, a strip of duct tape stuck to my jeans and peeled off the seat. The air conditioner above the next booth was padlocked to a steel staple bolted to the wall.

Billet stuck a toothpick in his mouth and looked at me across the wreckage of the feast he'd purchased on the city's American Express. "The weakest point in the St. Michael case was the lack of fingerprints," he said. "The only prints we got were from the victim and her husband. The bedroom and the front door had been wiped clean. You may not know this, but Adam never thought James did it. He always said if St. Michael had killed his wife, why wipe off the prints? He lived there. Of course we'd find his prints. But killers do stupid shit all the time. That's what makes my job easy."

He tapped his front tooth with the toothpick, waiting for me to say something. I ignored him, lit a cigarette and blew the smoke across the table into his face. He coughed slightly and set the toothpick on the edge of his plate. "What I don't get is how you figured out the deal with that spare key."

"I already told you."

"I know, I know. You found it because you looked for it. Little Miss Sherlock fucking Holmes." Billet swallowed a drink of iced tea. The air conditioner sounded like an old tractor trying to start after a long winter.

"It wasn't just that," I said. "There was also the key in the bottom of Endo's trophy drawer. At the time I didn't make the connection."

Billet nodded and sucked at a piece of meat stuck between his teeth. "Well, it doesn't matter. You found it and guessed right on the rest. The key in Endo's drawer fit the locks at the victim's house."

There was more that I didn't tell Billet, things Endo had said to me during our brief time on stage, things I'd never told anyone. From them I was able to build a picture of what happened that night. Maybe it was the right picture. I'd never know for sure.

Endo caught Ashley St. Michael at Playhouse on the Square after she took his picture stuffing Dick Buntyn into a wine barrel. He strangled her, then drove her body home. He knew where she lived because her house had belonged to Cole Ritter's mother. He used to play there as a kid. In particular, he liked to play behind the garage. It was a good place to hide things, he said, meaning he'd found that key frog years ago. He set the scene up to look like her husband had killed Ashley, not knowing James was a thousand miles away at the time, then locked the door behind him. He didn't stage her in his usual theatrical manner, first because it wasn't personal, she was just someone who was in the wrong place at the right time to get killed. But more importantly, he didn't want anyone to connect the Playhouse Killer to Ashley's murder, because her society photographs might link him to Richard Buntyn.

Next, he took the memory card from the Leica and set the camera on the top shelf in the closet. If he had taken the whole camera, the cops might have guessed Ashley had taken a picture of her murderer and tracked that back to him somehow. But by that time, Ashley's spirit had entered the camera, or attached itself to it, or possessed it, or something. I don't know what. Deiter was better at explaining this part.

So Endo only took the memory card and left the camera, but as he bent over her body to arrange the running shoes around her neck, the Leica snapped a photo of him. That photo went into the camera's internal memory.

As soon as the camera came into my possession, Ashley

started taking pictures trying to lead me to her killer—the photos backstage at the Orpheum, the ones at the Overton Park Shell, and the dark ones at Endo's studio. Maybe she was trying to lead me to the camera's memory—her memory, really. That was why Trey's diving rods kept pointing at me that night—because I was wearing her ghost around my neck, inside the Leica.

One thing that took me a long time to understand was why Ashley had waited to show her deadly secret to me. Why hadn't she shown herself to her husband? I realized that James probably never touched her camera until the day he sold it to me. That's why he hadn't known the memory card was missing. More importantly, she couldn't show herself without destroying him utterly. He was barely holding his life together as it was. Seeing her ghost would have killed him. She could show herself to me, because I was used to ghosts. I wouldn't fall apart. I couldn't fall apart, because I was already in pieces.

When I got out of the hospital, I went home to Mom and Dad to recuperate. It didn't take long to notice that I wasn't seeing my special friends anymore. Not while I was clean, anyway. The old man who lived by the elm tree was gone. So were the Indians in the backyard and my grandfather's ghost in the attic. The old house was still and quiet, probably for the first time in my life, and the only ghost I saw was my mother drifting in and out of my room to check on me.

I followed the story in the newspaper. It only lasted about a week before new murders took its place. The Playhouse Killer faded from the public mind, but not from mine. When I got back to Memphis, I obtained permission from Chief Billet to go through Endo's things. He signed the evidence form without a single question.

It took me about two months to watch all of Endo's home movies. The older ones were on video tape, the more recent digital files stored on his computer. Most were of him acting alone on his own sets. What Dave Straw had said was true. Endo was so Ed Wood awful, it made you laugh, even if you knew what a monster he was. I think he knew it, too. I think that's why he hung those Gacy paintings in his lobby, because Gacy recognized the ultimate comedy of his own monstrosity, the great cosmic joke played by God, not only on his victims, but also on John Wayne Gacy. And Noboyuki Endo. Gacy painted clown makeup on his own monstrous self-hating homosexual self, and so did Endo.

He also did a lot of monologuing. He never tried to justify his actions, he only wanted to document them as thoroughly as possible, for posterity. He thought the record of his deeds would be important one day.

Endo set great store by the fact he was born on Thespis Day. Because he survived his mother's attempted murder-suicide, he believed the gods of tragedy had chosen him for some special purpose, especially after he saw Adam on the news trying to link him to the Patsy Concorde murder. It was the strangest thing—all those theatrical coincidences really were coincidences. Endo had killed Patsy Concorde in a rage and set fire to her body to hide the evidence. He hadn't planned to link her to *Hippolytus*, yet everything seemed to fit together by design—Neptune Avenue, the Dionysian Theatre, Concorde's Mustang convertible. Endo said, from that moment he began to feel a greater power working through him. He had got religion at the church of Noboyuki Endo.

The only thing that didn't fit was the skull I'd found in the drawer. It pointed to a thirteenth victim, but when I mentioned it, Billet shook his head. "Wiley had it carbon dated. It's about four hundred years old. The teeth indicate archaic Native American. No telling where Endo got it."

"Alas, poor Yorick, it was probably a stage prop, lifted from a production of Hamlet," I suggested. "But what I don't get is why he kept it with the trophies of his killings."

"You know what I don't get?" Billet sucked his teeth and looked thoughtful for a moment, almost like he had a real brain in his head, knocking away. "He killed every one of them on a Monday. What's so special about Mondays?"

"Theaters are usually closed on Mondays. It was his day off."

"Christ." He leaned back in the creaking green leatherette booth. "What about the victims?"

"What about them?"

"Why kill them?"

"Does it matter?"

"It matters to me. I know you don't think I'm much of a cop, Jackie, but I'd like to know where I screwed up, so maybe next time I won't."

I never expected that out of Billet. I always figured him for a politician. "Some people he killed to cover his tracks. He killed one in a fit of rage. The ones he planned to kill—Krews, Buntyn, and the Simon Twins—all betrayed him, or he killed them to send a message to somebody who had betrayed him. Krews was his first real boyfriend, but they broke up. Buntyn abused him as a child. The Simon Twins caught him peeping in the boy's dressing room. With Hendricks, he was sending a message to Dave Straw. Cole was a message to his grandfather, and Michi, I think, was a message to me. Lucky for us he never got around to snuffing all the people he planned to kill. He had a list nearly as long as my leg."

"Lucky," Billet agreed.

The box Billet brought with him sat on our table next to the wall. It had been there the whole time we ate and he hadn't said anything about it. It looked like the kind of box that file folders come in.

A waitress came by and cleaned off our table. When she was gone, he leaned back and retightened his belt a notch, then glanced at his gold watch. "I'm not supposed to say this, but I'm glad you capped that boy. I'm glad his sick shit didn't get broadcast all over the news. It was better it ended this way."

"Better for you, maybe."

"I hope you don't feel guilty. Not for one God damn minute."

"I'm not losing any sleep," I said. "Not anymore. I just wish . . ." I couldn't finish.

"Wish what?" Billet asked. He wasn't even looking at me, and I doubt he really wanted to know.

I swallowed my pride and told him anyway. "I knew Endo was after me, but I let him walk right up behind me and hit me with a . . ." I choked my voice down to a whisper to keep from screaming. "He hit me with my own fucking baseball bat. Then I let him kill Adam. Back in the day, he'd never have got that close."

"You can't blame yourself. Endo took you, but he also took Adam . . ."

"Because of me," I interrupted.

He ignored me. "Adam was damned good. Better than either of us. When somebody's got your number, there's only so much you can do, especially when that somebody is a piece of work like our boy Endo." That sounded like something James would say.

Billet cleared his throat and smiled. "The thing is, Jackie, you did some good work. Damn good work on both of those cases. I'm not the only one saying it. Lots of people in the department have been talking about you." He reached into his pocket and laid his fist on the table.

"What's that?" I asked.

"It's a time machine. You want to see it?" Slowly, he opened his fingers. I dropped my cigarette on the floor and stubbed it out with my toe. I looked at the disk of shining bronze-colored metal lying on his palm.

"You can have it back, reinstated at your previous level and your original hire date. It'll be like you were out on medical leave."

"Back in vice?" I didn't think I could work vice again. Too many distractions, too many temptations. I was starting to think I could have a life and didn't want to ruin that fantasy.

Billet said, "Actually, I was thinking about putting you in homicide. But if you come back, you got to keep off the junk. I know you've been clean for a while now, and I commend that, but you skip one NA meeting without my permission and you're out. For good this time. You understand?"

"No, I don't understand." I hadn't seen this coming. He wasn't just being nice. He wanted something and I wanted to know what before I answered him. I smiled at him. "Explain it to me."

"I took the liberty of checking your mail for evidence. There was a card from the post office saying you had a package."

"From Michi?" He nodded and pushed the box across the table. This was the package Endo had been looking for in my apartment. It was also the reason Adam and James were dead. If I had never sold Michi those photos, they would still be alive.

But then again, so would Endo.

I pointed at the box. "I see you also took the liberty of opening it."

He shrugged and looked away. I lifted the top and set it aside. There was a letter, handwritten in Michi's tiny, precise, womanly cursive, about eight pages long, on blue-lined paper torn out of a spiral notebook. The first line said *Endo is the Playhouse Killer. When the police search my house, they will find these pictures, so I'm sending them to you so you don't get into trouble.*

I stopped reading. *That bastard*, I thought. Michi had tried to save me, too.

Beneath the letter were the photos of the Simon Twins. I looked up quickly, but Billet was smiling at a pair of good-looking black women in the booth across the way. They were smiling back at him, sucking their teeth and their fingers and rolling their eyes at each other. He held his hand to his ear like a phone. I shuffled through the other pictures, all the photos I'd sold to Michi over the years. Then I came across my pictures of the Buntyn murder, then the Krews murder, and dozens of other murders I'd never even shown the old pervert.

The only other person in the world who had copies of these pictures was Chief Billet.

"Why are you showing me this?" I asked.

He returned his attention to our table, still wearing his player smile. He picked up the box lid and laid it over the photos, just in case anybody walked by with a pitcher of tea. "Both of us were profiting off that old man's death fetish. You know how hard it is to get by on a cop's salary, even at my level. Why do you think I let Adam talk me into hiring you? I'd been selling crime scene pictures to Michi for years when Wiley got wind of it and cut off my access. I needed a new source."

"That's why Wiley hated me working his scenes." I had always thought it was because I was a woman, but it had nothing to do with me. It had always been about Billet.

"Pretty much. He couldn't prove anything, but he knew."

If this were true, then Michi had been paying me all along for copies of photos he already owned, the old liar. He'd done it for no other reason than to help me out. What a sad, sorry old man. Despite his perversions, I'd liked Michi, but he never gave anybody a chance to be honest with him.

Billet went on, "When I found this package addressed to you, I couldn't take a chance you already knew about me. I figured Michi had told you."

"He didn't tell me anything," I said bitterly.

"Well, now we both know something."

"So that's why you're giving me my badge. That way I'll have something to lose if I tell Wiley."

"That's one way of looking at it. Another is that you're a damn fine cop, even if you are a junkie. You proved that. I could use you, Jackie. We're a man down. A damn good one. Adam was my friend."

"He was my friend, too. What you're looking for is a new friend. Is that what you're telling me, Chief Billet?"

"Something like that," he said. Now I knew how he met Michi in the first place. Billet's door swung both ways.

"I'm not that kind of friend," I said.

"Honey, I'm a married man." He smiled like the politician he was.

"You and about a billion other guys."

I got up and took my box, but I left his badge sitting on the table. I was through with men. Every last one of them.

Acknowledgments

I would like to recognize the following people for their contributions, both deliberate and unintentional:

My agent, Peter Riva, and my editors at Minotaur, for their insight and wisdom.

Irakly Shanidze, for enthusiastically answering my photography questions, and for providing so much inspiration with his art.

My wife, for believing.

Everyone who ever scared me with their ghost stories. Thanks for the sleepless nights.

Everyone who ever haunted me, living and dead. You know who you are.